Braddock Heights

Marian,

To a Talented artist and good friend. I hope you enjoy the book.

Harold

BRADDOCK HEIGHTS

Harold J. Barend

Copyright © 2012 by Harold J. Barend.

Library of Congress Control Number:		2012910272
ISBN:	Hardcover	978-1-4771-2579-3
	Softcover	978-1-4771-2578-6
	Ebook	978-1-4771-2580-9

All rights reserved. No part of this book may be reproduced or transmitted in any form or by any means, electronic or mechanical, including photocopying, recording, or by any information storage and retrieval system, without permission in writing from the copyright owner.

This is a work of fiction. Names, characters, places and incidents either are the product of the author's imagination or are used fictitiously, and any resemblance to any actual persons, living or dead, events, or locales is entirely coincidental.

This book was printed in the United States of America.

To order additional copies of this book, contact:
Xlibris Corporation
1-888-795-4274
www.Xlibris.com
Orders@Xlibris.com
115838

Contents

Dedication 7
Explanation 8

Chapter 1	Harriet Bertrand...	11
Chapter 2	The Genealogy	14
Chapter 3	Reverend Kessler	21
Chapter 4	Let the Games Begin	28
Chapter 5	Only His Honor Left	34
Chapter 6	Otto Suhl Comes to America	39
Chapter 7	A Rough Voyage	43
Chapter 8	The Irish	49
Chapter 9	Mandels Come to America	51
Chapter 10	Castle Garden	53
Chapter 11	B. H. Barend...	59
Chapter 12	A Marriage Disavowed	62
Chapter 13	DWI Lift-Truck Operator	65
Chapter 14	The Early Years...	70
Chapter 15	A Family without a Home	79
Chapter 16	The Hotel Edison..	83
Chapter 17	Joe the Hobo	87
Chapter 18	Hope	91
Chapter 19	Parting Was Sweet Joy	94
Chapter 20	Anna and Henry Brown	99
Chapter 21	Coming Together	103
Chapter 22	Braddock Heights...	106
Chapter 23	Come to My House..	112
Chapter 24	IQ Tests..	126
Chapter 25	And the Years Passed	131
Chapter 26	Money, Money, Money	143
Chapter 27	The Clubhouse...	147

Chapter 28	Newspaper Boy	154
Chapter 29	Making Money	160
Chapter 30	Children of Revenge	163
Chapter 31	Hilton Central School	171
Chapter 32	High School	175
Chapter 33	Trashing the Neighborhood	181
Chapter 34	Summertime	186
Chapter 35	The Wawbeek Hotel	192
Chapter 36	The Fortunes of Life	198
Chapter 37	Crime and Punishment	210
Chapter 38	Have Wheels, Will Go	215
Chapter 39	Working the Graveyard Shift	221
Chapter 40	The U.S. Army	226
Chapter 41	Fort Slocum, NY	235
Chapter 42	Fort Hood, Texas	240
Chapter 43	Bremerhaven, Germany	252
Chapter 44	Coffey Barracks	255
Chapter 45	Basketball and Track at Coffey	266
Chapter 46	Seventh Army Headquarters	271
Chapter 47	Pyrenees	280
Chapter 48	Spain and England	285
Chapter 49	Dewayne Allen	288
Chapter 50	German, Beer, Wine, and Women	293
Chapter 51	Seventh Army Basketball	296
Chapter 52	Monroe Community College	298

Epilogue 313

About the Artists 317

DEDICATION

This book is dedicated to my children: David, Beth, and Samara. I pray that God blesses you. I am very proud of your personal strengths, character, education, athletic achievements, and the contributions you have made to your community.

There is an old Chinese saying that goes something like this: "You tell me what your children are, and I will tell you what you are." You are my legacy. I have been a fortunate parent who was able to enjoy the ride through life with three wonderful children. Remember to give your children all your love and most of your time. The rewards for the giving of your love far outweigh the negatives. According to Khalil Gibran in *The Prophet*:

> For even as love crowns you
>   so shall he crucify you.
> Even as he is for your growth
>   so is he for your pruning.
> Even as he ascends to your height and caresses
>   your tenderest branches that quiver in the sun,
> So shall he descend to your roots
>   And shake them in their clinging to earth.

Explanation

This book is a compilation of short stories. I have presented it in this format to give the reader a better understanding of the personalities and the forces of life that have affected the Barend and Suhl families. You can believe or disbelieve however much you desire.

It is not a book of judgment. In the course of my seventy-plus years, I have collected stories from my parents and grandparents, and remembered events from my life, which I have collected and recounted in this book. I cannot attest to the veracity of all the stories told to me when I was young—I can only assume they are true. How long these memories will remain with me is questionable. Consequently, I have taken the time and effort to record them.

An article in the November 2007 edition of *National Geographic* explains in one sentence my reason for compiling this book: "In the archives of the brain our lives linger or disappear."

While I still have recollection of my life, I hope to record it. I have been fortunate to have lived an exciting, colorful life; before God calls me away, I would like to share it with you.

My research indicates I am German, American Indian, French, and Jewish. I went from thinking I was 100 percent German to learning I could be a poster boy for cultural diversity in America.

When I realized my grandmother Rose Mandel was a German Jew, I recalled as a young boy searching through my grandparents' attic for lost treasurers and found a strange-looking star tucked away in an old trunk. When I mentioned the strange-looking star to my grandmother, she forbade me to go into the attic for future treasure hunts. She made me promise not to mention to my grandfather that I found the star.

I never made the connection until later in life. I have always appreciated the ability of the Jewish people to find a beauty in something or someone that most of us would miss.

In the summer of 1972, the Southern Tier of New York and Northern Pennsylvania experienced severe flooding from Hurricane Agnes. During this period, I owned a construction company headquartered in the Southern Tier.

I became friends with Ed and Annette Nezelek who owned a large construction company headquartered in the Southern Tier. Ed asked if I would accompany one of his construction managers in surveying the Hurricane Agnes flood damage in the Athens and Sayre, Pennsylvania. The Federal Emergency Management Agency requested his assistance in appraising the situation.

On our drive home from Athens, Pennsylvania, to Binghamton, New York, my companion asked me if I would reach into the backseat and hand him the book that was on the seat. When I grabbed it, I realized it was a Bible. After I handed it to him, he continued to drive with one hand on the wheel and one on the Bible. He told me this book was his most prized possession. It was evident that the book had been used on a regular basis. The pages were folded, and certain passages were highlighted. He told me he wanted me to have the Bible. I told him, "No thanks."

I did not want something that was so dear to him. Nor did I have any intention of ever reading the Bible.

He then proceeded with a psychological evaluation of me. He told me how I enjoy giving but that I have a problem receiving. "Take the book; someday you will read it," he said. I thought to myself, *Who the hell are you to tell me my shortcomings?* He repeated, "Take the book; someday you will read it."

For some reason, this time I did not argue or refuse to take the book.

That same book collected dust in my house for thirty years; I never opened it. I had no desire to read the Bible, even though I was always reading books. One evening, I was cleaning my nightstand and saw the Bible. I opened it and began leafing through the pages thinking, *What if the literary pundits are right?* I had the greatest book ever written resting for thirty years on my nightstand, and I never read it.

That night I pledged to read the book from cover to cover. It took me the better part of a year. I continued laboriously, page by page, until I had read it from cover to cover.

When I finished, I had a much greater appreciation for the Bible and the history of the Jewish people. If you doubt the accurateness of the Old Testament, read Numbers. Who would take the time and effort to fabricate a census of each Israeli tribe?

After reading the Bible, I recognized the importance of recording the history of our lives for future generations. A walk through any cemetery is evidence of the blank pages left behind: lives with stories to tell but no one left to tell them.

"Take the book; someday you will read it."

Chapter One

HARRIET BERTRAND

Lo, the poor Indian!
Whose untutored mind
See God in clouds,
Or hears Him in the wind.

—Alexander Pope, *Essay on Man*

Harriet Bertrand was born on October 5, 1869, and baptized five days later at St. Mary's Catholic Church in Clayton, New York. Her father, Oliver Bertrand, was born in 1837 in Cape Vincent, New York, and died in 1913 in Clayton, New York. Oliver was employed as a ship's carpenter.

Harriet's mother, Marie Genevieve (Jennie) Bazinet, was born in Canada in 1837 and died in Clayton in 1898. Harriet's mother was the daughter of Phillippe Bazinet and Genevieve Dupuis. Marie's mother, Genevieve Dupuis, was an American Indian; and her father, Phillippe Bazinet, was a French trapper.

Harriet's mother was a member of the Iroquois Federation, which encompassed six tribes of American Indians. Each tribe (Mohawk, Onondaga, Oneida, Seneca, Cayuga, and Tuscarora) played a major role in the French and Indian Wars and the Revolutionary War.

Just prior to the Revolutionary War, the Iroquois Federation unraveled because of a disagreement as to which side the tribes would join. Three tribes joined the English side, and three joined the colonialists in their fight for independence. Unfortunately, the Barend ancestors were Mohawks, who, along with the Oneida and Tuscarora, fought alongside the English.

During and after the war, the Mohawks felt the wrath of Washington's armies. When it became apparent the Mohawks had chosen the wrong side, Hetti's great-grandparents gathered their people and fled to Nova Scotia, Canada.

Years later, Hetti's parents and other members of their extended family returned to Clayton, New York, where they began a number of businesses. In 1897 Napoleon Bertrand opened the Herald House. For fifty years it remained in the Bertrand family. Over the years, the Bertrands expanded their business interests in the vicinity of Clayton, New York, to include a movie theater.

Genevieve (Jennie) Bazinet Bertrand, center, surrounded by six daughters and three sons.

Harriet Bertrand Barend

Harriet Bertrand Barend in her forties.

Harriet Bertrand Barend later in life: from a princess to a pauper.

Harriet Bertrand Barend died in 1934. Her funeral expenses at the time were $150.

CHAPTER TWO

THE GENEALOGY

*Life is a gamble at terrible odds
If it was a bet, you wouldn't take it.
Rosencrantz and Guildenstern are Dead*

—Act 3

The Barend/Bertrand Family Chart

Pedigree Chart

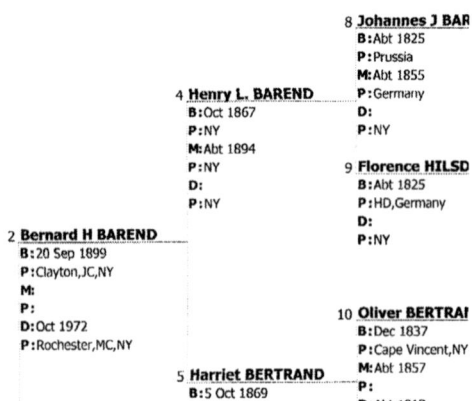

The Barend family history, according to my father, Bernard Harold Barend, begins in the mid-1800s when his grandfather, Johannes Behrend, at the age of six, immigrated to America from Germany with his parents. Johannes's father had been a high-ranking officer in the Prussian army who deserted the army and settled in a small scenic community called Clayton, New York. Prior to entry to Ellis Island, the name Behrend became Barend. Why? My dad believed it was because his great-grandfather wanted a new life.

The German Kaiser had powerful friends in the United States, and Johannes's father did not want to be found and shipped back to Germany. The Kaisers' friends did not look kindly on military deserters. The Behrend family arranged secret passage from Greenock, Scotland, to New York on a ship called *Susannah*. They arrived in New York City on June 28, 1833.

Johannes Behrend and Florentina Hilsdorf, born in Germany in 1825

Their son, Henry, born in Clayton, New York (1867)

Johannes Behrend was born in Prussia in 1825, and his wife, Florentina Hilsdorf, was born in Hess-Darmstadt the same year. They met in the United States and, after a short courtship, were married in 1855. Their son, Henry, my grandfather, was born in 1867 in Clayton, New York. In addition to Henry, Johannes and Florentina had four other children: Anna Barend, born in 1858; William Barend, born in 1861; John Barend, born in 1857; and Mary Barend, born in 1866.

Clayton, New York

When he was twenty-seven years old, Henry married Harriet Bertrand who was two years younger. Henry became successful in Clayton. He owned a sawmill, a general store, and many acres of farmland.

During the late 1800s and early 1900s, Clayton was the largest and most prosperous of the villages in the Thousand Islands area. Its commercial and industrial growth during this period was unmatched by any village or city within Northern New York. In addition to the industrial growth, its fertile soil and densely wooded forests provided a mecca for farmers and sawmill operators.

Henry was a gentleman farmer. A few years after his marriage, Henry purchased an elevated piece of land to construct his new home. It took three years to complete the six-bedroom, colonial-style mansion.

Henry's mill provided all the lumber for his house. The interior trim was mahogany, and the floors were oak. The sinks and bathroom fixtures were imported from New York City. Henry was adamant about having a functional bathroom rather than a conventional outhouse.

One of the European workers tried to convince him to install his toilet waste pipes so they would extend down the side of the house and exit into a wheelbarrow. The intent was to collect the human waste for crop fertilizer, a common practice at that time in Europe. When the worker couldn't explain away the smell, Henry asked for a trench to be dug on a slight grade so the waste would travel down a hand-installed pipe, which was connected to a large metal tank that was buried in the ground. The tank, ten feet long by eight feet in diameter, was part of an old boiler, which had been used at the sawmill.

With the building of his home and the rapid expansion of his business interests, Henry soon found himself short on cash.

An Ill-fated Partnership

John Barker, president and owner of the Bank of Clayton, felt Henry Barend had overextended. He refused to loan him any additional capital even though Henry had never been late on a bank payment. Barker always felt uncomfortable loaning money to entrepreneurial businessmen. The majority of the bank's money was invested in no-risk government securities or heavily secured business loans. The business loans were to men who had the same philosophy as Barker—squeeze the nickel until the buffalo shits.

Barker did suggest a solution, which in the end resulted in Henry's demise. He advised Henry to enter into a partnership with a wealthy Pennsylvanian named George Morris. After meeting with Morris, Henry agreed to Morris's conditions and made him a full partner in the sawmill and general store.

George Morris was a very studious-looking man. He was always impeccably dressed. He stood slightly below Henry but always positioned himself to be at the same level when discussing a point of business. He walked in an extreme upright posture. His vested suits were dark, and his shoes were always the shiniest in Clayton. The rumor had it that he graduated from an expensive college in Philadelphia. The men in town disliked him in every way, and some even thought he was gay. The ladies all greeted him with delight and giggled when he would step aside to let them pass. Morris was about as compatible with the Clayton men as a turd in a milk bottle.

Although they were partners in business, George Morris and Henry left their relationship at work. Morris attended to the books, and established and maintained the inventory and payroll system, while Henry was the manager and public front man—the customers and employees liked and trusted Henry but felt uncomfortable around Morris. Recognizing the situation, Morris did not attempt to push himself onto either. The men neither liked nor respected each other, which made for a very unsettling partnership.

One cold, wintry evening in January 1919, the two men were part of a large group that had gathered at the Walton Hotel in Clayton. It was a large old established hotel. Its owner, Samuel Johnston, was a popular figure whose family had been one of the original settlers of the area. Although attractive from a distance, up close, the hotel's facade gave it the appearance of the Old West. The siding around the windows appeared newer than the adjacent clapboards, and there was additional patched siding within the new siding, which indicated someone had shrunk the windows. Either the owner was concerned about heating the building or a body or two had exited the windows.

Besides dispensing the customary spirits, the hotel's tavern was the most popular gathering place for the Clayton men. Women, except for Molly O'Leary, were never seen frequenting the Walton—their social gatherings were planned around school or church activities where the men seldom participated.

Except on Sundays, the Walton far outdrew the school and the Baptist, Methodist, Episcopal, and Catholic churches in regular attendance. The people of Clayton worshiped on the Sabbath. Following Sunday services, they would devote the day to their spouses or children. There wasn't a store, shop, or bar open in Clayton on Sunday. The ministers and the priest knew their flock, and they administered to their spirits with tremendous gusto every seventh day.

Sam Johnston, the owner of the Walton, heard a rumor that the Temperance Reform Club was trying to bring the ax-wielding Carrie Nation to Clayton. Shortly thereafter, the governing board voted to impose a special tax on clubs whose purpose it was to influence or promote political change. Carrie Nation never arrived in Clayton.

On this particular winter evening, Henry and Morris were standing at the bar, a comfortable distance apart, when they both spotted George Dean about to exit the poker game—it was the only seat available. George was sitting at the large oak table where he spent the better part of two hours. He was ahead 50¢, and he knew if he didn't leave within the next fifteen minutes, his wife and children would appear at the door calling for him. As George began to rise from the chair, Henry and Morris both lunged for the soon-to-be-empty seat. George, realizing there was a contest for his chair, jumped to the side.

Morris grabbed onto the chair a second before Henry. Being very strong and of large build, Henry could not control his forward motion and body-checked Morris who went airborne and bounced off Sam Johnston, the owner of the Walton. En route to Sam, Morris knocked over a spittoon, which allowed a black liquid substance to quickly spread under the poker table. The men sitting at the table were furious with Morris even though it was Henry's fault.

While Morris was pulling himself up, one of the men sitting at the table cranked his head to the right and let fly a disgusting yellow-gray spit, which landed on Morris's suit coat. The player apologized. Morris's face had turned red, then a dull blue. Morris's blood vessels had swollen. His face turned flush red, and his muscles compressed his arteries so tight that it restricted his blood flow. He became dizzy.

There was a limit to Morris's rage. Physically, he was no match for any of the men in the Walton. These were mill workers, farmers, shipbuilders. They were big and muscular. Morris was unaccustomed to hard labor, and his physical appearance reflected his lifestyle. Even some of the patrons' sons could pummel Morris without much resistance.

Therefore, he straightened himself and quickly retreated in the direction of the sink, which hung on the back wall near the bar. Morris paused at the bar where Molly O' Leary, the bartender, gave him a couple of old rags to clean the tobacco juice from his coat.

Molly was the only woman unofficially allowed in the tavern area of the Walton. Ten years ago, Molly and her husband, Sean Kelly O' Leary, had come to America. They settled in Northern New York because it possessed all the beauty of Ireland. Sean died of pneumonia shortly after they arrived in Clayton. He left Molly with a young son.

She was twenty-five, blonde, and with physical features that propelled her far above the average Clayton woman. To go along with her physical beauty, she had a tongue that would make Satan proud.

Morris cleaned himself off at the sink. The only restroom was a coed outhouse about twenty feet to the back of the building, and everyone knew it was easier to hold it during the winter months than walk those twenty yards to the outhouse. If you had a weak bladder or diarrhea, the Walton was the last place you would want to be on a cold night. In the winter, each time a patron would exit the back door en route to the outhouse, someone would bang a large metal spoon against a frying pan. This signal was more a bell of courage than an indication someone was about to visit the crapper.

At this point, another story must be told that relates to this particular outhouse: Upon completion of the Emanuel Kessler story, I will finish telling the story about one of the most famous card games in the history of Clayton that forever changed the fortunes of the Barend family for generations.

Chapter Three

Reverend Kessler

Under a bad cloak there is often a good drinker.

—Cervantes, *Don Quixote*

Henry Barend loved to tell the story about Emanuel Kessler, the local Baptist minister. According to Henry, Kessler had an arrangement with Molly O'Leary. Three times a week, winter or summer, Molly would slip out from behind the bar with a bottle of whiskey. She would walk just beyond the back door and leave the bottle inside an old flower box, then retreat to the bar.

The minister would arrive at the flower box at exactly 10:00 p.m. every Monday, Wednesday, and Saturday. He would go directly to the bottle—place it to his lips and not remove it until the bottle was empty. He would then place the empty in the flower box along with the money for the whiskey plus a nice tip for Molly. After he left, Molly would retrieve the empty bottle, keep the tip, and return the cost of the whiskey to the Walton.

Sam Johnston knew about the arrangement, but he didn't mind. He was making a decent profit, and Molly was receiving a little extra. The patrons of the Walton knew about it, and every man kept the secret from his wife because every time the minister came on a Saturday evening, there would be a very short sermon on Sunday. No patron of the Walton wanted this arrangement disrupted.

In addition, Emanuel Kessler was a board member of the Temperance Reform Club, and the patrons of the Walton believed Kessler would do everything possible to protect the best interests of the Walton.

This cold windy Saturday evening, the minister made his pickup and then walked to the outhouse. A few of the men had been watching from the corner window. They were surprised when Kessler did not exit the outhouse. This was not Kessler's mode of operation.

Everyone speculated that despite the smell, Kessler had entered the outhouse for protection from the icy-cold wind. The men were sure the minister would emerge in less than a minute with the empty in hand, walk to his recycling bin, then say a good act of contrition.

It did not happen. The minister decided to plant his bare buttocks on the wooden toilet seat. With the wind-chill factor, the temperature was about twenty below zero. When Kessler finished the bottle and attempted to leave, his buttocks stuck to the toilet seat.

After sufficient time for most men and beasts to die from the cold, the men of the Walton decided someone had better check on the minister. By now, everyone in the Walton had taken an interest in the minister's plight. The back windows were full of faces and steam.

The Walton men became concerned and decided Molly should try to determine if Kessler was dead, sick, or drunk. Molly agreed.

She walked out the back door and straight to the outhouse door where she whispered, "Revered Kessler, are you OK?"

The answer came back with a sheepish, "No, I am stuck to the toilet seat."

Molly wanted to laugh, but held herself in check. She quickly said, "I will get some warm water and try to help you."

When she reentered the Walton, the men rushed to her. She explained the minister's plight, and everyone started laughing. Fortunately for Kessler, the wind was blowing, and the outhouse was located a good distance from the hotel, which made it impossible to hear the laughter from within the Walton.

Before returning to the outhouse, Molly made the men promise to move away from the windows. She very carefully wrapped a couple of towels around the long metal handle of the pan containing the hot water. It was very hot.

She then proceeded across the room, out the back door and directly to the structure that resembled four or five old pieces of barn board fastened together with a door.

Molly was smart enough to bring with her the broom that stood in the back corner of the Walton. She placed the broom under her arm and then returned both hands to the pan. Her worst fear was falling.

The short path to the outhouse was covered with ice and crusted snow. It was so cold the snow had crystallized. Each step was with caution until she arrived once again at the outhouse door. She slowly lowered the steaming pan onto the snow and then opened the door just wide enough to insert the pan containing boiling water.

The Walton Outhouse

Everyone in the Walton had crowded around the windows to experience the last morsel of this drama. Molly placed the steaming pan on the floor of the outhouse (the men felt it would be appropriate to make the water as hot as possible for the minister) and then used her broom to slide the pan to the minister.

Thankfully, their eyes never met. After she ensured the pan was within reach of Kessler, Molly quickly picked up her broom and returned, bone chilled, to the Walton.

After a few minutes the door slowly opened, and out popped the minister's head. His head, like a submarine's periscope, scouted the area before surfacing—he was trying to determine if anyone other than Molly knew of his situation. He looked straight at the windows of the Walton, but no one was there. In anticipation of his exit, the men had vacated the windows.

Kessler was comforted with his ignorance and felt confident Molly had kept his unfortunate condition a secret. Kessler's head emerged inch by inch from behind the door until finally he pushed the door open and walked quickly to the flower box where he placed the pan, empty bottle, and money.

Sam Johnston had gone upstairs to watch and report what the men could not see.

A few minutes after Kessler's departure, Charlie O'Hara hollered, "Tomorrow's sermon will probably focus on hard work and sticking to our goals."

Peter White remarked, "The minister's sermon will be on faith and how in the end everything comes out."

Back to the Walton Hotel

Once Morris had wiped the tobacco spit from his coat, he returned to claim the chair Henry now filled to capacity. Henry stood about five feet eight inches and was built like a lumberjack. His clothes seldom reflected his wealth.

Unlike Morris, Henry was a popular figure throughout the Clayton expanse. He extended credit to the farmers and a few of the fishermen. The only people he ever required a deposit or payment of in advance were ministers, lawyers, judges, bankers, and a few of the large business owners.

Ministers, according to Henry, could always rationalize their deeds or misdeeds in the name of God—so he knew in God's name he would get cheated out of his money.

Lawyers could always find a loophole—and if they couldn't find a loophole, they would attempt to legislate one. If you had to fight them in court, they were probably related to the judge or helped to get the judge appointed.

As for judges, they were too arrogant—they could strut from a sitting position according to Henry.

Bankers just weren't very popular anywhere—they always wanted to loan money when a person didn't need it but always refused to loan money to someone who had a real need.

Large business owners, according to Henry, had enough money they could afford to pay in advance, which helped Henry extend free credit to the less fortunate.

Children who accompanied their parents to the general store would always receive large sticks of peppermint or spearmint candy. This was as much a marketing tool as an act of kindness. Children could often be seen tugging on the clothes of their parents in an attempt to get them into the store.

On this day, Henry wasn't very popular with those who occupied the table where he sat. Henry had taken the only seat available at the table. Morris stood about four feet to the right of the chair in dispute. While motioning in the direction of Henry, Morris made a strong argument for the seat.

Sam Johnston motioned to the other three men at the table, excluding Henry, to join him for a conference. Grouped in the corner, adjacent to the back door, the four men discussed their dilemma: which of the two men should be allowed in the game.

Tom Rees remarked that Morris should be given the chair—after all, he reached it first, and if Henry Barend hadn't bumped Morris, Rees's boots would still be clean. Jeremiah Hall came up with the winning solution—why not add a sixth chair and permit both men to play? Just keep them separated.

Morris was happy, but Henry was very upset with the decision. Henry didn't like socializing with Morris, and a game of poker for him was socializing. The game began like any five-card poker game. The rules were the following: a player could draw up to a maximum of three cards, there were no wild cards, and a player needed a pair of jacks or better to open play.

Up to this point, there were no big winners or losers but a lot of talk, cigar smoke, and consumed alcohol. Anyone entering the room directly from the outside would need about thirty seconds to adjust his eyesight because of the thick haze of smoke throughout the room. The only ventilation system was the windows, and on cold nights the men preferred to choke from the smoke rather than freeze from the cold fresh air entering an open window.

Chapter Four

LET THE GAMES BEGIN

Never play cards with a man called Doc.
Never eat at a place called Mom's.
Never sleep with a woman
Whose troubles are worse than your own.

—*Newsweek*

Seated at the poker table with Henry were Tom Rees, the mortician for most of the area; Sam Johnston, the owner of the Walton; Dr. Benjamin White (the local physician who accepted payment for his services—depending on what his clients could afford); Oliver Crandall, a local farmer; and George Morris. With the exception of Crandall, any one of the other five men could lose in one night an average man's earnings for a year and have forgotten about it in a few days.

Morris seldom fraternized with the men or pushed his way into a poker game; he remained, everyone thought, because he was irritating Henry. Unfortunately for Morris, he was losing money. Each hand he would ante up and then fold, or bet once and then fold. Unlike some of the men, Morris never pretended a hand—he either had the cards, or he didn't have them—in which case he would fold. He knew the odds of attempting to reconstruct a bad hand. Therefore, he always folded unless he had a minimum pair of queens. Tonight, Morris's forehead was full of wrinkles, and his faint smile had become fainter.

When a man is forty years old and continues to live unmarried in a village like Clayton, rumors, like a cancer, begin to creep around about one's character or lack of it. Although churchgoing women, the Clayton ladies were professional storytellers—they were embryonic *Enquirer* staffers—but churchgoing women.

As he held his cards close to his large red plaid coat, Henry's expression—half glum, half serious—never changed during the last two hands. One he lost; one he won. He suddenly got lucky and won three hands in a row. The next hand, he was dealt three tens. He was a believer in running a lucky streak. He had accumulated a sizable stack of coins and currency, which was piled before him on the table.

Henry was an excellent poker player, and the men at the table knew he could be sitting with a royal flush or a royal bust. No one could tell the difference. Most of the men who frequented the Walton were aware he had bluffed his way to one of the largest poker pots in the greater Clayton area with a pair of threes. Four of the five other men who were playing that night held cards that would have beaten Henry, but none had the nerve to keep betting. Tonight, these were different players.

Henry knew the advantages of keeping the players in the game. He knew the probability of winning was very high when dealt three tens in the first five cards; each player had already placed 10¢ in the center of the table as a beginning bet before the cards were dealt. After the five cards were dealt, no one spoke. Henry hoped someone would open the betting before his turn—no one opened. He preferred never to show his hand unless he had to.

There was a gentleman's agreement at the Walton: no bet or raise could exceed $1, but there was no limit on the number of times the players could raise one another. Sam Johnston thought this policy to be fair for everyone and a good for business—the more exciting the game became, the longer the patrons stayed and drank.

After Henry reluctantly opened with a 25¢ bet, Oliver Crandall, the player to his right, matched the bet and then doubled it. It would now cost everyone 50¢ to remain in the game. Crandall was the only man at the table who really couldn't afford to be there. He had four sons and a wife. They lived on a modest farm just on the outskirts of the village. Whenever Crandall lost heavily in a poker game at the Walton, his boys would not be seen at school for a couple of weeks because they would be working to help their dad recover his losses.

Tom Rees and Dr. White both folded. This left Crandall, Sam Johnston, Morris, and Henry. Johnston placed his money in the center of the table. Morris then raised another $1. Recognizing the obvious, Johnston folded, but Crandall and Henry remained in the game. Henry then added another dollar. He felt very confident: he had drawn a fourth ten to go with his three tens. Crandall decided to cut his losses and leave the game. He couldn't be sure if Henry was bluffing or not, but he was confident Morris had something very good.

For the next twenty minutes, Morris and Henry continued to raise each other $1 at a time until the pot had grown to $140. Neither man would yield to the other. Finally, Sam Johnston broke the standoff and asked for one last bet of $5 each, after which both men would place their cards down simultaneously. About forty men had gathered around the table. Molly had left the bar and pushed her way to the back of the chair where Sam Johnston was sitting. She was leaning over Sam. If he turned his head quickly to the right, his face would be stuck in her left breast.

As each hand was placed on the table, no one made a sound. Henry glared at Morris's cards while Morris's eyes were fixed on the cards before Henry. This was one of the few times Morris allowed himself to express happiness and excitement. His four queens beat Henry's four tens. Henry's heart sank.

It was not the loss of the money, but the thought of losing to Morris that so repulsed him. Morris, on the other hand, was exploding with excitement. He hollered to Molly, "Drinks on Morris!" A few of the spectators took advantage of Morris's generosity and moved to the bar, but not one player at the table where the game was played asked for a free drink. Morris pretended he did not care, but he was insulted and hurt at a time when he wanted to celebrate.

Having experienced a degree of success and excitement that could possibly never again be repeated, Morris decided to leave the game and go home where he could quietly sit and relive this wonderful night. As Morris was putting his winnings safely into his pocket, Tom Rees commented how it was poker courtesy for him to remain in the game and give the other players an opportunity to win back some of their money.

Morris glared at Rees and then reluctantly slid back into his seat. The other players' silence was an indication to Tom Rees that maybe he should have just let Morris leave without saying anything.

What followed was the most talked-about story in Clayton for the next decade. As the game progressed, Henry noticed Morris was matching the opening bet and then folding almost immediately every hand. Morris was playing because he was embarrassed to leave. His strategy was play if need be but preserve the winnings—which meant risk-free poker. Morris would not bet unless he had an almost-sure winner. Henry kept trying to devise a strategy to entice Morris to continue betting, but all his efforts were fruitless.

Finally, out of frustration, Henry announced to everyone seated at the table how Morris and he, although partners in business, disliked each other. Henry said, "You are a cold, calculating son of a bitch, Morris. You have very little empathy for the poor or the farmer, and you are out of place in Clayton. These people don't like you any better than I do, and they know you don't like them. You might know how to squeeze a nickel, Morris, but you don't know anything about the people who live in Clayton."

Morris, in a very shaky voice, announced his mutual dislike for Henry, "Henry, you are a very lucky man. Your home and business are not a testament to your ability but to your luck. You married an Indian woman whose family has money. Her father and your parents set up the business. Anyone could have succeeded with the kind of assistance you received."

He continued in a monotone saying how Henry was ungrateful for the contributions Morris made to the success of their business. After each man denounced the other, Henry put forth a proposal. He asked Morris to play one hand of poker, just the two of them. The winner would be the sole owner of the general store—the loser would relinquish his 50 percent interest. Morris agreed. For both men, their word was their honor.

Sam Johnston was designated the dealer. Within minutes, word had spread throughout the hotel and the neighboring shops of the big game. People began pouring into the Walton before the first card was dealt. They filled the room ten deep. For them, this was more than a game. If Morris won, most people agreed, things would be very different at the Clayton General Store.

The game was played under the same house rules—five-card-draw poker—nothing wild, jacks, or better to open. Before cards were dealt, one card was drawn by each man to determine who would respond first. The person who opened would draw his cards second. The object was to give both players an equal opportunity to learn something of their opponent before drawing up to a maximum of three cards.

Henry drew a six and Morris a queen. Because Henry lost the draw, he was to announce first if he had had an opening hand. Morris was to replace his discards first. Other than the general store, there would be no additional bets or raises. The winner would be the player who held the five best cards. Sam dealt the cards very slowly. He kept the cards titled down as he gave each player his respective cards.

Ironically, the two men who disliked each other so much and had very little in common were reaching in unison for their cards. This involuntary act was the last thing Morris and Henry did together. They slowly slid each card from the spot where it had been dealt. With their right hands covering, they would slide the cards to their stomachs and then peek at the corner of each card. This ensured privacy from the spectators who surrounded the table.

There was really no need for secrecy. It didn't matter if you were a good poker player because the outcome would be determined by the draw of the cards. The poker skills Henry honed over the many years were useless to him in this game.

Henry acknowledged he had an opening hand. Morris then requested one card. Henry asked for three. It was obvious to Henry that Morris was attempting to draw one card for a straight, a flush, or a full house. The best possibility, he thought, was 30 percent.

Henry looked at each of his three new cards. His draw was worthless—the pair of queens remained his best hope. He laid his cards down. Morris smiled. He had two pairs and full ownership of the general store.

Within the next hour, Henry gambled away everything he had worked his whole life to attain—the general store, sawmill, his home and thousands of acres of land. Morris was now the sole owner of everything of substance Henry had owned. Although there wasn't an attorney present to confirm the contract, Henry gave his word, and his word was his honor.

After losing everything to Morris, Henry pushed his chair back from the table, lifted himself, and slowly walked to the front of the hotel. A lesser man would have had a heart attack and died on the spot. The Walton was eerie quiet. Not one person spoke as Henry walked past them to the front door—his head erect. Not a tear showed in his eyes. Everyone appeared as stunned as Henry.

For the citizens of Clayton, it was not unlike the assassination of a great man. Henry had been one of the wealthiest men in Clayton, a benefactor for the Clayton orphanage (one of the largest in the area), and a friend to the poor.

After tonight, Henry Barend would only be a memory.

Chapter Five

ONLY HIS HONOR LEFT

True tragedy may be defined as a dramatic work in which the outward failure of the principal personage is compensated for by the dignity and greatness of his character.

—Joseph Wood Krutch

A family photo during the good times. Harriet Bertrand Barend and Henry Barend with four of their seven children: Mary Portance (Marie), born 1894; Maud Cecelia, born 1896; Leo Dennis, born 1898; Bernard Harold, born 1899; Genevieve, born 1901; Henry Jr., born 1906; and John (Jack), born 1908.

Earlier that evening, Henry Barend entered the Walton a proud and wealthy citizen of Clayton. When he left the hotel at 9:30 p.m. on that cold winter evening in 1910, two and a half hours after he entered, he was sad, sick, and desperate. His world and the world of his family and friends had been shattered by a poker game. His blind dislike for Morris colored his vision and made his cerebrum malfunction. The effects of his actions would ripple through four generations of the Barend family. The question often arose: what if?

Without saying good night, so long, or any of the departing gestures friends normally use, he slowly walked to the door with his head down. Without looking up or stopping, he continued walking to his new black Lincoln. He drove directly home—the home he had just built.

Henry had his wife, Harriet, wake the children. One by one, they slowly drifted into the kitchen where Henry was standing. They were yawning, rubbing their eyes, and wishing they could go back to their warm beds. He stood beside the new oak table his workmen completed a short time ago.

When all the family was present, he explained, "Something happened tonight that requires us to leave Clayton and never return."

The family knew they would no longer be living in Clayton. Now they were about to make a long difficult night journey to New Hudson, New York, to stay with relatives. They knew something terrible happened but were afraid to ask. Six children squeezed into the backseat. Henry, Harriet, and the youngest child sat up front.

The Town of New Hudson was about thirty-six square miles, and the town population consisted of about one hundred families who were mostly dairy farmers with a few carpenters sprinkled in.

They arrived at Henry's brother's home the following morning. William's immediate thought was Henry and his family had driven from Clayton for a weekend visit. William was unprepared for his guests who became a part of his household for the next six months.

Within a month, Henry purchased the tools he needed to return to the trade he learned as a young man: masonry. He planned to work, save, then buy a home in Rochester.

Two years after they left Clayton, Henry received a box in the mail from Morris. The box contained a pearl necklace, Henry's birth certificate, his wife's citizenship papers as a member of the Mohawk Nation, two large gold bracelets, a marriage license, and a bank draft for $20,000. The note enclosed with the box read:

> Henry,
>
> I took the liberty of auctioning your personal items. Before the auction began, Mr. Davis, the auctioneer, and I appraised the merchandise to ensure you would receive a fair minimum bid. He and I both purchased a number of items prior to the auction. We both agreed to pay 50 percent above the appraised value. I have enclosed $20,000 from the proceeds of the auction and a few personal items, kept from auction, which I felt your family might want.
>
> George Morris

The money allowed Henry to purchase a small farm in New Hudson Township. About ten years after they bought the farm, they sold it and moved to Rochester. The Barend family bought a home on Brooks Avenue. A few years after they moved to Rochester, the Brooks Avenue home caught fire and was totally destroyed. Henry did not have fire insurance.

Although life became more difficult, the Barend family worked hard to rebuild their lives. Eventually, Harriet's jewelry was sold to help finance weddings and funerals.

Life was never the same for the Barend family. The children were asked to leave school and start work at the earliest possible age permitted by law. It was unfortunate because B. H. had been a very good student and would have had a very promising career. There was no longer a guaranteed future or the security of a family business.

The extended Barend family gathers for a reunion at Masseth Street in Rochester, New York.

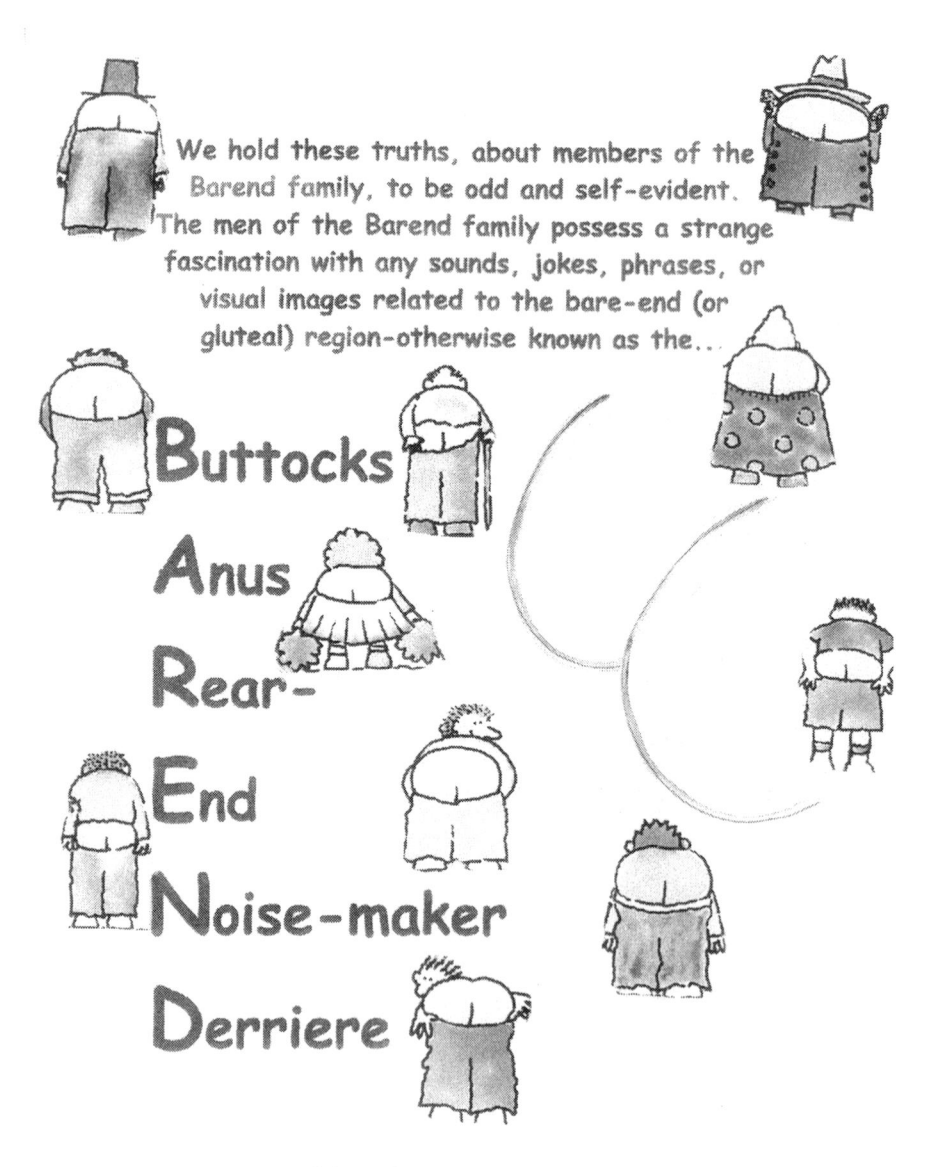

We hold these truths, about members of the Barend family, to be odd and self-evident. The men of the Barend family possess a strange fascination with any sounds, jokes, phrases, or visual images related to the bare-end (or gluteal) region-otherwise known as the...

Buttocks

Anus

Rear-

End

Noise-maker

Derriere

Artwork by Beth Barend. Rumps by Microsoft.

Chapter Six

Otto Suhl Comes to America

*Give me your tired, your poor,
Your huddled masses yearning to breathe free,
The wretched refuse of you teeming shore,
Send these the homeless, tempest tossed to me:
I lift my lamp beside the golden door.*

—Emma Lazarus, "The New Colossus"

Both of Otto's parents are buried in Steinfeld, Germany. Suhl is the name of a small city near the Rhine River.

During the reign of Kaiser Wilhelm I, Otto's father was a political activist who openly voiced his displeasure with the aggressive military policies of the Kaiser and Otto von Bismarck. As a result, he was removed from the government office and the city of his name.

Otto Suhl was born in Suhl, Germany, in the year 1878. Otto was ninety-four years old when he died in 1972. His grandfather was the Oberbürgermeister of Suhl, Germany—his mother's surname was Market.

Otto's parents resettled in the small farming village of Steinfeld, which is located about two hours' driving time directly north of Nurnberg. While serving in the U.S. Army, I was stationed in Germany. My grandfather had given me the names of some of his relatives and friends who he thought still lived in Steinfeld.

Undaunted by the fact I was unable make contact with any of my grandfather's relatives, I took a weekend leave during the summer of 1961 and hitchhiked to Steinfeld. I was fortunate to get a ride to the outskirts of Steinfeld.

With suitcase in hand, I walked into the village. It was a small remote farming community. About forty homes lined the one road that serviced Steinfeld. Each home had an assortment of hanging flower baskets or flower boxes. The colors were alive and greeted visitors with warmth.

I approached a woman who was hanging flower pots and asked if she knew the Suhl or Market family. I spoke broken German but enough to be understood.

She responded, "Yah, Yah." I explained I was Otto Suhl's grandson. She motioned for me to follow her. We walked past about ten houses, then up a dirt driveway leading to a two-story home sitting on a hill.

The lady hollered to one of the girls playing on the lawn. The girl went into her house and returned within minutes with her mother.

Addressing the mother, my escort pointed to me while speaking in German. Fortunately, one of the daughters had taken English lessons in high school. She explained I was Otto's grandson and I had come to Steinfeld to see his relatives.

The women hugged me and started asking me questions about my grandfather. My escort then handed me over to this wonderful family who was related to me via my great-grandmother whose last name prior to marriage was Market.

When I arrived, the women of the family were home, but the men were farming the fields. I stood with suitcase in hand and attempted to explain my being there.

Within a short time, a tractor came out of the field pulling a wagon. There were three men on the wagon and one driving the tractor. The tractor stopped about ten feet from where I was standing. The men jumped off and inquired about me. After they learned I was Otto's grandson, the oldest man pulled a jug off the wagon and began passing it around. After the four sweaty men drank from it, they offered it to me. I was tempted to wipe the top before taking a drink but quickly put the thought aside as a possible insult and placed the jug to my lips and drank some very strong homemade wine.

I stayed two nights with this wonderful, hospitable family. They showed me Steinfeld: the church where the Suhls and Markets attended, the graves of Otto's parents, and the home where his family had lived. I took pictures of the graves and his former home and gave them to my grandfather. My mother told me he rubbed the pictures so much he had put a hole in one.

When the Suhls arrived in Steinfeld, they built a new home. The house, one of the more attractive in the small village, had an extended front porch where numerous flower baskets displayed a rainbow of colors throughout the summer and fall. When I saw the house, it was still one of the nicest homes in Steinfeld.

Otto's parents loved wine. Shortly after their arrival in Steinfeld, Otto's father searched the hillside adjacent to the Main River looking for grapevines. When he located the proper vine, he purchased enough from the local farmers to provide a sufficient crop for his wine making—a talent Otto brought with him to America.

Otto's parents chose to have him leave Germany for America rather than enter the military. Consequently, at the age of twenty in the year 1897, he immigrated to America. Resolved their son would leave, Otto's parents secretly brought him to Rotterdam, South Holland, Netherlands.

His mother gave him sufficient money for his passage and subsistence for one year. She also bought him a new pair of shoes and told him, "Otto, do not wear these shoes until you leave the boat. If other passengers see you wearing an expensive pair of shoes, they will assume you have money, and you will become prey for robbers. Once you get to America, take some of the money and buy a new suit. You will need to wear the suit, Otto, when you seek employment."

After his parents left him to return to Steinfeld, Otto found lodging for the night at a hotel owned by the British Ship Owners Limited. Shortly thereafter, he walked to the ship's office.

The ship he would be sailing on was named the *British Queen*. It was subsequently sold to the United States government and renamed the U.S. *McPherson*. The ship was 410 feet long and 40 feet wide. It could carry 940 passengers: 80 first-class, 60 second-class, and 800 third-class.

He knew most of the ships in harbor would leave early the next morning. Instead of purchasing a ticket, Otto inquired at the main office of the British Ship Owners Limited with regards to employment. The clerk told him to return in about an hour and he could speak with the captain.

Exactly one hour later, Otto returned and met with the captain who told him, "I will hire you but not for wages. You must work for your passage and meals. You will be part of the crew. You will be required to do what we ask of you. This can sometimes be hard work. You look like a strong lad. Do you think you can handle it?

If for any reason you don't feel like working, someone else will be required to do your work, so they will get your food serving for that day."

Chapter Seven

A Rough Voyage

Roll on thou deep and dark blue ocean-roll!
Ten Thousand fleets sweep over thee in vain;
Man marks the earth with ruin—his control
Stops with the shore.

—Lord Byron, *Childe Harold's Pilgrimage*

When he reported to the ship the morning of departure, he was greeted by the first mate who told Otto he was responsible for helping in the kitchen and cleaning any mess the passengers made. Otto never envisioned "mess" to mean vomit. The voyage lasted just short of two weeks. It was the worst time Otto had ever experienced.

After the first three days at sea, the water began to get rough, and the boat bobbed and bucked as the big waves showed little intimidation of the huge black sailing ship that carried Otto and the other 939 passengers plus the crew. The majority of the passengers were jammed into steerage bunks.

The bunks were made of wood. Each bunk was about three feet wide by five and a half feet long. Resting on each bunk was a pillow, blanket, and sheet. Third-class passengers were in the basement of the ship—no ocean view.

Their food was given in rations, and disease was a frequent visitor. In addition to small-scale outbreaks of typhus and smallpox, there was also a major cholera problem. Some of the passengers occasionally walked onto deck where they hung over the rail barfing their guts out while others were not as considerate and spread their meals across the deck, in the nearest corner, or under their steerage bunks.

Some passengers were sick because of the constant movement of the boat, but others fell victim to the ship's food or lack thereof.

After six weeks of cleaning puke, Otto smelled like a fish cannery. His mother told him to make as many friends as possible on the voyage to America because they will be the only friends he will have when he got there. Instead of taking her advice and booking passage, he wanted to save the money. Otto would undress and remove his money belt, then dry himself, and return the money belt to his waist. His routine eventually took its toll. Otto caught a cold and had a terrible cough.

Give me your tired, your poor
Your huddles masses yearning
Yearning to breathe free.

After almost two weeks cleaning vomit from passengers, Otto stood at the ship's rail along with hundreds of other passengers. They were mesmerized by the coastline of the United States and the flickering light from the torch held high by Ms. Liberty. When the boat passed Ellis Island, it appeared as a collection of many buildings.

The captain's voice came began shouting to the passengers via a large amplifier he held to his mouth, "You must leave the ship at this Hudson River Pier. From here, you will be ferried to Ellis Island. I am told you will be processed through the new facility, Ellis Island. Before entering the United States, you must be approved for citizenship. Once you are approved, you will be permitted to leave. If for any reason, you are not approved for citizenship, this boat will be returning to the Netherlands in two days, and your fee will be half of what you paid coming over."

The mention of possible denial for citizenship caused a considerable amount of confusion among the passengers. About 80 percent of immigrants coming to Ellis Island were passed by both medical and immigration inspectors. A large number of people were held for long and short periods. Many women and children were detained until money arrived from a relative to prove they had support.

Unfortunately for the passengers, the captain ignored their pleas and questions for additional information and continued, "Be sure to keep your children with you. There are many people on Ellis Island, and they could get lost or fall into the ocean. There is considerable amount of construction taking place. Be careful where you walk. Now, I wish you all a happy new life and a safe journey wherever you are going. May God go with you."

While the captain was addressing the passengers, Otto sneaked into the captain's room and stole a bar of soap. Despite his lingering cold and loud cough, he then went to the men's room where he thoroughly cleansed himself and put on new clothes. Otto took the clothes he had been wearing for the whole voyage (same shirt, pants, socks, shoes, and the money belt) and threw them in the garbage area. Then he walked barefoot to his sleeping area and found his socks and the pair of shoes his mother had bought him.

When this clean, well-dressed tall strapping young man was noticed by the crew, they realized he had traveled incognito without anyone realizing he probably had a considerable amount of money with him.

Upon leaving, Otto turned to the men who had been ordering him to clean vomit every day for two weeks and said, "I will say a prayer for this boat to sink on your return to Deutschland. Guten Tag."

Wearing an identity tag, Otto was in a single file and directed into a seating area, which was divided by iron railways that made the huge hall resemble a maze of open gangways.

When Otto stood before two uniformed doctors employed by the U.S. Public Health Service, he coughed continuously. The two doctors spoke to each other and then shook their heads at Otto, indicating he could not enter Ellis Island. The captain of the ship was standing off to the side watching as each passenger passed the doctors.

When the captain realized Otto was being taken aside for return to Germany, he pushed his body through the line to the doctors and asked, "What is the problem with this young man? Why are you questioning his entry to the island?"

One of the doctors replied, "He is very sick. His cough sounds like the plague. We cannot endanger everyone else."

"Nonsense!" replied the captain. "He is very strong and a good worker. Besides, look at his clothes—he comes from an important family. He got sick on the boat coming over. He just has a cold. Keep him in one of your hospital buildings, and he will be better soon."

After a few words, the doctors decided to examine Otto's eyes. The doctor took a buttonhook and lifted his eyelids looking for trachoma. A chalk letter was marked on his arm, and he was taken to a building that was under construction and would eventually become the infirmary.

The decision to allow Otto to remain was made based upon the captain's remarks and the possibility Otto might have influential friends.

A United States emigration employee was asked to accompany Otto to the makeshift infirmary. In the building, a nurse and an assistant welcomed Otto. After being informed as to Otto's condition, they showed him to a room and asked if he would partially undress for them to examine him.

Otto was concerned about the safety of his money. In broken English, he asked the nurse and her assistant who were speaking together where he could safely keep his money. He had with him about $100 in German marks.

If he had arrived a few years earlier, Otto would have been free game for the money exchangers, tavern owners, merchants, and everyone else attempting to entice the naive immigrants to part with their money.

The nurse told him, "I will have one of the assistants give you a receipt for your money; then he will put it in the security bank on the island. You will eventually need to exchange your money for American currency. When we determine if you are able to become a citizen, we will take you to the currency exchange area."

For the next four days, Otto slept in a bunk bed with clean sheets and without any motors humming. It was wonderful but unsettling. Once his appearance improved and his cough was nonexistent, Otto was permitted to take his German marks to the bursar's office where, accompanied by an immigration official, he exchanged his money for U.S. currency.

With suitcase in hand, he was accompanied to the waiting ferry, which took him to the Island of Manhattan. He walked from the dock to Grand Central Terminal where he boarded a train to Rochester, New York.

Otto Suhl prepared to journey to a young city founded by Nathaniel Rochester in 1812. Compared to the cities of Europe, which dated back four and five centuries, Rochester was a child. The Genesee River, the Barge Canal, and abundance of water power were helping to make Rochester, New York, a major manufacturing city.

When he arrived in Rochester, Otto located the geographical area that had the highest concentration of German immigrants: Germantown. Here he found temporary living quarters.

He soon learned construction jobs on the Barge Canal were no longer available until the spring of the following year. Consequently, Otto had to find some type of employment until the Barge Canal work became available.

Chapter Eight

THE IRISH

Everyone is a prisoner to his own experiences.
No one can eliminate prejudices—just recognize them.

—Edward R. Murrow

After two days of searching for work, Otto finally found a job with a road building company. He was hired on the spot and asked to report to work within a few hours.

Along with another man, Otto was responsible for lifting large bundles of red bricks from the back of a horse-drawn wagon and placing them on the dirt road. The bricks were then tapped into place in the dirt by four other men. At the end of each day, the men were expected to have completed at least 150 feet of road.

After a week of this work, Otto was sore and feeling pain throughout his whole body. He had no social life; when he returned to his room after work, he was exhausted. Each night, after he ate his dinner, he went to sleep until another day. He missed his mother, father, and his Germany.

During his fourth week of employment, Otto was lifting a bundle of bricks along with his companion, a young Italian. When they grabbed onto the bundle and began lifting, the horse, attached to the front of the wagon, jerked and caused the bundle of bricks to shift, pinning Otto's hand between the bricks and the oak sideboards of the wagon.

The foreman was a large stocky Irishman who continuously smoked cigars and indiscriminately puffed his smoke in the faces of his employees. Otto disliked him and did not keep his feelings secret.

The four men who were pounding the bricks into the ground hurriedly grabbed the bundle and slid it away from Otto's hand. When the hand was freed, blood poured profusely over the bricks and onto the ground. Otto's little finger had been almost ripped off.

His Italian helper quickly took the scarf from his sweaty neck and fashioned a tourniquet to stop the bleeding. After the bleeding had stopped and Otto began to regain his composure, the foreman walked to the gathered men, looked at Otto's hand, and then barked at the men, "I want everyone back to work immediately. You are not getting paid for standing around. We have a quota to meet, and we must keep working."

Then he turned to Otto and said, "I suggest you go to the hospital and have your finger taken care of, but make sure you return to work tomorrow morning. Otherwise, I will replace you with another. Here is your pay for what you worked today."

With his good hand, Otto took the money. He then looked at the mangled hand. It was already beginning to swell. The small finger was hanging via skin and cartilage. The bones had been severed. He looked at the Irish foreman with fury and hate. Then, he turned and began walking two miles to the nearest hospital.

At the hospital, the medical staff gave him a sedative and then amputated his finger. He was crippled before his twenty-first birthday; he knew his dreams of working on the canal were history. If there was a beginning to Otto's hate for the Irish, it was probably this incident.

Chapter Nine

MANDELS COME TO AMERICA

I am a Jew. Hath not a Jew eyes?
Hath not a Jew hands, organs, dimensions, senses, affections, passions?

—William Shakespeare, *The Merchant of Venice*

Rose Mandel, her sister, and three brothers immigrated to the United States from Alsace-Lorraine, Germany. Alsace-Lorraine is located on the French-German border and covers approximately twelve thousand square miles.

Most of the inhabitants of Alsace-Lorraine are bilingual and were occasionally forced to shift their loyalty from France to Germany or Germany to France depending on the outcome of a war. Sometimes there was religious tolerance and sometimes not.

Although records have not been located to confirm the suspicion, from my conversations with my mother and grandmother, I suspect my grandmother was born into a Jewish family. The Mandels could have been Jews who converted to Christianity in the late 1700s.

Unlike Otto, the Mandel children came to the United States via a steamboat during the summer months and were processed through Castle Garden, the predecessor of Ellis Island.

Rose Mandel, her sister Barbara, and three brothers—Gustave, John, and Lawrence—arrived in the United States in 1883, three years before Otto. Their boat trip, as passengers, was a considerably better experience than Otto's.

At this time, the passenger business to America was becoming very profitable. Intense competition developed, and fare wars became common. Recognizing this, Mr. Mandel was able to book inexpensive passage for his sons and two daughters. The parents did not accompany them at this time but hoped to save enough money to join them later. It never happened.

Ships from Le Havre, France, often returned from the United States with cotton from New Orleans. Many German families took a ship from Le Havre to New Orleans and then traveled the Mississippi a bit farther to St. Louis or Cincinnati—two cities with strong German culture.

Rose, who completed eight years of schooling, spoke French as well as German. There was a necessity to know both languages because of where they lived. In addition, they each had a working knowledge of English from school. Those who chose travel on a French ship and could not speak or understand French were often exposed to insults, mistreatment, and a difficult voyage.

Chapter Ten

CASTLE GARDEN

*A nation like a tree does not thrive well
Till it is en-grafted with a foreign stock.*

—Ralph Waldo Emerson

"For thirty-five years," according to author Barbara Benton, "Castle Garden operated as the receiving station in New York whereby, at the end of the nineteenth century, 75 percent of all immigrants to the United States landed."

Rose Mandel's parents had saved their money in preparation for their children's voyage to America. Once they arrived in America, arrangements had been made for the children to stay with relatives. After most immigrants paid their fares to America, they were left hoping for a miracle because they were immobilized by their poverty. Consequently, New York City became a depository for many immigrants who could go no farther. In 1824, the State of New York passed a measure requiring captains to report the names of their passengers to the mayor and post a two-year $300 bond for each to ensure they would not become wards of the state.

Like Otto, Rose and her sister and brothers relocated in an area heavily populated with people of German descent. Rose and her siblings were divided between four different families (relatives) all living in the Rochester area. They planned to stay with the families until their parents arrived from Germany. Once it became apparent the Mandels could not save enough for the trip, Rose and her siblings were encouraged to find suitable partners for marriage.

Four years after Otto arrived, he and Rose met at a German club in Rochester. He was twenty-three, and she was twenty-five. Two years later, they married in a Catholic ceremony.

Otto had been hired by George Eastman who began his Rochester-based photographic plate-making business in 1880. Otto began as a pan cleaner and then moved to machinist and then plate making. During his forty-five years with Eastman Kodak, Otto lost two fingers and accumulated millions of dollars in Eastman Kodak stock.

A decade after their marriage, Otto and his wife, Rose, purchased a piece of farmland on Myrtle Street in Rochester, New York. It was a small parcel of land but big enough for a two-story home, a garden, and chicken coop. Otto and his two sons Albert and Raymond built the home. They constructed the foundation, framed the house, and installed the electrical and plumbing—they did it all. It was the first home in the City of Rochester to have a permit for a chicken coop.

Otto was afraid of electricity and did not want to put any electrical wiring in the house when it was being built. Unknown to him, while he was sleeping, his two teenage sons Albert and Raymond burned holes in the rafters at night to install electrical wires.

When the house was completed, it was all wired without Otto knowing. When the timing was right, the boys energized the house, much to everyone's surprise and happiness. Eventually, his neighborhood became populated with new families moving in from Germany, Italy, and Ireland.

Otto and Rose Suhl's Children

Raymond Suhl

Albert Suhl and nephew Raymie

Raymond Suhl married Elsie. He and his wife were godparents to my brother Raymond. Before death, Raymond Suhl suffered a stroke which left him disabled. They had one son: Raymie. Raymie graduated from Eastman School of Music. He married a Hawaiian who also graduated from Eastman School of Music. They live in Hawaii. After Otto died, Raymond and his wife moved to Hawaii to be with their son and daughter-in-law.

Albert Suhl finished high school. He left Rochester to take an executive position in New York City with Federal Express. He was married to Ceil. They lived in a brownstone in the Bronx. After his wife and Otto died, he also moved to Hawaii.

Rose Pauline Suhl

Rose Pauline Suhl married Bernard Harold Barend. She completed grammar school, but her father would not allow her to continue beyond grammar school.

She found employment at a book bindery. She was an excellent tennis player in her younger years. She never mentioned her accomplishments—we learned about them from her brother Albert and from her mother.

Rose suffered from epilepsy at an early age. It continued through adulthood. Medical examinations determined it was caused by head trauma. Her father, Otto, would hit her on the head because he hated her red hair.

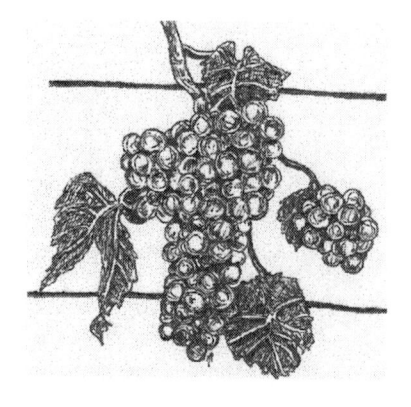

The Grapes of Wrath

Like his father and grandfather, Otto enjoyed making his own wine. Consequently, he needed an abundant supply of grapes.

He decided to build a chain-link fence on his property line. The plan was to have the grapevines grow on the fence. He spent hours digging holes, mixing concrete, and erecting the metal fence. Once the fence was in place, he planted the vines, which he collected from the Finger Lakes area.

After four years, the vines were producing an abundance of Concord grapes.

Unfortunately, Otto never planned on his neighbor's children acquiring a taste for grapes. Each time he would see the children picking his grapes, he would scream at them, "Get out of there, you little bastards! Don't your parents teach you not to steal? Leave my grapes alone, or I will have you put in jail."

The neighbors eventually learned Otto's schedule. Every Sunday morning at 8:30 a.m., Otto, Rose, and their children would get into their black Model T and travel five blocks to St. Peter and Paul's Church. This was the only day Otto would drive his Model T.

The Suhls would be gone for an hour, and the neighbors knew it was grape-picking time. Knowing how much Otto hated the spitting of grape skins onto his property, the children peppered his driveway and lawn for almost the whole time he was in church.

Each Sunday, when the Suhls returned from church, the whole neighborhood would have their quiet pierced by a symphony of backfires complimented by a series of *ugahsssss, ugahsssss*, coming from the Model T. The horn-blowing was to make people aware he was coming.

The six children who lived in the two-family home adjacent to Otto and Rose would gather at the windows and watch the Model T move slowly along the two narrow strips of concrete, which constituted the Suhls' driveway.

After two years of Otto's relentless screaming and threats to shoot the grape poachers, he hired an attorney. The attorney advised him to move the fence far enough inside his property so the neighbors would be trespassing if they took his grapes.

Unlike his father, who shared the cuttings and grapes with his neighbors, Otto refused to give anyone anything. He took nothing from anyone, and he expected the same in return.

When he told Rose of his intent to move the fence, she said, "Why are you doing this, Otto? Let them have the grapes. If you didn't holler and scream, they will probably leave you alone. How many grapes can you eat? What you don't take, the birds will only eat. Let them have the grapes and save yourself the work and expense of moving the fence."

Otto could not understand his wife. She was always willing to find good in people even when there wasn't any.

He told her, "They never once asked me if they could have the grapes. The grapes are mine, not theirs. I planted them. Why must I give to someone who steals from me? I would sooner move the fence."

The following spring, the fence was moved, and Otto's problem with the neighbors dissolved.

Unfortunately for Otto, the moving of the fence and disturbance of the vines caused a loss of about 75 percent of his grape crop the next year.

Rose and Otto Suhl—their fiftieth wedding anniversary.

Rose Suhl is sitting with her two brothers.

Two Roses and their dog.

Chapter Eleven

B. H. Barend

Schoolmasters and parents exist to be grown out of.

—John Wolfenden, *Sunday Times London*

Despite being an excellent student and the urging of his teacher to remain in school, Bernard Harold Barend left school when he was fourteen years old.

In the early 1900s, only the rich could afford to educate their children beyond grammar school.

At age fourteen, Bernard was told to get a job and contribute to his family. He was one of seven children: three brothers—John, William, and Leo—and three sisters (Maud, Marie, and Genevieve).

During his teen years, Bernard learned the mason trade from his father. However, he never found satisfaction in patching sidewalks, building walls, or repairing chimneys.

Bernard's father often took him and his brother Bill with him when estimating a job. After listening to the prospective customer, Henry Barend and his sons would each estimate the job independent of the other. Whichever son's estimate was closest to his, that son would be assigned the easiest task on that particular job. The fact that Henry Barend's estimates could have been wrong was never questioned.

Many of the buildings built by Henry Barend still exist with grandeur in the Rochester area. After his daughter Maud died in her teens, he constructed a masonry angel for a headstone. Decades later, he was informed by the cemetery that the headstone needed repair. He offered to do it for free. The cemetery personnel informed him only they could make the repairs; Henry Barend told them to go to hell.

B. H. stood about five feet seven inches. His complexion was always darker than his peers. He had sharp features, dark brown hair, and wore glasses. According to Rose, he was very handsome as a young man. His worst character flaw, like his father, was his love of gambling. Unlike his father, he never had the resources to become a big loser.

After only a few years, B. H. decided against the brick-and-mortar trade. Henry Barend was shocked when he learned his son would no longer be his employee. The uncertainty of work and not knowing if he would be outside in the cold or dripping wet in the heat contributed to his decision.

In addition, his hands would always crack when the weather turned cold, and they would stay that way until spring. At both corners of his thumbnails, the skin would split apart, leaving a very sore crevice. When mixing the cement, his fingers would feel like someone was poking them with a needle, and the needle kept digging through deeper and deeper. When working with his father, he suffered excruciating pain every winter.

To alleviate his pain, once a week, his mother would take a trip to a wooded area about three miles from the Barend home. There she would search for a specific pine tree. It was a practice she had learned from her parents. When the proper tree was found, she would remove from her apron a small knife. With the knife she would strip bark and needles from the tree. Upon her return home, she would take a stone and pulverize the bark and needles.

The smashed pieces were then mixed with a small amount of water, which formed a pasty substance.

The paste was applied to B. H.'s hands each evening during the winter months—the remedy worked. His hands would be almost painless for a short time. When he resumed the masonry work, the skin would reopen, and the healing process would have to be repeated.

Chapter Twelve

A Marriage Disavowed

Find what revenge of old
Tese angry sires did find
Against their children that rebelled
And showed themselves unkind.

—William Shakespeare, *The Tragedy of Romeo and Juliet*

After two years of covering pipes with asbestos at Eastman Kodak Company and saving his money, B. H. asked Rose Pauline's parents if he could marry her. Rose's mother had no objection and gave them both her blessing.

But when Rose's father, Otto, was told of the request for his daughter, he became enraged. He cursed at B. H. and chased him around the dining room table. Otto grabbed an oak dining room chair and hurled it at B. H., striking him across his shoulder and back.

While B. H. was attempting to raise himself from the floor, Otto grabbed him around the neck with both hands, trying to choke him. B. H. flung himself at Otto in an attempt to escape.

Rose's mother screamed at Otto to leave him alone, "Otto! Otto! Are you crazy? Stop it! Stop it!" Then she hollered at her two sons to help. They were standing beside their mother, watching in shock.

Uncharacteristic of herself, Rose's mother hollered at Otto. She placed her face within inches of his—almost nose to nose. Here was this small, five-feet-four-inch frail courageous lady who never raised her voice, ready to combat a man who loomed over her in size at six feet two inches and 225-plus pounds.

She pushed him away from B. H. Rose's two brothers remained frozen with fear as they watched their mother rebuke Otto. B. H. quickly found his way to the door.

Otto screamed after him as he left the house, "No stinking lousy son of a gambler is going to marry my daughter and ruin her life. Don't ever come back here! I will shoot you if you ever step on my property again!"

Otto told Rose she could not marry him or ever see him again. If she disobeyed, he would disown her, and she would never receive any financial help from him or ever be welcome in his home again. She left home that evening and never saw her father again for almost fifty years—when her mother died.

In a Catholic wedding ceremony at St. Peter's and Paul's Church in Rochester, New York, Rose Pauline was given to Bernard Harold by her two brothers, Albert and Raymond. Her mother attended the wedding, but her father did not.

While employed at Eastman Kodak, B. H. married Rose.

Their first child, Norman, had died shortly after birth. A year later, their second child, Alberta, was born.

Bernard Harold Barend in his twenties.

Rose and B. H. just prior to their wedding.

Chapter Thirteen

DWI LIFT-TRUCK OPERATOR

There's been an accident, they said
Your servant's cut in half; he's dead.
Indeed said Mr. Jones, please,
Send me the half that's got my keys.

—*Ruthless Rhymes for Heartless Homes*

Shortly after their marriage, B. H. took a job at Bausch & Lomb Optical Company in Rochester, New York, covering large heating pipes with asbestos. Edward and William Bausch, two sons of John Jacob Bausch, a founder of the company, and his grandnephew, Carl, were responsible for managing Bausch & Lomb when B. H. began and ended his employment with the company.

Working with asbestos was a dirty job that required some knowledge of masonry or plastering. Fibers of nonspinning asbestos were mixed with a binding material and formed into sheets, which were formed around the huge heating pipes that snaked throughout the Bausch & Lomb factory. Although doctors in the 1920s knew that asbestos particles damaged the lungs of many of the people who worked with it, nothing was done to stop corporations from using the material.

For seven years, B. H. worked about fifty hours a week shaping asbestos around huge heating and ventilation pipes. The work was dangerous, unhealthy, and filthy; but the money was good, and the possibilities for advancement were promising.

One morning during the Christmas season, a drunken lift-truck operator turned a corner in the factory too fast and lost control of his machine. B. H. was working on a six-foot ladder, applying the asbestos to a three-foot-diameter heating pipe.

The truck operator never saw B. H., who was standing two rungs up on the ladder. The truck crashed into the ladder and slammed B. H. against a concrete wall. He had the distinction of being the only person to have been struck by a DWI lift-truck operator.

The foreman called two men to carry B. H. to a small room, which functioned as the company medical room, coffee-break room, and storage room. The company doctor was immediately called to examine B. H. In those days, you didn't stay sick or on coffee break very long—and when you did, management assured you would not be too comfortable. After being examined, the doctor decided to send B. H. home for the remainder of the day.

Upon leaving, his foreman reminded him to make every effort to return to work the following day. The next morning, the pain shot across his whole back. Tears would form in his eyes when he tried to walk. B. H.'s father Henry drove him in their old Lincoln to the Strong Memorial Hospital.

B.H.'s wife, Rose, never drove an automobile because of her epilepsy. She occasionally had grand mal seizures.

A few days after the accident, when it became obvious B. H. was seriously injured, Bausch & Lomb provided a severance package for the lift-truck operator, and he disappeared.

Months later, a lawyer for Bausch & Lomb argued at B. H.'s workman's compensation hearing that the accident was minor and the steel brace the doctors at Strong Memorial asked him to wear was part of a charade to cheat Bausch & Lomb out of workman's compensation money. B. H. would wear the steel back brace for the rest of his life.

The Bausch & Lomb attorney claimed B. H. had walked in front of the operator. The fault of the accident was with B. H., according to Bausch & Lomb, and not the lift-truck operator. The Bausch & Lomb attorney argued B. H. was capable of returning to work immediately based upon information provided to Bausch & Lomb by their company physician. No mention was ever made at the hearing with regards to the medical reports from Strong Memorial Hospital.

When the judge requested the driver of the lift truck to testify, he was informed by the Bausch & Lomb attorney that the driver had quit work and the company could not locate him. The hearing judge ruled B. H.'s condition did not prevent him from returning to work. Consequently, he would not be entitled to workman's compensation. Bausch & Lomb's decision to fight B. H.'s compensation claim resulted in a mortgage foreclosure on a home they had just purchased.

After the bank foreclosed, B. H. and Rose relocated to an apartment on Masseth Street in the German section of Rochester. In 1941, at the age of forty-three, B. H. had three children, lost his job at B&L, lost his home, and was crippled.

Bernard Harold Barend in his forties.

Barend family portrait.

Harold (a bit unkempt) Ray (the perfect angel).

Bedtime for Harold and Ray.

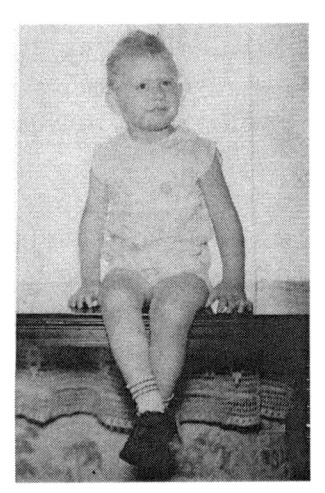

Angelic pose.

What preceded were stories told to me by my parents and grandparents. At the age of four, this is where my memories began.

Chapter Fourteen

THE EARLY YEARS

*Children are like flowers to share
To see them blossom we must
Give them love and care
Or the weeds will be there*

—H. J. Barend

By the time I reached my fourth birthday, my parents, Bernard Harold and Rose Pauline; my brother Raymond; sister Alberta; and I relocated to a new address.

Prior to apartment living on Masseth Street, my parents had owned a home in a middle-class residential section of Rochester, New York. It was always referred to as "the other house." I was too young to remember, but the stories made it sound like a wonderful place.

Shortly after my fifteenth birthday, I saw the house for the first time; my dad pointed to it as we quickly drove past—he never slowed. It was an Ozzie and Harriet three-bedroom house in a neat, quiet neighborhood. My parents never spoke of the house—perhaps it was a bittersweet memory—like something wonderful you possess for a very short time. I am sure they felt the magic of that moment. Unfortunately, they were never able to recapture the dream. After my parents lost their home in

1941, we moved to a large apartment that housed two families in an area of Rochester called Germantown. As the name indicated, mostly German families lived in the ten-block area.

There were many cities like Rochester that encompassed ethnic strongholds. It was safer and easier to live with people you felt you had something in common with.

Within the City of Rochester were small communities of Italians, Germans, Irish, and Poles. All had their geographical areas. They even retained their traditions, patron saints, and native languages. The only vehicles of integration were the churches and schools—which very often only serviced two or three different nationalities.

Shortly after moving to a rental (double) in Germantown, my father was hired as an Electrolux salesman. Electrolux salesmen had to be very good to convince people to pay five times more for their product. My dad worked from 8:00 a.m. until 8:00 p.m. Times were bad, money was scarce, and people were buying very few Electrolux cleaners.

During this period, prejudices were as free as water. There were no organizations such as the National Association for the Advancement of Italians, Germans, Poles, or Jews. This could be why fusion has taken place with most people from diverse backgrounds. There was no busing and no quota system but plenty of discrimination.

When the Jewish rag peddlers came through the streets of Germantown guiding their horse-drawn wagons and crying out, "Rags, rags, I will buy your old rags," the neighborhood children would run alongside the wagon and holler, "Jew! Jew! We are going to get the screw."

The first few times I was with the group, I knew something was wrong because the man would just lower his head and keep moving along with his horse and wagon. The kids who were doing the taunting would holler the words and then run away. After I heard them holler their litany a few times, I was confident my courage was sufficient so I could verbally participate.

Following my first attempt, I had a strange feeling. I knew I did something wrong, but I couldn't understand my feelings. Why did it feel so wrong to me when the other children were having so much fun? I asked my mother what the words meant. She addressed the question without specifically answering it.

She explained, "It would be like someone calling me a Nazi." Even a five-year-old living in 1943 knew being a Nazi was not a compliment.

She told me, "The Jews were being persecuted by the Germans in Germany, Poland, Austria, Norway, and France. They are being forced to live in ghettos and sent to concentration camps just because they are Jews. Would you want the same thing to happen to you just because you are a German or a Catholic? They don't need the same thing happening to them in America." I never forgot this short speech about respecting another person's beliefs.

In September, my mother walked the two miles from our house to Holy Family School with my brother, Ray, and my sister, Alberta, for their first day of school at Holy Family. The school was a combination parish church and school. The whole complex consisted of a red brick church and a parking area adjacent to the church, which also served as a playground for the red brick school. My mother was a fervent believer that all children should have a religious education and the discipline it brings.

I was five years old, and I should have been walking to school with my brother and sister and entering kindergarten. But my mother, at the encouragement of the school principal, kept me home until I was six. She was concerned my stuttering would encourage abuse from the other children. To some extent, she was right—but to a much larger extent, she was wrong.

My stuttering had "almost" disappeared by the time my sixth birthday arrived. There was still enough stutter left to provoke criticism from my first—and second-grade classmates. One of the students prided himself on finishing my sentences or fishing for the missing word whenever I was having difficulty. I wanted to hit him so hard but knew he was fatter than me and probably would have whipped me.

In the second grade, another boy, Tommy O'Hara, would make an announcement regarding me each time I would have to read aloud in class.

My reading skills were excellent, but my confidence was terrible. I would practice the chapters over and over. I was always three chapters ahead of the class just in case the teacher jumped a chapter or two. I knew the words inside and outside, backward and forward—for hours I practiced reading aloud. No stutter. Everything was perfect until it came my turn to read aloud in class; my sweat glands would work overtime.

Each time a student was asked to read, they would stand beside their desk and read about three paragraphs. The girls always seemed to read the best; they had a perfect knack at knowing what to emphasize, where to stop, where to pause, and how to smile at the nuns.

The teachers at Holy Family were all nuns. They would randomly select students to read aloud. At least three times a week, I would be called on—this was the teacher's idea of doing me a favor. I hated this part of the day. I worried before and during class that my name would be called, and Tommy O'Hara would shout, "Harold is having a problem."

In addition to harassing me in school, Tommy was my nemesis after school. He and his brother would await my arrival about two blocks from school. Like clockwork, three times a week, they would hide in the bushes of one of the homes I would walk past. When I would approach the area they normally attacked from, I would run as fast as possible. After my first bloody nose, they only caught me once. They had learned at an early age to hate everyone who was German.

My problems ended after I explained to my brother Ray about Tommy O'Hara. Initially, I felt bad involving him because my dad taught each of us to fight our own battles. Ray usually left school about fifteen minutes after me, except for this one day in March 1946. Ray walked about a hundred yards behind me and told me not to look back. If Tommy chased me, Ray told me to stop and put my hands up like I was going to fight. He promised he would be there to protect me, and he was.

Just as Tommy was about to grind me into a pulp, Ray grabbed his arm from behind and proceeded to toss him into a snow bank. I smacked tough Tommy's brother a couple of times, and he ran for home, crying. After pushing Tommy's face in the snow three or four times, Ray told him, "If you ever chase or hurt my brother again, you'll get worse."

For about a week after that incident, I continued to accelerate my pace when I approached the houses where Tommy and his brother launched their attacks. No one chased me.

As the weeks proceeded, my fear lessened. I could now walk home with a secure feeling. I never had another problem.

I can't remember which of us, Tommy O'Hara or I, was the first to acknowledge the other with a nod in the school hallway. We never really became good friends, but we were no longer at war.

Learning to read and write was easy. Doing my homework was the most difficult part of school. After dinner, each of the Barend children had a cleanup detail—then homework.

During the homework phase, my mother patrolled the kitchen and living room with a large wooden stick. She ensured there would be no disturbances, and everyone would be prepared for the next day.

I was assigned the kitchen table as my homework station because no one else wanted it. I was normally the last one finished when red cabbage or Brussels sprouts were served—which was about four times a week. Each evening, I was remanded there until I finished my food, spelled every word perfectly, completed the math, or claimed to understand various parts of Catholicism—which to this day, I still do not.

If an episode of *The Lone Ranger* was being listened to by my brother or *Gang Busters* by my dad, my concentration level was nil. I would be listening to the radio, and while my mother was asking me questions, my mind was everywhere except on my homework.

I would think about the times I went with my brother and Sue Guetner to the railroad yards where we collected old cigarette butts. Then, we climbed into the center hole of stacked railroad ties and smoked them. The ties were placed in a square, which gave us a secret hiding place where we could experiment with the used cigarette butts. When the stick made a loud snap on the table or I felt a sharp pain on my hand or arm, I knew my focus had shifted in the wrong direction.

Although my parents never visited Rose and Otto Suhl (my mother's parents), Alberta, Ray, and I were encouraged to visit our grandparents. My grandmother wanted to see us either together or individually—my grandfather just tolerated or ignored us. I enjoyed walking the two miles from Masseth to Myrtle Street to visit my grandparents, listen to them speak in German, and have lunch or dinner with them.

My grandfather's table manners were from the Flintstones. During one meal, he shoved a whole baked potato into his mouth. It was too hot. I watched in amazement as the potato shot from his mouth across the table. I started to laugh, but my grandmother immediately told me to stop, and my grandfather Otto swore at me in German.

If I got lucky and happened to arrive when my grandmother was baking, I would get to taste fresh bread, plum küchen, or an apple pie. My grandparents' house always had the fresh smell of a bakery.

Occasionally, I spent the evening with my grandparents. After dinner, I helped clean the dishes while my grandmother prepared dessert and Otto located the cards, pad, and pencil for a game of pinochle. After observing many evenings, I was eventually invited to become a participant in three-handed pinochle.

Thirty-seven Stitches

During one of my visits to my grandparents when I was six years old, Otto asked if I would walk about three blocks to the bakery and get him a loaf of pumpernickel bread. He gave me a 50¢ piece and said, "Be sure to tell them you want the loaf of bread for Otto."

I began walking on the sidewalk, which continued up to a busy intersection. At the side of the road, a milk truck was preparing to leave the curb. I ran to the truck and jumped on the back platform. I rode the truck to the intersection where the bakery was located and then leaped off. When I jumped, a car following the truck never saw me. The car hit my body and tossed me to the side of the road.

Within minutes a huge crowd gathered, and an ambulance arrived. Blood covered my clothes and the road. My head had been split, but I was still conscious. The doctor asked where I lived. I screamed that I did not want to go to the hospital. I eventually told him my grandparents' address.

While they drove me in the ambulance to my grandparents, I was still screaming, "Don't take me to the hospital! I don't want to go to the hospital! Please don't take me to the hospital!"

On my grandmother's living-room sofa, the physician and nurse put thirty-seven stitches into my head. The nurse told my grandfather, "When we arrived, your grandson was still clutching the 50¢ piece he had been given to purchase the bread."

Otto was pleased that I still had his money.

Ray standing at attention and Harold with his head in the clouds.

Eviction

Toward the middle of our third year in the Germantown apartment, my parents were asked to leave. My dad couldn't earn enough money to feed his family, pay rent, and keep the lights on. He was in and out of hospitals because of his back pain.

My sister recalls coming home from school and seeing all our furniture on the sidewalk in front of the two-family we lived in. We were evicted, and there was no mercy for the poor.

My mother, not wanting to separate the family, begged my father to try anything. "Keep the family together," my mother would say over and over again.

After we left the apartment, we stayed with my uncle Henry and aunt Anna who were distant relatives, but out of respect, we called them "Aunt" and "Uncle."

After a few days with the Browns, we moved to Bea Fisher's home. Bea was my mother's psychic friend. Before my mother got married, she worked about a year with Bea at a book bindery in Rochester. We stayed with Bea for about a week. It was here, via a deck of strange-looking cards, that I was told how my life would be. Fortunately, or unfortunately, most of her predictions have come true.

At age ten, after I took my brother's new Schwinn bike for a ride without his permission, my mother was quick to remind me about one of Bea's early predictions.

The bike was going top speed when I approached an intersection. As I went around the corner, I came face-to-face with a car. I don't remember much, except that it happened so fast.

I flew about eight feet into the air. The bike was destroyed, and I was tossed over a hedgerow. I landed on a lawn and incurred a broken leg and arm, minor bruises, and the wrath of my brother.

Bea had predicted, before I was a teenager, that I would have an accident on a bicycle that did not belong to me.

At eight years old, Harold makes his first communion at Holy Family. Alongside is dapper Ray. Ray's good-looking suit will eventually be handed down to Harold. This was the last function at the Masseth Street apartment before our eviction.

Chapter Fifteen

A Family Without a Home

It is a most miserable thing to feel ashamed of home.

—Charles Dickens, *Great Expectations*

While the Barend family was exhausting its stay with Bea Fisher, my dad was fruitlessly attempting to provide a life preserver. In a last desperate attempt to keep the family together, he visited David Cassidy, a friend and employee of the Monroe County Welfare Department.

Mr. Cassidy told my dad, "I do not have anything at this moment where you could live safely as a family. We do have a home that has been bequeathed to the Welfare Department. We have been informed by the family of the deceased that she asked the home be deeded to the Monroe County Welfare Department with the specific provision to provide shelter for a family in need. If it becomes available, I'll let you know."

My dad questioned Mr. Cassidy as to how long it would take, but he was not given any positive assurance or timetable. Mr. Cassidy told him, "If you can place your children with relatives, I can arrange a room for you and your wife at a hotel in downtown Rochester. The county has an arrangement with the hotel owner for a few rooms at discounted price. It is not in the best section of the city, but if you can live there for a few months, maybe this house will become available."

That afternoon when I returned from Holy Family School, my mother and dad, Ray, and Alberta had everything packed. We were moving again. It would be the third move in less than three months.

When my dad returned from meeting with Mr. Cassidy, my mother decided to take control. She called her mother to beg for help in housing Alberta and possibly me. My grandfather agreed to permit Alberta but not me.

According to my grandmother, who always told the story with a smile, Otto told her if I lived there, he would go crazy and so would his chickens. He would never have any eggs from his chickens, and I would probably befriend the Irish hooligans next door. According to him, "I was very much like them."

My mother felt his concerns were baseless. It was, she told me, because my dad's middle name was Harold. Otto, to his death, never spoke to my dad after he ejected him from his house. Alberta, on the other hand, was named after his favorite son, Albert.

My mother then called her brother, Raymond, and asked permission for my brother, Ray, to stay with his godparents—Raymond and Elsie Suhl.

After their housing was arranged, my mother determined it was time to leave Bea. We had overstayed. I'm not sure how it was possible, but after our three-week stay with Bea, my mother and Bea still remained good friends.

We loaded my dad's black four-door Buick, and we were off for my grandparents' home on Myrtle Street. When my father turned onto Myrtle Street, he drove past the first three houses and then pulled the car to the curb and stopped.

He asked Raymond and me to help Alberta carry her things the half block to my grandparents' white, two-story home.

When we arrived, my grandmother was waiting for us. She asked us to put down the items we were carrying and then hugged each of us. Ray and I thanked her for taking Alberta. She then walked into the kitchen and got us large pieces of warm bread smothered with butter. With bread in our mouths and butter on our faces, Ray and I waved good-bye to Alberta and then ran back to the Buick.

It was Ray's turn to be dropped off. The twenty-minute ride to Raymond and Elsie Suhl's residence in Greece, New York, was long. We sat in the backseat of the Buick, unusually quiet. He was nervous and somewhat scared. I was worried because something told me I would not see my brother and sister for a long time.

Raymond and Elsie Suhl's home was a perfect middle-class house in a perfect middle-class neighborhood with a perfect one-child family—until my brother arrived.

From the surface, everything appeared too nice. In time, we realized Ray had it worst of all. He was the victim of mental and physical abuse by both his aunt and uncle. According to my mother, he often went without a lunch at the Catholic school he attended because his aunt refused to give him money unless my mother gave her the lunch money in advance. There were many times when my mother did not have the money to send to Ray. Consequently, Ray would not eat lunch.

What appeared to be the perfect family was really a strange coming together of three very strange people. They were sneaky, scary, and unethical. If Elsie had something to say, and she did not want everyone to hear it, she would whisper in the ear of a person in front of everyone.

A Will In Question

When Otto died, he left an estate worth, by his own estimate, over a million dollars. After my mother disobeyed him and married my father, he disowned her. Following my grandmother's death, he was helpless. My mother offered to help him clean his house and do his laundry. Eventually, he moved to a small room at my uncle Raymond's home, where he remained until he was transferred to the Lake Shore Nursing Home in Rochester where he died.

He was so grateful for what my mother had done he demanded his son and daughter-in-law (Raymond and Elsie) take him during the early 1960s to his attorney's office (Knauf & Knauf).

While there, he requested a new will that included his daughter Rose for an equal share. At the time, Elsie Suhl caused a terrible fight, but Otto insisted Rose be put into the will for an equal share. Otto told me when I visited him that the change had been made. He said he would not let the devil prevail.

After Otto died, the original will was probated—not Otto's last will. Why? The reason for the switch was never made known to my mother's family. The Barend children each received $1,000, and the balance of Otto's estate went to his two sons Albert and Raymond. The will that was probated was dated October 1953 and witnessed by Andrew Knauf and Margaret Scipioci.

In 1973, the psychic Phil Jordan told me about a conspiracy regarding my grandfather's last will. I asked Phil Jordon two questions: "May I tape-record this session?" To which he responded, "Yes." My second question was, "What can you tell me about a recently probated will that was left by my grandfather?"

He said a relative of no blood relation had worked as a secretary for the law firm that prepared Otto's will. While working for the lawyers, she learned information that, if made public, would have been very damaging to the law firm. According to Phil Jordan, after Otto died, she threatened to disclose the information unless the attorney discarded Otto's last will and probated his original will.

After my visit with Phil Jordan, I called my sister Alberta to try to better understand the physic's story.

I asked her if Elsie Suhl ever worked as a secretary for a law firm. She responded yes. I asked if the firm was Knauf & Knauf in Rochester—she was quite sure it was. She asked me how I learned this, and I told her a psychic.

She was shocked.

Chapter Sixteen

THE HOTEL EDISON

All saints can do miracles but few of them can keep a hotel.

—Mark Twain

HOTEL EDISON
ELM NEAR MAIN STREET EAST

I very seldom cried when I was a child, but tears flowed in my eyes when the car pulled from the driveway, and I waved good-bye to Ray. For a long time, I sat on the backseat in silence, wondering what was going to happen to our family. At eight years old, I had just lost my best friend and my sister, and I would be living in a strange hotel.

As the car approached our final destination, the neighborhood just kept getting worse. The Hotel Edison's entrance faced Elm Street, a very poor section of Rochester's inner city. Above the entrance was a neon sign that read Edison Hotel.

Adorning the entrance and sidewalks on both sides of the hotel were shabbily dressed women with very short skirts and lots of coloring on their faces. The men wore old coats and shoes with holes in them. Empty liquor and wine bottles, small used cans of a heating liquid, cigarette butts, and miscellaneous garbage were scattered across the concrete sidewalks at the hotel's entrance. My mother was aghast.

"Harold," she addressed my dad, "this is awful! Why are these people surrounding this hotel? What kind of place are you taking us to?"

I will never forget my dad's answer. It was the first time I had ever heard the expression used, and it told me things probably could not get worse.

"Beggars can't be choosers," he said. "Those people are here because they have nowhere to go. We are here for the same reason. The biggest difference between them and us is we are on the inside and they are outside. But the most important thing is we have hope."

While my mother and dad registered at the hotel desk, I unloaded our few bags and pieces of bedding, pillows, blankets, sheets—the hotel didn't supply them. A few of the homeless men watched as I emptied the car. No one moved to help or say hello. They just watched with blank stares as I kept walking from the car to the lobby.

My mother stood by the door watching the car for fear someone might steal what little we had. When I was almost done, a black lady named Mary walked up to me and said, "Hey, kid, are you and your parents staying here? This is the Statler Hilton of Rochester. They save this place for the best white families in Rochester. Maybe you come and see me sometime, and I'll help that weenie of yours grow."

An older black man, whose name I later learned was Joe, was sitting on the sidewalk with his back propped against the hotel wall. He called to the woman who was talking to me and said, "What's the matter with you, woman? Leave that boy alone. He done nothing to you. Go peddle your pussy and get before you give this place a bad reputation." His last remark brought a chorus of laughs from his peers.

Just then I heard my mother hollering from the doorway, "What do you want? Leave my son alone, and get on with your business. I know your kind." My mother hurried to the front door and pulled me by the arm back into the hotel. I had just met our neighbors.

The lobby of the hotel was filled with old Salvation Army—type furniture. I sat on a large chair and waited while my parents were being grilled by Mr. Murphy the desk clerk. He asked if they smoked, drank, or had reason to use the bathroom frequently.

Even though Mr. Cassidy had made an arrangement with the hotel, my parents were still responsible for paying a portion of the hotel bill.

Our room was on the third floor. The hotel did not have an elevator. There was a drab hallway leading from the stairs to our room. The hallway wallpaper was peeling, and the lightbulbs were so dim you could barely see. The hallway carpet was dirty. I doubt if it had been cleaned once in the last ten years.

When my dad opened the door to our room, it wasn't much better. There was a large old dirty double-paned window for ventilation but without a screen. With a tug, it opened from the bottom up. There was a double bed and an old army cot.

My mother told me to pretend I was in the army and it would be more fun sleeping on the cot. At night, I would usually roll on the cot for hours before falling asleep. The sounds of sirens, loud voices, screeching tires, and an occasional scream would keep me awake. The people in the rooms adjacent to ours would begin making thump, thump noises at about 2:00 or 3:00 a.m. and wake me.

If there was ever a jungle for humans, this was it.

Joe the Hobo

Chapter Seventeen

Joe the Hobo

Do not judge, and you will never be mistaken.

—Emile Rousseau

For nine months, the Hotel Edison was our home. Each morning during the school year, I would awake at five thirty; hurry to the bathroom, which was at the end of the hall; and lock the door. For the next twenty minutes, I was commander of the room. I unleashed my bodily functions, washed my body, and combed my hair. The one bathroom served everyone who had a room on our floor, and getting to use it between six and eight in the evening meant waiting in line for about an hour.

The room contained an old round iron bathtub, which was elevated off the floor by four iron legs; a white porcelain toilet with a cracked wooden seat; and a small mirror over a wall-mounted soiled white sink. The back of the toilet faced a small window that had been painted opaque. The bathroom wallpaper had disappeared in a number of places; and the vinyl tile on the floor was ripped, dirty, and swollen in spots. The only time the toilet got cleaned was just before my mother would use it. I always brought a roll of toilet paper with me because at 5:30 a.m., no one cares if you have a problem.

By 6:30 a.m., I had to be at the bus stop a block from the Hotel Edison. After I dressed, my dad would take me to a nearby dinner for donuts and hot chocolate. At eight years old, I took the bus to downtown Rochester and then transferred to another bus, which eventually deposited me about two hundred yards from Holy Family School.

Each morning, as I approached the school parking lot, which was located in front of the school, all the children would be in formation like a military review. I would always be the last to arrive, and the nuns would complain aloud about my tardiness.

The girls wore plaid skirts with white blouses, and the boys looked like little clones in their white shirts and ties. I hated the shirt and tie.

After roll call, the nuns would parade us into school and begin another day. By the time I returned to the hotel, it was 5:30 p.m. and I was exhausted; often I would fall asleep without an evening meal.

Two days after our arrival at the Edison, I ventured into the lobby; spoke with Mr. Murphy, the desk clerk; and then sat and watched the events unfold outside. The following weekend, I ventured outside. I sat on the concrete sidewalk with my back to the building for about ten minutes before anyone acknowledged my presence.

I saw the same black man who intervened on my behalf when we arrived. He was still sitting in the same position. I later learned that each homeless person laid claim to their own place on the sidewalk.

When he saw me looking at him, he asked me what I was doing there by myself. "This ain't no place for little kids," he told me, "especially little white kids. Where's your mamma, boy?" he asked. Then he blurted out, "These people don't take kindly to kids sitting staring at them."

I told him my mother was upstairs. Then I asked, "Why can't I be here? We live here." After that question, Joe just smiled. He knew I was honest, innocent, and colorblind. When he smiled, Joe had about four of his most visible teeth missing. In his left hand was a bottle of Mogen David wine.

It was the end of summer when I first spoke with Joe. I noticed his hands were worn, and there was a large slit on one shoe, which exhibited the whole side of his foot. As the year progressed, I learned, unlike most people, Joe seldom changed his clothes. His changes only occurred when someone died or an empathetic person gave him some second-hand clothes.

Four or five times a week, I visited Joe. I timed my visits when my mother was either sleeping or gone. I always sat a few feet away from Joe because of his terrible body odor. Saturday mornings were the best. I would slip out the front door of the hotel before Murphy was at the desk and my mother awake and then find a spot next to Joe. We did not have much food to share, but sometimes I would bring crackers or potato chips.

Occasionally, Mary and a few of her friends would join us. Joe explained that Mary was really a nice lady, but life had been hard to her. He told me how Mary was in business for herself. You know, he said, like the man who owns the restaurant where you go with your dad almost every morning. I asked him what she did and what she sold. He replied, "You just wouldn't understand, but it's nothing like hot chocolate and donuts."

A few weeks later, Mary told me she was a prostitute. When I got older I would understand, she said, how that thing between my legs would make me want things I shouldn't have.

The next morning when I locked the door to the bathroom, I examined my penis. I wondered what was so special about this thing that always dribbled when I urinated in the bathroom at school. The small wet spot on my pants, a result of it, would cause me great embarrassment when I returned to the classroom. It also was a nuisance when I put my underpants on and sometimes pinched it.

Joe, Mary, and her friend Elizabeth taught me life from a much different perspective. We talked about my school, the president, the Hotel Edison, their families, my family, the weather, how children are born. About the only thing we never discussed was their future.

Joe would tell me stories of his life wandering from state to state. He spoke about the redwood trees that were the tallest in the world and how they stretched from San Francisco to Oregon. He described Mount Whitney and how sometimes you couldn't see its peak because it was in the clouds.

He told of how he lived by begging or working in menial jobs—how he traveled for free across the United States. Most often, he was lucky; but the few times he wasn't, according to him, made up for the hundreds of times he was.

Joe's missing teeth were the result of a railroad policeman's club striking him across the face. If he wasn't able to keep on his feet, Joe claimed, he would be dead and no one would be the wiser. No one cared about the poor, the tramp, or the migratory worker. Even the hospitals didn't want to treat them in their emergency rooms because no one would pay.

The only people he ever spoke badly about were the Gypsies. Sometimes, he said, they would enter a camp comprised of homeless wandering men and women like Mary and him. The Gypsies would come in bunches and pretend to be your friend. They would entertain you and then steal everything of value—a few dollars, a piece of jewelry. It was very sad, he claimed.

Chapter Eighteen

HOPE

If winter comes, can spring be far behind?

—Shelley, "Ode to the West Wind"

In March 1947, my dad picked me up from school and took me to a late-afternoon meeting with Mr. Cassidy from the Monroe County Welfare Department. My mother had been constantly complaining about the Hotel Edison and wanted us out. My dad wanted to inquire about the possibility of moving out of the Hotel Edison. I was his witness to make sure my mother knew he was there.

During their meeting, Mr. Cassidy told him the house had been bequeathed to the Monroe County Welfare Department. He believed our family met the requirements stipulated in the transfer of property. Then he asked my dad if he would drive to Braddock Heights and inspect the house with him. He insisted the house be livable before he could allow anyone to occupy it.

Three weeks later, Mr. Cassidy and my father drove to the house in Braddock Heights. Mr. Cassidy thought the cottage, with a bit of work, could be a home for our family. It needed a considerable amount of work. When they arrived, Cassidy and my dad inspected the house, and both agreed some work would have to be done on the front porch to make it safe.

The foundation of the house was comprised of eight cement block columns, which supported the house about three feet above ground level. There was no basement or crawl space. Consequently, the winter would be difficult because there was no insulation under the floor. In addition, someone had removed the sideboards, which protected the perimeter of the house and kept the wind from blowing under the house.

With the exception of the toilet, there were no fixtures in the bathroom. A number of windows had been broken by rocks, and there was no insulation in the sidewalls. After they inspected the dwelling, Mr. Cassidy told my dad he felt it was not fit for immediate occupancy.

Mr. Cassidy indicated it would take about ten months before the house could be in livable condition. He felt there was no other recourse but to wait. Any intention of living there should be postponed until spring 1948. This ten-month delay would give the Welfare Department sufficient time to insulate the cottage, replace the broken windows, and install support for the floors.

On their return to Rochester, Mr. Cassidy questioned my dad about his employment. He wanted to know what if any plans he had made for an income. My dad had already spoken with a banker who was a good friend. He knew him through the Knights of Columbus. He had no money for a down payment, but the banker was willing to have my father sign his Buick as collateral for a loan to cover the full purchase price of a used truck. My dad planned to use the truck to procure odd jobs cleaning attics and removing debris.

Until now, other than the bank foreclosure on their first house, my mother and father never borrowed money or accepted any money as charity from anyone.

After they returned to the County Welfare Department, my dad asked Mr. Cassidy if it was possible for us to accept the house the way it is. He and my mother wanted to reunite our family and move in immediately. He believed our family could make the house livable.

Mr. Cassidy was stunned when my dad refused his offer of free help in lieu of a chance to bring his family together sooner. Mr. Cassidy knew the additional nine months would be a hardship but no worse than enduring a winter in a cottage built without insulation, broken windows, and faulty plumbing.

With a puzzled look, he asked my dad, "Are you sure you can prepare that cottage for winter? Wouldn't you prefer knowing your children were safe for the next nine months? They could freeze or get pneumonia living in a building without insulation. If you are sure you want this, I will review the bequest and have the rental agreement prepared so you and your family can take possession next month."

The terms of the bequest of the house to the Monroe County Welfare Department were as follows: The home could only be rented to a family qualified for public assistance. The family must provide labor for maintenance and improvements. In return, the monthly rental was to be adjusted. There could be no discrimination with regards to color, nationality, or religion.

On July 1 my dad was told the house in Braddock Heights was available. He immediately drove to Mr. Cassidy's office. A rental agreement had been prepared, which required the Barend family to pay a minimum monthly payment in exchange for work on the house.

My mother and father, too proud to accept charity or welfare, fit the terms of the bequest perfectly. Mr. Cassidy structured the agreement to provide modest shelter for the Barend family, give my parents an opportunity to financially recover, and provide the Welfare Department with a tenant willing to pay rent and put forth labor.

Unbeknown to my parents, Mr. Cassidy called an oil company and had them install and fill a new oil tank with enough heating fuel to last the first winter.

Chapter Nineteen

Parting Was Sweet Joy

In human affairs, the best stimulus for running ahead is to have something we must run from.

—Eric Hoffer, *The Ordeal of Change*

During the nine months of our stay at the Hotel Edison, my mother never realized my only friends during that time were the people who greeted us on arrival. My dad knew but never told my mother. He figured because my friends were poor, it didn't mean they were mean or incorrigible. He knew first-hand the prejudice greetings bestowed on the poor by those who were "holier than thou."

Two days before our departure from the Hotel Edison, I spoke with old Joe. It was the second weekend in July, and the weather was hot and sticky. Joe was still dressed in the same clothes he wore in December.

After we had solved many of the world's problems and discussed how wine and cigarettes were made, I asked Joe if there was one thing he could have, what would that be?

Dad often asked me this question, and I always had fun thinking about what I wanted most. I sometimes hoped for things that were really unattainable but mostly responded with items like a new pair of shoes or socks that were not darned and redarned fifty times. I did not want to feel ashamed if I took my shoes off and my socks had holes sewn from heel to toe.

Joe thought for a few minutes and then completely surprised me by saying, "I would love to sit in a bathtub for about an hour. A nice warm bath with no one to bother me would be wonderful."

Forgetting about Joe's color and financial status, I replied that it didn't sound like it would be too difficult to arrange. I asked Joe why he couldn't ask Mr. Murphy, who managed the Edison, if he could take a bath.

Joe laughed for a long time. He pointed to one of the other men who frequently adorned the sidewalk and said, "This kid thinks Murphy will let us take baths in his hotel. I guess you haven't learned to read the signs behind the counter that say No Niggers or Pets Allowed. Murphy would shoot us if he caught us taking a bath in his hotel. He hates everybody, but he saves a little extra for black folks. Did you know sometimes in the winter, he walks out of the hotel and throws a bucket of dirty water onto everyone out here? That man don't want us taking a bath—he wants us to die."

Joe Takes a Bath

The next day, I devised a plan to arrange a bath for Joe. It took me ten minutes to convince Joe everything would be fine. I knew Murphy was never at the desk when I left for school. In the early morning hours, the front door would be locked from the inside, and a small light would provide minimum visibility in the lobby. My plan was to sneak Joe into the bathroom the Saturday morning before we left.

The Friday evening before my plan was to be activated, I waited until my mother was asleep, then made a sign, Out of Order. I shoved the sign under my covers and then slipped a pair of my dad's pants, underwear, shirt, and socks into bed with me. I put my pajama tops on but left my underwear, pants, and socks on.

When my dad arrived back at the room that evening, as I expected, he pulled my covers around my shoulders and kissed me on the forehead—I didn't want him to know I had my clothes on or his clothes under the covers.

When 6:00 a.m. Saturday arrived, I automatically awoke. I slipped into my T-shirt and then very quietly grabbed the clothes that were stuffed under my covers and slowly tiptoed from the room. I was excited. I was to direct a covert plan so Joe could have his wish.

I immediately walked to the bathroom at the end of the hall and placed the sign on the exterior of the door with tape I stole from the front desk. Knowing how dirty Joe was, I borrowed a few extra bars of soap. I left my dad's clothes on the bathroom floor for Joe.

A few minutes later, I was walking outside between the bodies of sleeping hobos. When I saw Joe, he was sound asleep. I gently shook him on the shoulder, and he murmured something and then opened his eyes and looked at me startled for a few seconds.

"Joe, I've got everything ready," I said. "Come on, you have to hurry. Just follow me into the hotel and then up the stairs. Go to the third floor. The bathroom is at the end of the hall. Make sure you lock the door. I'll try to position myself outside the door—this will discourage people from going to the bathroom."

I stopped talking for a moment while he was picking himself off the sidewalk. Then I continued, "I heard black people like to sing when they bathe—please don't make any noise. If I rap three times, you had better hurry out. I think we can get you a nice long bath. Oh, by the way, I put some clothes in the bathroom for you—my dad was going to throw them out," I told him.

After Joe scurried up the stairs to the third floor, I relocked the hotel's front door and then remained for about ten minutes to see if Murphy was awake. The place was eerily quiet except for Joe's water running.

When I returned to our room, my mother was awake. She began one of her interrogations, which normally lasted for an hour or until she was satisfied. Fortunately, my dad asked her to please leave me alone and let him sleep for a few more minutes. He told her it was my last day here, and I was probably a little nervous.

About ten minutes later, I grabbed a towel and some soap and told my mother I would be in the bathroom. I waited at the bathroom door for about twenty minutes and then knocked on the door as planned.

I quietly opened the door and in a very hushed voice said to Joe, "You have to hurry. I think Murphy might be getting up. My mother will be coming to use the bathroom in a very short time."

From the time he heard my voice to the opening of the door, it took Joe about three minutes. Joe was washed and had dressed in my dad's clothes. Except for the shoes, he looked like a totally different person. I forgot about shaving, but a beard doesn't show as bad on a black person. At eight years old, I had no idea what was needed to shave a beard.

Joe followed me at a distance down the steps. I kept motioning for him to come forward, but he moved very slowly. When I got to the hotel lobby, Murphy was nowhere to be seen. I walked to the front door, unlocked it, and stood where Joe could easily see me. He moved quickly down the few steps then shot like a bullet across the lobby to the front door and out. When I walked outside to say good-bye, he shook my hand and hugged me. I felt really good—and for a change, he smelled good.

That morning when my mother returned from the bathroom, she was complaining how she wanted to take a bath but someone left it filthy. It would take at least twenty minutes to clean the bathtub, she claimed. I laughed inside.

A few hours later, my dad pulled the Buick to the front door. My mother and I carried our three suitcases, four blankets, and three pillows to the lobby. These constituted the total net worth of the Barend family. My dad opened the trunk.

While we were loading the items into the trunk, a number of people who lived outside the Edison came to say good-bye. My mother was in shock.

This was the first she realized the only friends I had to play with during nine months at the Edison were the men and women who lived on the corner sidewalk surrounding the hotel.

Joe stood in the background, probably knowing I stole from my dad the clothes he was wearing. The two prostitutes I became friends with hugged me and made me promise I would return when I was eighteen.

My parents sat in the front seat and I in the back. As the car was pulling away from the hotel, I leaned out the window and waved. Joe, who had been leaning against the building, stepped from the shadows, waved, and hollered, "Good-bye, my friend Harold."

Joe never walked to the car. His right hand waved as the car pulled away. I never saw Joe again. He is probably in the Kingdom of Hobodom, where the sun always shines and there are warm baths for everyone.

My mother turned around in order to see who was hollering to me. She wanted to hear what they were saying. She asked me, "Who is that man? Why did he call you his friend?"

I responded that he was just a friend. I said he told me about his wife who died and his two daughters and their families. I tried to explain he was really a nice person—she didn't buy it.

She looked at my dad and said, "It is really too bad the only way those people can live is to beg or steal."

My dad replied, "If they are poorer than us, then they really need to steal." As the car moved away from the Hotel Edison, I saw the poor, seedy side of life from a different perspective. I learned much about life—much more than my parents would have wanted.

Chapter 20 is a slight diversion from the story sequence of the Barend family's transition to Braddock Heights. Chapter 20 is a story about love and kindness expressed to my family and me during a very difficult time in our lives. People like Anna and Henry Brown are the reason why this country is one nation under God.

CHAPTER TWENTY

ANNA AND HENRY BROWN

*He that is thy friend indeed,
He will help thee in thy need.*

R. Barnfield, "Address to the Nightingale"

During all the moving and resettling, I missed about three months of school.

My mother had made arrangements with Anna and Henry Brown, the family we stayed with for a few days, to have me eat lunch at their home every day when I attended Holy Family School.

At lunchtime I walked about ten minutes to their home in good and bad weather. Each day Anna Brown would prepare two poached eggs on toast with a dessert. It was the best meal I would have the whole day. She and her husband refused to take anything from my parents for feeding me.

When Henry Brown died, I drove from Seneca Falls to Rochester to attend his funeral in a new Dodge convertible. En route to the funeral, a speeding ten-wheel dump truck entered the I-490 Expressway just east of Rochester. It slammed into the back of my car and smashed my car into a guardrail. My car bounced off the guardrail and shot back across the expressway. It flew off an embankment and landed thirty feet below the road.

Under normal conditions, I would have been killed. Fortunately, the Highway Department dumped about fifteen feet of snow where my car landed.

The car and I were bruised and banged up. I had been knocked unconscious. When I regained consciousness, I heard a man digging the snow from around my car and attempting to pry open the driver's side door. Fortunately, I was not wearing a seatbelt. Two of the motor mounts broke when the car hit, and the steering wheel slammed into the driver's seat.

Within minutes of the accident, an ambulance and four police cars arrived. After my car was pulled by cable to the road, the mechanic realigned the motor onto the broken mounts. I refused to go to the hospital and asked if the car was drivable. The mechanic told me to try to start it.

"If it starts," he said, "I'll check to see if there are any leaks. You know, buddy, there are no lights on either the front or back, and the front seat is broken. The back looks like an accordion." He continued, "If this moves, I want a picture of it." The impact from the truck pushed the trunk almost to the back window.

After I started the car, the mechanic checked the brakes, the steering column, and tires to ensure everything was OK to go. The attending police motioned for the mechanic to join them in a private conversation. After it was determined the car could be driven, the passenger's side door was tied shut with a rope, and the front driver's seat was pried up with a board.

The police and the mechanic warned me if I had to drive the car not to drive it over ten miles per hour. My only intention was to drive the car one mile at a time. I told the police I wanted to continue to a funeral. My intent was to attend the funeral and then get a ride home with someone.

If possible I would return to Seneca Falls after the funeral. I explained to them that my wife was pregnant with our first child and due anytime. I was concerned for her welfare and did not want to leave her.

The medics checked my eyes and patched me up. I had a large bump on my head and about a two-inch cut on my arm. The front of the car was damaged slightly. Amazingly, the car still moved. But the muffler was very noisy.

A sheriff's deputy said he would provide me an escort almost the entire distance to the funeral parlor. About a block from the funeral parlor, he waved good-bye.

When Anna and her daughter saw me, they couldn't believe I was there. Anna told me that her husband would have been so pleased that I came.

"Dear Jesus," she said, "you look worse than my dead husband. Don't walk past the undertaker, or he will be measuring you for one of his caskets. Please let me make arrangements to have you stay at the house until tomorrow."

I thanked her but politely refused. I stayed for about an hour and then began my return trip to Seneca Falls. It took me almost four hours to drive what normally was a one-hour trip. The last mile was driven at dusk and without any lights. In addition, the pain medication administered at the accident site by the medics had begun to decrease in effectiveness—my head and arm were throbbing.

When I pulled the car into the driveway at Ovid Street Extension, Seneca Falls, I was exhausted. For about five minutes, I sat in the car while it was parked in the driveway. I was trying to collect enough energy to walk my body into the house.

When Sally saw me, she hollered, "Oh my god, oh my god, what should I do? I am going to call an ambulance. We need to take you to the hospital!"

I pulled myself out of the car, walked into the house, and went to sleep.

In a short time my wounds healed. Unfortunately, the back injury would plague me for years.

My insurance company was also the insurer for the truck that hit me. In addition, the insurance adjuster (we thought) was a friend of ours.

Sally pushed for a quick settlement without going to an attorney. I agreed to the insurance company's settlement terms. They would replace the car and pay all my ongoing medical expenses for my back injury. It seemed fair.

About three months after our insurance settlement, I was waiting at a red light in Seneca Falls when a woman drove into the back of my car. She was uninsured. My insurance company used this as an opportunity to escape from their prior agreement to pay for any future medical expenses.

Hit by a ten-wheel dump truck.

Chapter Twenty-One

COMING TOGETHER

All children find chaos congenial.
Any unruliness, even by nature,
Advances the child's program of subverting authority.

—George F. Will, *Ideological Storms*

The previous day, my mother telephoned her mother and brother to tell them Alberta and Raymond would be picked up on Sunday. The car stopped, as it did nine months ago, a block before my grandparents' home.

I was sent to collect Alberta and help carry her suitcase and bedding to the car. I ran to the house, anxious to see my sister and grandmother. I hadn't seen either of them for months. It would be the last opportunity I would have to see my grandmother for quite a while. With some luck, she would be baking.

When I arrived, my sister was packed and anxious to leave. Otto had left before I entered the house. My grandmother said he was meeting with his friend Frank Keller. Frank was going to help Otto restore the grapevines he lost when moving the fence. I asked if he left because my parents were coming to get Alberta. She just smiled.

The house had the most wonderful aroma coming from the kitchen. Along with the bread, there was a plum küchen and a crumb cake in the oven. Grandma Suhl announced they were for us, but they could not be removed from the oven for another ten minutes.

I asked Alberta to tell Mom and Dad that Grandpa had left and we would be delayed for a few minutes. Knowing the coast was clear, my dad drove the car to the front of the house. He pulled alongside the curb. Alberta, dressed in a plaid skirt and brown-and-white shoes, was riding on the running board. She jumped off when the car stopped.

My grandmother stood inside the front door watching as the car arrived. She opened the door, carefully grabbed the black iron handrail, and slowly walked down the three wooden steps leading to the sidewalk.

I watched as my mother and grandmother ran to each other and embraced. They hugged and cried for a long time. Like the movies, it gave me goose bumps. I had taken my mother and her mother's relationship for granted.

Whenever I wanted to see my grandmother, I would walk the two miles from Holy Family School to her house. Some nights I would stay with my grandparents until 6:00 or 7:00 p.m. or until my dad would pick me up at a prearranged time and location. I realized now how difficult it was for my mother and grandmother to see each other.

Their reunion gave me ample time to slip out the back door and play havoc with my grandfather's chickens. I loved to go into the chicken coop where Otto kept about twenty egg-laying chickens and a couple of roosters. The coop always smelled like someone had plastered the floor with shit.

As soon as I unlatched the homemade wire door, the chickens started to move and make noise. I made crazy noises, and the chickens started flapping their wings and flying inside the small coop. I jumped and hollered; and the chickens started flying in every direction, quacking, and flapping. Big white feathers filled the air like snow. I ran and ducked while anarchy ruled the chicken coop.

A rooster tried to attack me, but I darted to the opposite side of the coop's wire door and slammed it while he was half out. I had to take my foot and push him back in order to latch the door. Otto often complained after one of my coop invasions how his chickens were not laying as many eggs.

I learned to become a good listener. I am sure my grandmother knew about my backyard adventures, but she never told Otto. She probably saved my life.

A few months prior to this adventure, my grandmother advised me to stay away from the chicken coop because the chickens were not laying eggs. My grandfather suspected I was the cause and wanted to wring my neck.

With my sister came the much-appreciated baked goods. As the Buick pulled away from the curb, my mother, Alberta, and I stuck our bodies out the windows and waved good-bye to the sweetest, most wonderful grandmother. She stood at the curbside and cried, "Auf Wiedersehn." My mother would not see her mother again for ten years.

We were once again beginning to feel like a family. Alberta and I shared the backseat with the warm bread and kuchens nestled between us.

The next stop before Braddock Heights was to get my brother Ray. When we arrived at Raymond and Elsie Suhl's home, my brother had carried his things to the side door of the house. His possessions were parked on the driveway, and he was sitting on the sidewalk with his back resting against the house. The Suhls had told Ray to wait outside while they had a private family conversation.

Elsie Suhl was the kind of person who enjoyed whispering in front of others. When my dad drove into the driveway, the Suhl family emerged from their house. Ray was more than prepared to leave. He had some bitter memories from his experience; it was a difficult time for all of us.

Chapter Twenty-Two

BRADDOCK HEIGHTS

At a certain season of our life we are accustomed to consider every spot as the possible site of a house.

—Henry David Thoreau, *Walden*

During the eight-mile ride from Rochester to Braddock Heights, my dad told us the house was in a community of summer homes. It was located on a peninsula, with Braddock Bay on the west, Lake Ontario on the north, and Cranberry Pond on the east.

I had never thought about the cultural composition of Braddock Heights until I was in high school. There were no Negroes, Asians, or Jews. Everyone who lived in Braddock Heights was white and either Protestant or Catholic.

The house we were about to call home had been built as a summer cottage about twenty years prior to our arrival. It lacked many of the basic necessities most homes had: no basement, no shower or bathtub, no insulation. My dad promised he would do whatever was humanly possible to make the house livable for us—he never mentioned comfortable.

As the Buick moved along, Beach Avenue melted into Edgemere Drive. We passed large lakefront homes. We stared in amazement as the car went by English Tudor homes, large stone mansions, plantation-style white two-story homes with large columns at the front.

The homes on Beach Avenue and Edgemere Drive were grand displays of wealth. Rochester's wealthy boarded up many of these homes for six months each year. What most people dreamed of living in permanently, for Rochester's chosen few, it was a few months of splendor at the lake.

About two miles from Braddock Heights, a large sign announced the Crescent Beach Hotel. The hotel was located about five hundred feet back from the road. The hotel's large parking lot was immediately adjacent to Edgemere Drive. The hotel was situated to take full advantage of Lake Ontario. A long canopy-covered walk directed guests to the main entrance of the hotel. This hotel made the Edison look like an outhouse. In its prime, the Crescent Beach Hotel was a favorite hotel and restaurant for the famous and infamous of Rochester.

About three months after we took residence in Braddock Heights, Ray and I were given one-year memberships to the YMCA compliments of the owners of the Crescent Beach Hotel. We never learned how Mr. and Mrs. Ray Guise heard about us, but the memberships were wonderful.

Every Saturday morning in the fall and winter of our first year, my dad would drive Ray and me into downtown Rochester. He would leave us at the YMCA for about two hours so we could learn to swim.

A mile northwest of the Crescent Beach Hotel was Grandview Heights. As the Buick made an *S* turn along Edgemere Drive, we saw men, women, and children fishing. They were leaning over a white concrete bridge with their fishing poles extended. The small bridge marked the entrance to Grandview Heights. Instead of driving across the bridge into Grandview Heights, the Buick veered right onto a two-lane gravel road.

This road was the exit and entrance that connected Braddock Heights to the southeast. On the north side of the two-lane road, modest summer homes kissed Lake Ontario while the south side was open to Cranberry Pond. There was a four-feet tapered stone bank, which began at the edge of the road's south side and continued into the pond—no shoulder, no guardrails.

There was little traffic on this portion of Edgemere Drive. Consequently, the Town of Greece could not justify spending money for guardrails along the exposed side of the road leading directly into the pond. Prior to the erection of the guardrails, it was not uncommon to see a vehicle go over the bank and into the pond. The pond had a way of taking care of DWIs.

Alberta, Ray, and I were leaning out the windows of the old black four-door Buick. We were capturing all the delights of this new neighborhood that I would call home for the next fifteen years. At the entrance to the hamlet called Braddock Heights, the Buick came to a Y; the car veered to the left. We passed First Avenue, Second Avenue, and then turned right onto Third Avenue. Other than Edgemere Drive, Third Avenue was the longest street in Braddock Heights. It extended two blocks from Cranberry Pond to Braddock's Bay. The homes built along Second and Third Avenues were more inland and less exclusive. There were some year-round homes but mostly middle-class cottages.

Approaching the entrance to Braddock Heights with Cranberry Pond on the left. Edgemere Drive continues straight. We turned left onto Cranberry Pond Road. Sixty years ago, this portion of Edgemere Drive was not paved, and the guardrails were not in place.

The Buick passed four or five houses on Third Avenue and then slowed and made a left turn into a dirt driveway. I didn't realize we had arrived.

When I collected myself, I began to focus on the surroundings. The driveway was banked on the side adjacent to the house. High grass and weeds had captured most of the front lawn and driveway—it was a battle lost years ago. The base of the house was elevated about eight feet above the road, which contributed to the steep bank where the front lawn met the street. I sat in the car staring, not knowing if I should cry from happiness or disappointment. The house was in bad shape. What made it appear even worse was our recent sojourn past the monuments to Rochester's rich.

Some of the local hooligans had taken the liberty of dropping stones through three windows on the north side of the house. The garage, which stood facing us, appeared worn and tired. The whole structure was leaning to the right. It looked almost like one of those funny mirrors at the carnival, except when you walked away from the mirror you knew everything would be fine because it was an optical trick. The garage may have looked like an optical trick to a passerby, but to us it was real.

The steps going to the front porch had been stolen, removed, or just rotted away. My dad found a wooden box at the back of the house and placed it between the ground and the house. He helped my mother step onto the box then onto the front porch.

The porch extended the width of the house and projected about eight feet out. It had a half wall extending up about four feet, which permitted some privacy. There was indication that during the better days of this house, screens had enclosed the porch. The front door, which opened to the living room, was enclosed by the porch.

As my mother began her precarious walk across the porch, two boards cracked, and she let out a scream. Our neighbors knew we had arrived. Ray and I laughed hysterically, but Alberta kept calm. She grabbed my mother so she didn't fall and chastised us.

My dad had preceded everyone and unlocked the front door. He was already inside checking to ensure the electricity and water had been turned on. Fortunately, everything was working.

By a midget's standard, the house was small. To the left of the living room was a ten-feet-by-ten-feet bedroom. Immediately behind the living room was the kitchen—an eight-feet-by-eight-feet space. From the kitchen, a small hallway led to the second bedroom, which was also ten feet by ten feet. The only toilet was at the back of the house, a few feet from the second bedroom.

We had no furniture, no carpeting (all the floors were covered with a cheap one-piece rolled vinyl). There was a stove and a refrigerator.

Ray and I shared one bedroom. Alberta had the living room by night, and my mother and dad had the other bedroom. When the family split, my dad had given away or sold everything except my parents' bedroom furniture, two lamps, a card table, and four chairs. During the next two days, the whole family slept on the floor. Ray and I pretended living at Fifty-ninth Third Avenue was a campout.

Despite all the hardships, we found a way to have fun. Alberta would stay for the summer and then return to our grandparents, where she lived while attending St. Joseph's Academy in Rochester.

The Braddock Heights marching band was an integral part of the community. Ray played the trumpet and Harold the drums. The band performed at fireman's festivals throughout the Greater Rochester area.

The next morning, my dad arranged for his brother Bill to drive him to an auto dealership in Rochester where he picked up an old green truck with removable wooden sides. It looked like a truck used in movies when migrant workers were transported from field to field. According to my dad, for being seven years old, it was in very good condition.

We were the only family living in Braddock Heights that had a car and a truck but no furniture, no food, and a garage that was falling down. Before he bought the truck, my dad exhausted every possible opportunity for work in the Rochester area. Furniture, he said, would not buy us food. He needed the truck to make money to support our family. He had no choice but to try to find work on his own.

There was no telephone in the house. The telephone company required at least a month's advance notice for rural installations. If you lived in Braddock Heights in 1947, it was rural. If you were fortunate enough to have a telephone, you were on a party line with four other families.

Until our telephone was installed, Mr. Cassidy agreed to allow B. H. to put in his classified advertisements the telephone number for Cassidy's office at the Monroe County Welfare Department. Mr. Cassidy personally spoke with everyone who called in response to the ad. He was responsible for many of B. H.'s new customers and was the best salesman my dad ever had.

When B. H. completed everything required to put the truck on the road, there were six jobs waiting. After the first week, he earned enough money to get the furniture out of storage, purchase a very large comfortable sofa from the Salvation Army (Alberta's bed), and buy enough food for the week.

Beds for my mother, father, and Alberta had been resolved. Ray and I remained bedded down on the floor.

Chapter Twenty-Three

Come to My House

A boy is a piece of existence quite separate from all things else, and deserves separate chapters in the natural history of men.

—Henry Ward Beecher, *Proverbs from Plymouth Pulpit*

The third day in Braddock Heights, Ray and I toured the hamlet on foot. He was twelve, and I was nine. Ray wasn't keen on having his little brother tag along wherever he went. He knew no one else; therefore, I was invited to accompany him.

As we walked, we were cognizant of how the houses were nestled close together, unlike the ones on Edgemere Drive. There was not one house that looked as bad as ours. The population of Braddock Heights was about two hundred, excluding children and dogs. I had already decided if we met anyone, I would not tell them we lived at Fifty-ninth Third Avenue.

We walked north on Third Avenue past where East Manitou Road crossed. We continued to the end of the street. In front of us was a large marsh area with hundreds of cattails. The marshland was part of Braddock Bay. To the right of the bay was the beautiful blue water of Lake Ontario. We then turned right to circle home via Second Avenue.

As we began our trek up Second Avenue, two boys on bicycles came toward us. They stopped a few feet in front of us. One of the boys had an old beater bike—no fenders, no chain guard. When he stopped, he lowered his body onto the support bars—his legs straddled the bike between the handlebars and the seat.

The other boy stood with one foot on the ground and the other on a pedal with his shiny new Schwinn leaning into his body. The Schwinn rider was about Ray's age. They stared at us for what seemed like minutes. The fellow on the Schwinn asked, "Did you guys just move into the neighborhood, or are you just visiting . . . or what? We've never seen you here."

Before I could tell them we were just visiting, Ray said, "Yeah! We just moved here. We live on Third Avenue."

I was cringing with embarrassment. I thought how stupid my brother could be. The last thing I wanted anyone to know was where we lived.

Ray asked, "Do either of you go to school at Our Mother of Sorrows?"

The boy on the beater introduced himself as Ronnie Lupo. I sized him up quickly—he was about three inches shorter than me, dirty blond hair, blue eyes—and I knew if we ever got into a fight, I could create a lot of damage for him.

The other boy, who addressed all his remarks to Ray, was just about Ray's height, dark brown hair, and a rugged build. He looked like he could run you over and not even feel a thing. I knew if he ever got mad at me, I would have one of two choices: run or be killed.

He said his name was Earl Vokel, and he lived on Second Avenue. Earl acknowledged he went to the Catholic school. Ronnie was about my age and was quick to inform us that he lived on Edgemere Drive (which in my mind meant his house was more expensive). Although Catholic, Ronnie did not attend Catholic school. He proudly boasted that public schools were much better. "We have real teachers who know how to teach. You have nuns and priests who are always mean and cranky," Ronnie said. "I've heard how the nuns hit the kids—even when they are not doing anything. My dad says it is because they don't have anyone else to take their frustrations out on. You don't have any gym, art, or good food. Plus, they can't beat the shit out of us in public school like they do to the kids attending the Catholic school. Besides, who wants to wear a stupid tie to school every day?"

When I heard Ronnie talk, I thought, *Why can't we be like everyone else and not wear a stupid shirt and tie?* My worst fears had been realized—I hated wearing those ties.

They proceeded to tell us that only a few kids from Braddock Heights and Grandview go to the Catholic school. The Catholic school was called Paddy Hill because it was located on a hill, and it was named after the priest who originally founded the church. According to Earl, Father Daniel O'Rourke, the pastor, was a big fat priest who came after the church was built.

Earl announced, "I'm an altar boy—there is good money in the funerals and weddings. You really have to be a favorite of O'Rourke's to get the best jobs as an altar boy. Tim Flynn told me Father O'Rourke was serving mass last week, and Flynn was responsible for bringing the wine to O'Rourke and pouring it. He said the bottle was almost full when he started mass and empty when he finished."

Ray and I looked at each other a bit puzzled. We had never heard anyone speak so ill about a priest, and I never thought being an altar boy was a paid job. Ronnie broke in, "My parents and I sometimes go to church on Sundays. The church is miles away, and it takes forever to get there. Who wants to ruin your whole Sunday morning by just going back and forth to church? My parents told me it couldn't be possible for everyone who missed Sunday mass to be condemned to hell—if it were true, there would be no one in heaven."

My mother's warnings regarding public school kids sure did fit Ronnie. It had been ingrained in me from as far back as I can remember that the priest was sacred, nuns were the next level down, and missing mass on

Sundays was second only to shaking hands with Satan. When I asked her once why Alberta, Ray, and I had to attend Catholic school, she said, "The devil controls the public schools. If you want to be close to God, you need as much help as you can get. The Catholic schools teach you respect for yourself, for others, and for God. In addition, a good swat every now and then will do you good."

Earl straightened his bike and said, "I've got to go now, but we'll see you around. Oh, by the way, Saturday and Sunday afternoons a number of us meet on the big open field beside the restaurant on the hill. We play baseball in the summer and football in the fall. The volunteer firemen play softball games there every Sunday afternoon. Each team brings a keg of beer, and by the fourth inning, half the guys are so drunk they ask us to play for them. Maybe we'll see you this afternoon or next Saturday."

We watched as the bikes disappeared down Second Avenue and around the corner. Ray explained as they rode away how Earl demonstrated his strength. "There aren't a lot of guys who can hold a bike with one leg like Earl did. He didn't even shift the bike or his legs. I was watching him while he talked with us," Ray said. "His legs didn't even move. I wouldn't want to fight with him."

A few minutes later, we were walking toward our house. As we approached Fifty-ninth Third Avenue, we could see a number of workmen installing a new blacktop driveway at the house directly across from ours. We turned and walked up the narrow one-lane dirt driveway that serviced Fifty-ninth Third Avenue.

Ray and I were unable to play baseball that afternoon or any afternoon for two weeks. My father asked us to help him make our house livable. My father had purchased a new hand mower so we could cut the grass and trim the weeds around the house. The mower was sharp, but it was a real chore trying to push it through the tall grass and weeds. We made very little progress until my dad decided to give us each a hand scythe. We cut the lawn first with scythes and then raked the portions we had cut. After three passes, we mowed the grass with the lawnmower. After the weeds were removed from the front lawn, two large pink peony plants were uncovered; they were beautiful.

When Ray and I finished the first day, we both had huge blisters on our hands. While we were punishing the lawn, my dad was replacing the broken windows, and Alberta and mom were cleaning the inside.

Within a short time, dad promised Ray and I would be sleeping in our own bed and we would have carpeting for the living room and bedrooms (what we got were remnants). The house was beginning to appear like someone was planning to live there.

The backyard was postage-stamp size with a hedgerow separating it from an open area of about two square miles. The open area was a boy's paradise. Trees, weeds, wild raspberry bushes, wild strawberries, a big old walnut tree, a number of apple trees left from an abandoned orchard, wild turkeys, pheasants, deer, frogs, rabbits, and an occasional fox were all there depending on the time of year. In addition, there were lots of old tires, wooden barrels, and other trash the Braddock residents had decided to store there.

Alberta's friends on the front lawn of Fifty-ninth Third Avenue. Harold is front and center.

This is the 2007 version of Fifty-ninth Third Avenue. On my return to Hilton High School for my fiftieth class reunion, I stopped at Fifty-ninth Third Avenue.

Quite a few changes had been made to the house: a dormer and new windows had been installed, the front porch had been enclosed, the yard had been regraded, and the garage had been removed. The new owners of the vacant property behind Fifty-ninth Third Avenue erected a chain-link fence, which divided the homes on Third Avenue from the wonderful fruit and wild life habitat behind the houses.

While I was staring at the house, the owner of the home walked over to me and asked if he could help me. After I explained who I was, I told him the Barend family had been the poorest family in Braddock Heights. He looked at my BMW convertible, smiled at me, and said, "It appears you have come a long ways."

*Alberta, **left**, and two of her friends adorn the back steps at Fifty-ninth Third Avenue, Braddock Heights. To the right is a milk box. Twice a week a milkman would make home delivery.*

After a few weeks, Earl and Ronnie came to our house. They learned where we lived from the girl who lived in the house across the street. They knocked loudly on the back door. My mother was baking a large batch of chocolate chip cookies. She walked to the door and invited them in. As part of her welcome, my mother offered them cookies and milk.

Once they were seated at the kitchen table, she called to Ray and me. Ray had been in the backyard helping my dad attempt to straighten the garage. They had concocted a Rube Goldberg system of pulleys and jacks and appeared to be making some progress when my mother hollered out the back door to Ray, "Raymond, two of your friends have come to visit. Come in and have cookies and milk with them. That garage can wait another ten or fifteen minutes," she told my dad. "Let him have a rest; he's worked hard enough," she continued.

I was in the bedroom reading one of my brother's classic comic books. I remained silent, hoping they would forget about me. No such luck. A second later my mother's voice came rolling down the hall, "Harold, you have friends here. Come out of the bedroom and say hello."

She couldn't comprehend the complexity of my anxiety. Earl, Ronnie, and Ray sat at an old kitchen table my dad had picked up from a used furniture dealer. Unknown to me, Earl and Ronnie didn't care about the table or our lack of furniture.

They sat gorging themselves on the warm soft chocolate chip cookies. I could hear them dunking cookies into their milk and then slurping them down. No one seemed to miss me. When I realized all the cookies would be gone in a few minutes, I swallowed my pride, came out of hiding, said hello to Earl and Ronnie, and then pulled a seat to the table.

Within ten minutes, all my mother's work had been devoured, and we proceeded to grab the hot cookies as they were exiting the oven. After the cookie feast, I knew Earl and Ronnie would be good friends. Our mother was the perfect hostess.

A few weeks later, Ronnie came to invite me to go swimming. I told him I was just learning how to swim. He said, "Don't worry, there are plenty of us who know how to swim. There are about four very wide sandbars where we will be swimming. You don't have to go very far to be in shallow water. It's about ninety-five degrees and all the kids will be there. I think your brother is already down there."

The Point

Walking paths meander through the peninsula (the Point) where children from decades ago enjoyed clear blue waters, muskrat, fox, beaver, pheasant, and birds. Lake Ontario lies on the north side of the Point. Jetties extending out from the Point were constructed by the Corp of Engineers to enhance the sandy beach area.

I ran to my room, slipped into my swim trunks, grabbed a towel, and within minutes I was walking with Ronnie down Third Avenue heading toward Braddock Bay. When we arrived at the sandy peninsula (the Point), which separated Lake Ontario from Braddock Bay, about ten kids were swimming in the bay.

Although the bay water wasn't quite as clean as the lake, it was always warmer and very sandy near the north end of the peninsula. The Point measured about a hundred feet wide and a quarter mile long. The trees and high weeds in the center of the Point provided coverage when we had our BB gun fights.

In Braddock Heights where Edgemere Drive ends, the Point begins. During the summer, the children who lived in Braddock Heights visited the Point almost on a daily basis. At the end of the Point, the waters from Lake Ontario and Braddock Bay kissed.

It was a place to swim, picnic, have BB gun fights, and just fall in love with nature. During the summer, we could choose swimming in the lake, bay, or pond. The waters in the lake and bay were crystal clear. Cranberry Pond was a little murky.

Today, man's influence on nature can be seen in the mucky waters of the bay and the silted opaque waters of Lake Ontario. Within sixty years, man had severely damaged this natural beauty.

Shortly after entering the water, Ronnie left me and grabbed one of the girls. He swam underwater through her legs and lifted her onto his shoulders. He then proceeded to entangle himself and his partner in battle with three other boys who had girls mounted on their shoulders. The object was to be the last standing.

I saw my brother splashing water at two boys and girls his age. When he noticed me, I could sense a bit of disappointment. He walked to me and said very low so no one could hear him, "Harold, what are you doing here? You don't know how to swim, and I am not going to ruin my whole day by having to watch you."

I really wanted to tell him to blow it out his ass, but I knew he would embarrass me in front of all the kids, so I responded with temper in check, "Ray, nobody has to take care of me. I'm not going swimming. Ronnie asked me to come. I'll just go a little way into the water. I want to cool off. I'll go over where they are playing chicken. Ronnie told me the water is only four feet deep as long I stay on the sandbar."

Ray wasn't convinced. He quickly turned away from me when one of the girls came toward us. It was obvious he did not want her to know I was his little brother. I ignored him and moved in the direction of Ronnie and the other three couples. They were furiously pulling and screaming at each other in an attempt to knock the riders into the bay—thoroughly enjoying the game of chicken.

While I was watching, pretending to be engaged in the battle, a beautiful, long-haired blonde ten-year-old named Annie asked me if she could get onto my shoulders and join the battle. It was love at first fight.

When I attempted to lift her and place her onto my shoulders, Annie laughed hysterically and asked, "Haven't you ever played water chicken before? I get on your shoulders when you swim between my legs—but no funny stuff."

After I lifted Annie, we galloped along to the sandbar where the four other couples were jousting for the winner's rights. When we got there, Annie reached out and made a major miscalculation of our combined athleticism and strength.

She grabbed Gail Robbins, who was sitting atop Earl Vokel. Annie pulled her arm backward, forcing Earl to stumble. They both went down. I was beginning to believe in divine intervention.

Annie was patting my shoulders, saying, "Good, Horsy! Good, Horsy!" and I was pumped with confidence.

Within seconds my confidence disappeared like a penny in a whirlpool. I saw Gail, who was on Earl's shoulders, rise out of the water. When they stumbled and fell, she never left his shoulders. Earl was strong enough to recover his balance underwater without dumping Gail. He was standing upright and glaring at me—ready for war.

He looked just like the mammoth wild bull that charged through our yard when we lived on Masseth Street in Rochester. The bull had broken loose from a railroad car and invaded our side yard where Ray and I were playing. It came with the force of an army. The bull plowed through an iron fence as if it were paper. We were close enough to see steam pouring from his nose.

Without caring who I was or how many chocolate chip cookies he ate at my house, Earl came charging at us. Gail's arms were flaying like a puppet without direction. I quickly sidestepped.

Earl grabbed my leg with one hand and held his rider with his other hand. His hand quickly moved to the top of my bathing trunks; then he attempted to pull them down. Earl had every intention of embarrassing me in front of the girls—he wanted payback for being knocked off balance by a nine-year-old. I was scared of being humiliated in front of my peers and kids I hadn't even met.

While I kept trying to spin away, unaware of my plight, Annie kept pulling on Gail's arm. She was trying to pull them off balance while pulling them toward us. She had no clue as to our desperate situation. When I finally broke loose, I had moved to the very edge of the sandbar. My feet teetered on the edge. I wanted to scream for help but knew it was too late. I desperately moved my feet trying to find the sand. The sand was quickly disappearing. Within seconds, we slipped off the edge, and we were in twelve feet of water instead of four. Annie was still mounted on my shoulders.

I tried to push her off with both hands. She was grabbing my head and face while I was pushing and pulling at her legs.

When Earl and Danny saw both of us go underwater and neither of us surfaced, they both ran to the spot where we slipped off the sandbar. They jumped in and grabbed us. They knew Annie couldn't swim. I kept pushing to get Annie off while she was using me to keep herself from sinking.

Finally, Earl pulled Annie off me, and Danny pulled me out of the water. I was unconscious, and my lungs were full of water. Danny and Earl proceeded to invoke rescue techniques they learned in the Boy Scouts. They dragged my limp body to the shore where Earl laid me on my stomach—my head was motionless and titled down. He leaned over me and proceeded to count as he pushed forward.

Within seconds, water began to pour from my mouth. I remember coughing water and staring at my brother who was standing over me, asking, "Harold, are you OK? Harold, are you OK?"

For a few minutes I was the center of attention. All the attention vaporized when my big-mouthed brother told everyone he knew something was going to happen to his "little brother." Ronnie, who had been standing beside Annie, began hollering at her and asking her why was she trying to kill me.

"Annie, why did you keep pushing Harold down? Do you hate him already? Is it because you attend the Catholic school and you get all hot when he put you on his shoulders?"

Annie's face was flush. She was embarrassed and hollered at Ronnie with her face inches from his, "You sick little boy, I don't get turned on by little pigs like you. You and your friend should play in the shallow part where the little kids go."

If there was ever a time I wanted to kill my brother, it was at this very moment. I knew his remark about his little brother destroyed any chance I had with Annie. As for Ronnie, he was just being Ronnie.

Ronnie and I melted away from the group and quietly walked to his house. We didn't need that group. We knew we could have fun by ourselves. We both agreed all the older boys pretended they were hot shit when the girls were around—they just liked to pick on us because it made them look better. At nine years old, we had isolated the variable that caused us the most havoc and motivated the older boys to act stupid: girls!

Ray and Harold life, discussing how not to drown.

Sundays were a day for church, ice cream—and then a pony ride.

David Lyons with Harold and Ray in Detroit, Michigan, where the Lyons family hosted Harold and Ray for a month during the summer of 1949. It was a wonderful summer experience.

The picture on the right was taken three years later in Braddock Heights by Mrs. Lyons who experienced a summer with the "dead-end kids." Michael Lyons is standing in front of his brother David, Raymond, and Harold. The picture was taken in Braddock Heights at the home of the Ackermans (grandparents to David and Michael Lyons) who lived adjacent to Fifty-ninth Third Avenue.

Chapter Twenty-Four

IQ Tests

With respect to wit, I learned there was not much difference between the half and the whole.

—Henry David Thoreau, *Walden*

In 1884, visitors to the International Health Exhibition at London's South Kensington Museum were invited to pay three pence each and enter Francis Galton's Anthropometric Laboratory. At the end of the exhibition, more than nine thousand men and women had been enticed to take what were designed to be intelligence tests.

Not unlike Galton's tests, in the third grade no one explained to me the real significance of the tests I was required to take. No one said anything about being branded as a human being who has the capacity for learning on a scale of below average, average, above average, or just plain genius.

Not until I transferred to public school was it explained to me the significance of the tests that had been administered to me at Our Mother of Sorrows Grammar School. If a three-year-old solved problems normally reserved for a five-year-old, his mental age would be five while his chronological age would be three. A bright child would have an IQ over 100, dull children under 100, and the average child has an IQ of 100.

The only IQ test I remember taking was in the third grade. It was administered by Ms. Marguerite McShea, my third-grade teacher at Our Mother of Sorrows. It was a very controversial test only because I scored the highest of anyone in the class.

The nuns were sure the kid who transferred from the city schools found a way to cheat. The question remained: how could a child of poverty score higher than a child who was groomed by a family of wealth and expected to become a shining star?

The morning after taking the Stanford-Binet tests, Ms. McShea sent me to Sister Agnes Cecilia's office. She told me to wait outside the door until I was called. When I arrived at Sister Cecilia's office, there was a chair adjacent to the open door. I sat on the chair without entering the office or announcing I had arrived.

The principal, Sister Agnes Cecilia, SSJ, was speaking with her secretary who had been reviewing the Stanford-Binet test results. When I heard my name mentioned, I realized they were discussing my test results. I was all ears.

Sister Cecilia did most of the talking, "I am convinced the test results are flawed. Either he cheated or he just got lucky by guessing. There are a number of children in that class who are much smarter than Harold. Based upon his upbringing and environment, I doubt if he has any moral guilt about committing a dishonest act."

Harold in third grade at Our Mother of Sorrows.
Second testing: IQ score 130 and holding.

The secretary said, "Yes, sister, I agree with you. I didn't think there was anyone in the room smarter than Tommy." Tommy was a grade behind me, but his parents requested he take the tests early.

"I was not happy with Tommy's scores," Sister Cecilia continued. "I think we will arrange for both Barend and Tommy to retake the examinations before we submit them. Please prepare notes that I can send to their parents informing them, because of a problem with the testing, we would like to have some of the students retake the examinations tomorrow. We'll just backdate the examinations."

I was listening to the whole conversation. The acoustics in the Quonset school building (a half-moon metal building), which resembled a metal airplane hangar, were very good. The Quonset hut replaced a building called the Beamish House. The Quonset hut was built during the tenure of Father O'Rourke in 1945 and remained in use until 1953.

I listened until Sister Mary Magdalene walked past. She did a double take when she realized the office conversation was about me. She stopped, looked at me, and asked, "Does anyone know you are waiting here?" I replied, "No, sister. I was told by Ms. McShea to report here because Sister Cecilia had sent for me, and I should wait outside the door until I was called."

She gave me a strange look and then turned and walked into the office where the conversation was unfolding. Sister Magdalene asked Sister Cecilia and her secretary if there was some problem of which she should be informed.

Sister Cecilia told her, "We have the results of the Stanford-Binet third-grade test, and the Barend boy scored the highest of anyone in the class. The results cannot be valid. I do not believe he honestly scored higher than Tommy or a number of the other children in that class. I am planning to have Tommy and Barend retested. Tommy scored well but not as good as he should have, and his father was quite concerned about the results of these tests."

"Sister, I don't understand what the problem is," Sister Magdalene interjected, "Harold is an A+ student. He has done exceptionally well since coming here, and you should know he is sitting outside the door as we speak."

With those words, Sister Cecilia lurched forward as if she had been shot from a sling and rushed to me. With her face inches from mine, she hollered, "Why are you sitting there listening to our conversation? I knew there was something I did not trust about you. Now tell me quickly—why are you sitting here?"

I was scared. I had just listened to them discuss how they believed I cheated. I didn't think I had done anything wrong, but now I was wondering if maybe I did. I wasn't sure what it was except I scored too high on the tests.

"Sister," I responded, "I was sent here by Ms. McShea. She told me to go directly to your office and sit here until you discussed a matter of importance with me. I came here and have been waiting for you. You were talking, and I did not want to walk into your office and interrupt you. I am sorry about listening to the conversation, but I was told to come here, and I did exactly as I was told."

"Maybe you did score high on the tests," Sister Agnes Cecilia replied. "You have a very smart mouth. Would you like it washed with my bar of soap? Did you cheat on those examinations? Who were you sitting beside?"

Each time she asked a question, I tried to answer, but my answer was cut short with another question. I realized she really didn't care about my answer because she already had her answer.

The next day, the tests were retaken by Tommy and me. A note had been sent to my parents informing them that because of a clerical mistake some students would be required to retake the IQ examination. It would be beneficial, the note read, to have me get a good night's sleep.

It was probably the first and last time an IQ test was given with the hope one student would do exceptionally well and the other average or less. A month after the examination my parents were sent a form that showed how I scored and my aptitude ability. My test score on the second set of tests was 130.

After my mother read the information, her only comment was, "You see, because I delayed your starting school a year, it must have helped you taking the tests. You tested high because you are older than most of the kids in your class."

I wondered why the nuns couldn't have figured that out if my mother resolved the problem so easily. I did not start grammar school until I was six years old. My mother was concerned the other children would make fun of me because I stuttered—a well-intentioned mistake.

Chapter Twenty-Five

AND THE YEARS PASSED

Time in its aging course teaches all things.

—Aeschylus, *Prometheus Bound*

Most of the bad habits I nurtured in Ms. McShea's classroom, I retained throughout my years at Our Mother of Sorrows. The five years, which brought me from the third to the eighth grade, were filled with colorful events somewhat uncommon to boys my age. I became acclimated to the regimentation of a Catholic school and developed into an excellent student but a bit of a disciplinary problem. My grades were all A or in the high 90s.

Ms. McShea was one of the teachers for the third, fourth, and fifth grades. I had managed to discover why she called me the wrong name whenever I sat in the back of the classroom—she was almost blind. I became friends with Joe S. who lived in Grandview Heights and was also a disciplinary problem. There was a major difference between Joe and me: his father owned a department store, and his family had plenty of money to smooth over any of his indiscretions.

I never took advantage of Ms. McShea's handicap until the fifth grade. When I got to fifth grade, Joe and I had become friends. He was every bit as adventurous as me. Each day, Joe and I would play our game in Ms. McShea's class. While she was teaching the class, Joe and I would sneak along the side of the classroom wall inching our way to the door. The kids in the class would giggle and laugh, but Ms. McShea would never see us unless we moved too fast. We relished in the adventure—thinking we were too smart to get caught.

Joe and I would compete each day to be first out of the room and into the safety of the boys' room. Once we arrived in the boys' room, we began a game of pitch (whoever tossed the penny closest to the wall would win the other person's penny). We would play this game until we got bored and then sneak back into the classroom.

My dad knew how much I hated being in the Catholic school. He also had difficulty with the Catholic "way"—he could not understand why the church put so much emphasis on money and discriminated so much against the poor.

My dad was a good Catholic and a better Christian. He volunteered his time at church functions, donated his services to help poor families, served as an usher, and even helped to organize the first chapter of the Knights of Columbus at Our Mother of Sorrows.

At the beginning of my sixth grade, Father Daniel O'Rourke decided to publish a weekly list of all the parishioners and how much they donated. My mother and dad bristled when the list was published. Every Sunday it would be folded into the bulletin. My parents always gave money to the church even when we had little or next to nothing. That was between them and God. Now Father O'Rourke made it a public humiliation—my parents were always at the bottom of the list.

When my sister, Alberta, finished her second year of high school at Saint Joseph's Academy in Rochester, she was sixteen. She worked all the while she was attending school to pay her tuition.

Ray had turned thirteen on December 25, 1948. He was about to complete his last year at Mother of Sorrows and graduate from grammar school. He was a favorite of Sister Agnes Cecilia. As much as she saw the angel in him, she saw the devil in me.

During this year, a problem arose, and there was some consideration with regards to Ray's being able to graduate. An incident took place while Earl Vokel, Ronnie Weins, and Ray were instructing me in the ritual of being an altar boy. The four of us walked the short distance from the school building through the church cemetery to the red brick church, which was built in 1878. Ray, Earl, and Ronnie were there to ensure everything was correct for the forthcoming Easter mass.

I was to be instructed as to the duties of an altar boy, but I knew it was doubtful that I would ever serve as an altar boy. Father O'Rourke would never accept the idea of me being on the altar with him.

One of the assistant priests, Father O' Brien, had taken an interest in me and convinced Father O'Rourke and Sister Agnes Cecilia that it would be good discipline for me. He believed I would become closer to God if I practiced to be an altar boy. They both went along with Father O' Brien, but I am sure neither one ever bought into his idea of bringing me closer to God.

We went to the church to practice for the forthcoming Easter mass. Earl had already served at a number of masses at Mother of Sorrows and at the Star of the Sea (a summer-only Catholic church located on Edgemere Drive that offered mass only on Sundays).

I accompanied them because it was mandatory, and I enjoyed getting out of class. It was about 1:00 p.m. We were the only ones in the church. After practicing for about thirty minutes, Ray decided to climb the stairs to the balcony and pound on the organ. Earl and Ronnie mounted the pulpit to give a sermon. I sat in a pew about halfway up the center aisle.

Ray banged on the organ, and Earl and Ronnie Weins stood in pulpit, hollering, "We want money! We want money!" Over and over again, they shouted it, and I laughed and laughed and laughed. They just kept hollering, "We want more money! We want more money!"

I hollered from my pew, "You can only have one more wine. You drink too much. You're too fat. You don't need money. You need to eat less."

Ray kept banging on the organ. He didn't have the slightest idea how to play, so he made a lot of noise.

Then, in a moment I will never forget, Father Daniel O' Rourke appeared in the center of the double doors at the main entrance of the church. It was like a bad dream.

His voice boomed at peak volume, "Who dares to commit this sacrilege in the house of the Lord? Who are these evil boys entrusted with the sacred positions of the altar? Get out! Get out! The devil has found its way into my church! I never want to see your faces again." He was screaming, but he had no idea who was in the church.

Earl and Ronnie saw Father O' Rourke first, and they were gone in a flash. They jumped off the pulpit and ran out the back door of the sanctuary. Ray stopped playing the organ just as soon as Earl and Ronnie took off. Ray ran down the balcony stairs and out the side door. I realized there was a problem when Earl and Ronnie ran from the pulpit as the church doors opened. And just as suddenly, the organ music stopped.

I was sitting in a pew with my back was to the church door entrance. When I turned to look at the entrance, it was too late. O' Rourke was moving.

Father O' Rourke's voice was booming, and I was the only one left in the church for him to chase. All 350 pounds of him rumbled down the center aisle.

I was on my feet, half scared to move and half scared to stay. I knew he already recognized me. O'Rourke grabbed me as I struggled to get out of the pew. While I was tripping over the kneeler, he pulled my shirt so hard it ripped the sleeve. Then with his right hand, he blasted me across the head. With his big fat red face inches from mine, he screamed at me, "You disgraced God! You have sinned in the house of God! I should have known it was you! Who was helping you do this awful thing? Who are they? Tell me and be quick about it, or I'll have you back in kindergarten. You are a disgrace to me, to your teachers, and to your parents."

With each word he spoke, his big hand would find a spot on my body—the majority of the blows landed above my shoulders. He kept staring at me with eyes so full of hate and hitting me with his right hand while squeezing my ripped shirt with his left hand.

I realized he did not have his glasses on. Without them he would not have been able to see who was in the pulpit. I would never tell on Ray or Earl, and the Weins family lived directly across from us.

Things had become a bit complicated. I was now in the sixth grade, and there was a certain amount of respect and honor that came with courage. In addition, it never left my mind that Ray and Earl would beat the hell out of me if I told on them. This was the time I had to be courageous.

I told him, "I only know the boy in the pulpit because I never turned around to see who was on the organ. The person on the organ was probably one of the girls practicing."

"You're lying in the house of God!" he barked. "Who was in here with you? God will punish you for lying in church. I know someday you will burn in hell."

I looked him straight in the face and said, "The boy in the pulpit was Tommy. He was the only one I could see. I can't even be sure it was him because he was pretending to be a monk and he had his face partially covered."

I knew when I said Tommy, it was stupid, but I couldn't resist saying it because Tommy was the pet student of all the nuns and priests. I resolved myself to getting belted again. It was worth it to see the expression on Father O'Rourke's face.

"Tommy! Tommy! It was not Tommy!" Father O'Rourke barked. "Tommy would never do anything like that. You are lying before God. Get out of this church! Go back to your room immediately. No! I want you to report directly to Sister Agnes Cecilia and tell her exactly what happened. I'll give you one more chance as an altar boy, but you must confess who the other two boys were. I do not want you serving on the altar with me until you confess your sins. I want to see you in confession soon. Now get out of here!"

With the last command, he swung his foot in an attempt to kick me, but I moved too fast. His foot caught the hem of his black cassock. His big body teetered off balance. If it had not been for his proximity to the pew, he would have plopped in the aisle. Even in church, I was hoping for him to fall flat on his ass. I pushed open the big oak doors and was on my way back to the Quonset-hut metal building that served as a school for about 150 students from grade one through eight.

That was my last practice as an altar boy.

The quickest route from the church to the school was the diagonal walk through the cemetery. I choose to walk down the road and enter the school from the street. This took about five minutes longer. I had fifteen minutes before the school buses arrived, and I wanted to avoid Sister Cecilia who often patrolled the cemetery looking for students who might be skipping class. The upper-class students, of which I considered myself, stayed clear of Sister Cecilia when she wasn't teaching. The students nicknamed her Novena Punch. She carried a large silver key ring, which contained about nine or ten keys. When she was particularly annoyed with a student, she would rap the student across the head with her hand—the hand holding the keys. You prayed when she was about to hit you—thus Novena Punch. She knew more about brass knuckles than the mafia.

When the bell rang for dismissal, I moved quickly into line. Sister Cecilia was nowhere in sight, and I wasn't about to look for her. I hurried to find a seat on the bus and then slithered down. I held my breath while the bus began its slow movement away from the school. Earl and Ray had boarded the bus a few minutes after me and were anxiously waiting to hear my story. I was comfortably nestled in a seat beside Joe.

The bus slowly moved past the waving teachers and nuns. Coming toward the bus was Father O'Rourke. His big arms were flopping like a large seal. I scrunched down farther for fear he would stop the bus and pull me off. I wanted to ensure my invisibility from him and his inquisition team.

As soon as the bus left the parking lot, Ray and Earl moved to my seat, and I sat upright. It didn't make any difference to them that Joe was sitting next to me. They just moved in and moved him out. They told him to find another seat.

"Tell us what happened," Earl asked in a rush.

"I didn't know I was so popular," I responded. "Are you sure you want to sit with me today?"

"Ray," Earl said, annoyed as hell, "tell Harold to cut the shit and tell us what happened. I want to know why they didn't send for either of us."

"Come on, Harold, don't jerk us around," Ray said. "Just tell us what happened. Mom is going to kill me if she hears about this."

"Nothing happened except Father O'Rourke smacked me about fifteen times. He called me a devil and told me I was going to hell. I was the only one who didn't do a thing. I should have told him who was really in the church. Then you guys would take the same beating as me. He was crazy, you know. I tried to get out of there, but he was quicker than I thought. His face was so red I thought he was going to explode. I put my hands over my head and face, but he kept wailing on me."

I paused for a few seconds and took notice that all the kids around us were listening to my story. "He told me I have to go to confession this week. He's crazy if he thinks I will confess to him. I didn't do anything. When I go to confession, I'll tell Father O'Brien that O'Rourke hit an innocent altar boy, and O'Rourke should be confessing to someone."

When they realized I hadn't told O'Rourke, and he never recognized them, they were elated. They immediately began planning a strategy for the time when they would be called to the principal's office to answer questions as to their whereabouts. They knew there would be many questions for them to answer the next day. They had to explain their absence from altar practice during the time the disturbance took place in church and why they left me in the church.

As expected, the next day Earl and Ray (for some reason Ronnie Weins was not questioned) were called to the principal's office and questioned individually and then questioned together. Under the threat of bodily harm, they lied to Sister Agnes Cecilia.

She could easily believe them because they were her angels. As previously rehearsed, they said they left the church a little early to go into the cellar under the church and check the wine. Father O'Rourke had asked Earl and Ray, a few months prior to the incident, if they would periodically check to ensure there was enough wine for the masses.

Sister Cecilia, no dummy, asked after she heard their story, "Did you hear any disturbance in the church? Was anyone playing the organ?"

Earl answered, "I didn't think there was a disturbance. We heard some voices."

Ray nodded in agreement, "Yes, there were voices."

"With regards to the organ playing," Earl said, "someone was playing the organ. It sounded really nice. I thought it was the regular organist practicing for Easter."

"Well, was there enough wine for the weekend?" Sister Cecilia asked sarcastically.

Both Earl and Ray responded yes. We had been in the cellar before going up to the church. While Ray, Earl, and Ronnie indulged in the wine as if it were the Last Supper, I sipped it because I was anxious to join their fun.

For the next two months, they both brownnosed so much I thought their whole upper bodies would become turds. Consequently, they were both allowed to graduate that June. My parents had a party to celebrate Ray's graduation. Many of our relatives attended, and Ray received a considerable amount of gifts and money—an opportunity that would pass me by.

The evening after our altar exercise, I decided to tell my dad what had happened. I told him the true story and included the part Earl and Ray had played. Prior to telling him, I offered to help install the new screens he had made for the front porch. My mother had gone for a walk, Alberta was out with her boyfriend, and Ray was playing baseball at the fireman's field. My timing was perfect. He had a good laugh after I replayed the story. When I finished, he said, "Please, for your mother's sake, try not to upset the teachers anymore. After this year, you only have two more years at that school. It sounds like you already received enough punishment for one day. I won't say anything to your mother unless she hears about it from someone else. You had better tell your friends not to discuss this in our house because your mother will be very upset."

In their own way, Ray and Earl thanked me. They said it was unfortunate I got caught. They felt bad I took the beating, but according to them, it was my own fault for not leaving the church when they did. They both agreed my getting caught almost ruined them.

The following September I was standing in the hall at Mother of Sorrows School when Tommy's sister, Charlene, walked up to me laughing hysterically. Charlene was in the eighth grade, one grade ahead of me. Father O'Rourke and some of the nuns were frequent guests at their home during the summer. Charlene's father was a well-respected and very successful physician who practiced in Rochester. The family lived in a very upscale home on Edgemere Drive.

Charlene overhead Sister Agnes Cecilia telling her father how this wild Barend boy, who will probably be in prison someday, said it was Tommy in the pulpit. According to Charlene, they all had a hearty laugh except Tommy. Charlene was a really nice person. She was so different from her brother.

She asked me with a big smile, "How could you even think Father O'Rourke would believe you when you said it was Tommy? All the priests and nuns know Tommy, and they know he would never have done such a thing."

"I didn't know who to say, and Tommy's name was the first that came to my mind," I told her. "I knew Father O'Rourke wouldn't believe me, and I really didn't care. I just wanted to get away from him. He was hitting me on the head. Your brother can be such a jerk. Why is he like that?" I asked. She never answered.

One morning, before the eighth-grade class began, I, along with a number of classmates, was in the boys' room playing pitch with nickels (which was now forbidden at Our Mother of Sorrows) when Tommy walked in. Tommy always did everything right, except for this day. While standing at the urinal, he turned his head to watch us, and he wet his pants. It wouldn't have been bad, except Joe and I couldn't stop laughing.

Tommy got mad, started crying, and told us, "I'm going to tell Sister Cecilia you are playing pitch with nickels. You wait! She is going to get you, guys."

At the time, Sister Cecilia held dual roles. She was the principal of the school and the seventh—and eighth-grade teacher. I didn't want any problems with Sister "Novena Punch" or Tommy, so I said, "Tommy, if you tell Sister Cecilia about us, we'll tell the whole school you pissed your pants."

A few minutes after Tommy left and before the bell rang, Joe and I quickly went to our classroom. We were concerned as to what might happen regarding Tommy. Class went as usual—the same people were holding their hands in the air, hoping to be called to prove how smart they were.

I slipped into my seat while Sister Agnes Cecilia was standing at the front blackboard explaining how a sentence was to be diagrammed. On the right side of the board, she had written our spelling words for the next day. I hurriedly wrote them in my notebook along with a comment to myself, "Tommy is a big problem. Be Careful!"

A few months later, while four of us were practicing our pitch skills in the boys' room, Tommy walked in again. He looked at us playing pitch and snidely commented how we were going to be in big trouble. He proceeded to a toilet stall.

Within minutes, Tom Hoadley stepped outside the room and, without saying a word, motioned for us to join him and close the door so Tommy could not hear us. He whispered how we should foam him with the fire extinguisher, which hung adjacent to the door of the boys' room. I tried to convince him not to do it. He blurted out, "If you don't want me to do it, you do it. He'll see me if I do it, but, Harold, you are a lot taller than I am. You can stand on the wastebasket and spray over the top of the stall, and he'll never see who is doing it." He convinced me it was for the good of all.

While Tommy was still sitting on the toilet, I took the fire extinguisher and walked into the boys' room. Joe flipped the metal wastebasket so I could stand on the bottom. I stepped onto the metal wastebasket, pulled the pin from the fire extinguisher, and raised my arms, extending the big black plastic funnel-shaped cone over the top. I squeezed the trigger for about a minute. I sprayed so much foam that it was oozing out of the open area on the bottom side of the stall.

Tommy was screaming and hollering. I was afraid someone would hear him. There was so much foam in the stall that he couldn't find the door latch to exit the stall.

I quickly handed the fire extinguisher to Joe and then jumped off the wastebasket. As we ran out the door, Joe returned the fire extinguisher to its original position. Unfortunately, before we could leave the area and reenter our classroom, we saw Tommy emerging from the boys' room crying—and he saw us. His head and shoulders were covered with foam.

This time, I knew the line had been crossed—but it was worth it.

Harold in seventh grade.

Chapter Twenty-Six

MONEY, MONEY, MONEY

Some men worship rank, some worship heroes, some worship power, some worship God, and over these ideals they dispute—but they all worship money.

—Mark Twain

Our Mother of Sorrows Church, located on the corner of Latta Road and Mount Read Boulevard in Greece, New York, was originally named Our Mother of the Seven Sorrows. A French priest named Father Jacques Maurice founded the church.

The old basement furnace room of the church had a unique history for storage: wine was kept there in the early 1950s and runaway slaves in the 1800s. To this day, there are rumors the building is haunted by the spirits of young children who had been molested, hurt, or killed underneath the church. Even though the building has been converted to a town library, Father Maurice remains there. His body is buried in the graveyard adjacent to the Paddy Hill Library.

Each Sunday, the weekly bulletin listing the amounts each parishioner gave the previous week began to take its toll on my family. The first listing of contributors to Mother of Sorrows was published during the summer prior to my beginning the seventh grade. During that summer, one of my classmates sent my family their used clothing.

When I returned to school that September, I was still angry and humiliated. We had been sent clothes in the form of charity. I told Molly, the daughter of the family who sent the clothes, that my dad planned to return the clothes. We did not want them or their charity, I told her. I was angry and hurt. Unfortunately, Molly, who may have been innocently attempting to help, took the brunt of my anger. I hated being poor and having people feel sorry for my family.

She ran from me, crying. Within a few minutes, I was called to the principal's office to explain why I was so rude to the nice student who offered my family help. It was a true act of charity according to Sister "Novena Punch," and I was an ungrateful person who was the antitheses of what a good Catholic student should be.

Two days later, while I was talking with some of my classmates, an eighth grader walked up to me with a few of his friends and said, "You can have my old white dress shirts if you want. I know your parents are poor and might not have enough money to buy you new shirts."

I glared at him with so much hatred that I could not speak. I just punched him as hard as I could in the nose and broke it. There was blood all over the playground. When the nuns ran over to see what happened, he was so embarrassed he told them he tripped and fell. His offer to take the blame didn't carry much weight with the nuns.

They immediately established their inquisition and determined the smart-mouthed, ungrateful, habitual troublemaker was involved. Of the five nuns and three priests at the school, only Sister Magdalene, Father O'Brien, and two lay teachers came to my support.

The following evening, my parents were asked to attend a meeting with Sister Cecilia and Father O' Rourke. Sister Cecilia suggested when it came time for me to attend high school that my parents should consider Boys Town because it had an excellent football team. According to her, it would give me an opportunity to take my aggressions out in a more constructive manner.

Father O' Rourke suggested they have me enlist in the army as soon as possible even if they had to lie about my age. I was suspended again from school for a week. I was now on probation. Another miscue and I would be with all the devils in the public school.

When I returned, I became something of a big man at school. Sister Magdalene told me Father O'Brien was quite impressed that I would slug this boy who was considerably bigger than me.

She said he told Father O' Rourke, "Despite Harold's untimely nature, he is quite intelligent and has a lot of courage. He took on a boy considerably bigger than himself. He has pride, and I think that is good in a young person."

When I asked her what Father O' Rourke said, she smiled and replied, "He said, 'God has given us a mission to save souls and to educate the young, not to mold or encourage pugilists. Too much pride is a sin.' He said you could spend every day in confession and not be done."

I really wasn't too concerned about Father O' Rourke's opinion of me. I had already formed my opinion of him: he drank too much wine, he was too fat, and he published that list. I knew all I had to know about Father O'Rourke, and I could not see Christ in him anywhere. Sister Mary Magdalene was a wonderful teacher, a friend, and a beautiful person.

A few weeks later, Betsy asked if I would walk with her after school to the ice-cream stand. I accepted her invitation even though I would miss the school bus and would be walking home six miles.

When we finished our ice cream, Betsy asked if I would like to go with her to the Riviera Theater on Lake Avenue on Saturday. Being a bit flustered and without much thought, I said yes. I regained my composure and collected my thoughts enough to suggest we meet inside the theater at the popcorn machine. This was my first date.

I had no idea how I would go from my house to the movie theater, which was seven miles away, or how much the movie would cost. At least I had enough moxie to maneuver myself into a position to pay for one admission.

Chapter Twenty-Seven

THE CLUBHOUSE

I know only what is moral is what you feel good after, and what is immoral is what you feel bad after.

—Ernest Hemingway, *Death in the Afternoon*

According to the World Book Encyclopedia, "People join clubs for a number of reasons. Sometimes they merely believe in or favor the purposes of the club." The boys from Braddock Heights certainly did believe in the purpose of the Club.

The Club was a place where a select group of teenagers could meet, compete, and learn. Shortly after the altar-boy incident, Ronnie Lupo and I were invited to join the exclusive Braddock Heights Clubhouse.

The land on which the clubhouse was constructed was approximately four acres. The land bordered all the properties on the southern portion of Third Avenue. It was a wonderful place to catch frogs, hunt pheasants, pick berries, or just wander through studying the science of life. There were bushes and trees, rabbits, squirrels, skunks, foxes, pheasants, and wild turkeys.

Even though the land was privately owned on which the clubhouse was to be constructed, no one bothered to get the owner's permission to construct the building. We were kids. What did we know about permits or permission?

The property had been dormant for more than a decade. It provided the residents of Braddock Heights with a bounty of wildlife and wild berries.

It was something the residents had been using for decades. As far as we could determine, it would remain vacant. We felt as if we had a God-given right to use the property—it was a part of Braddock Heights—or so we thought.

Unfortunately, time does not stand still. During a recent visit to Braddock Heights, I observed a chain-link fence that enclosed the whole property where our beloved clubhouse once stood. The property where we climbed trees; picked strawberries, blueberries, and apples; played horseshoes; hunted pheasant and rabbit; and accelerated our transition from boys to men.

Adorning the fence were No Trespassing signs. The previous owner had died and willed it to a relative who immediately decided to change the status quo. How sad. The children living in Braddock Heights no longer had the opportunity to explore that wonderful habitat for learning.

Our clubhouse was an actual one-story wood building approximately twenty feet by thirty feet. It was constructed of discarded building materials, which were collected from trash heaps and junk piles.

With the help of our fathers, we leveled an area of about thirty feet by thirty-five feet. Then we dug holes in the ground for the four corners of the building and two center holes for the center support. Concrete was mixed and poured into the holes, which were about six inches above ground and served as the foundation for the building.

My Dad, Ronnie's father (Carl Lupo), and two other fathers got wheelbarrows and taught us how to mix the concrete and construct the foundation. Two days after we cleared the ground, we had constructed a solid floor with six concrete support columns. The floor was built of three-fourths-inch plywood. The sidewalls were erected of conventional two-inch-by-four-inch studs covered with plywood. We hammered, nailed, and sawed, without any power equipment until the building was completed.

The clubhouse was originally planned to be one big room. Earl and Ray had different thoughts about the floor plan. Within a week of the house being erected, interior partitions were installed for two bedrooms. Eventually, two old discarded beds with mattresses were dragged from a trash heap to the clubhouse. A couple of pieces of carpeting, an old wood-burning stove, and some doors were eventually found. There was no running water or electricity. If you used the clubhouse in the evening, you had to feel your way—which we normally did anyway.

Club members were always on the lookout for discarded building materials and good furniture that could be salvaged. Via our newspaper routes, Ronnie and I monitored everyone's trash in Braddock Heights.

Ronnie and I were invited into the clubhouse as half members. It was built to be a social gathering place for a select few. According to Ray and Earl, Ronnie and I were the youngest; therefore, we were responsible for doing most of the work: collecting bottles, rags, newspapers, and anything else that could be turned into cash for the club.

There was a code of honor: each member was sworn to secrecy. Nothing could be told to our parents or to nonmembers with regards to the activities of the club. The only nonmembers were the girls, who could come and go as they pleased, but they were also sworn to secrecy.

By the completion of seventh grade, I had learned the techniques of winning at strip poker. Earl and Ray always had extra cards hidden, and they seldom ever lost. At thirteen, we were frequenting the library more than ever to study the human anatomy of girls, and we were enjoying every minute.

Once Ronnie and I had become full-fledged members of the club, life became full of surprises. Every weekend, we would invite two or three of the girls to the clubhouse to play horseshoes, teach them how to trap shoot, and then complete the day with a game of strip poker.

The following year after my attempt to be an altar boy, another incident took place, which further convinced the powers that be at Our Mother of Sorrows that I was incorrigible and should be dumped on the trash heap of public education.

One of the girls who frequently visited the clubhouse confessed to Father O'Rourke about the various clubhouse games she had played. The Saturday morning following her confession, O'Rourke led a group of our fathers into the field, and they tore down the clubhouse.

The same fathers who helped to build the clubhouse realized their mistake and dismantled it within an hour. After the walls were down, just to ensure they would never rise again, everything was burned.

Ronnie, Earl, Ray, and I stood at the hedgerow in our backyard watching the destruction of our clubhouse. We were in shock. We concluded there was only one way our parents could have learned: Father O'Rourke. Someone within our group confessed to Father O'Rourke. Almost in unison, we hollered, "It's a sin to repeat what someone tells you in confession. You committed a sacrilege against God."

It didn't faze Father O'Rourke or our fathers. By demolishing the clubhouse, our fathers acknowledged the wrongs their children had committed. After the incident, I was put on probation from school for the second time that year.

When my father returned from dismantling the clubhouse, he wouldn't discuss the problem with my mother. She was not one to be kept in the dark about anything. All he would say was "The problem has been taken care of—it is gone. Now, let's move on."

He continued telling her, "There were quite a few of the neighborhood kids involved. I do not know what involvement Raymond and Harold had. It is best to just leave it alone. The boys have lost their clubhouse, and Father O'Rourke is satisfied. If Ray and Harold want to tell you what went on, it is up to them. I really don't care to know."

I knew my mother wanted to scream at both of us, but she didn't know what to scream about, and neither Ray nor I was about to tell her. If we told her the truth, it would be like opening the doors to hell. She would have pulled our hair out—if she could catch us. She glared at me, her blue eyes almost popping out of their sockets and her red hair bristling.

"Harold, tell me what went on in there. Were there girls involved? Oh my god! There were girls involved! That is what this is all about, isn't it?"

"Mom," I responded, "I wasn't one of the big guys in the club. I didn't go there very often because the older guys were always there. You very seldom ever saw me go there. I went when Ronnie's dad came over to give us boxing lessons. I played horseshoes and sometimes brought my shotgun to practice shooting clay pigeons." It was a lie for survival, and I knew God would understand.

That evening when our family sat down to dinner, my dad said the following prayer, which I will never forget, "Dear, Lord, bless this house and everyone in it. Let the sins of the past be forgiven and help us to remain in your path."

I knew the part about sins in the past would tickle my mother's interest. As soon as the last word rolled out of my dad's mouth, she looked at Ray and me and asked, "Is what you did so awful you can't tell your own mother? Never mind! I don't need to know what went on in there. I just make the meals, wash the clothes, and try to keep the house nice for the family. I do not want to be embarrassed by either of your actions. Nor do I want to feel ashamed when I kneel at the communion rail. This Saturday, I want both of you to go to confession."

Father O'Rourke not only demolished the clubhouse, but he scared the hell out of most of the girls in Braddock Heights. For the next four months, all invitations to assist the baby-sitters were canceled—except for the non-Catholic girls. Thank God for the Protestants.

Ronnie and I became good friends. Each evening after dinner, we would meet on the steps of the only store in Braddock Heights: Vokel's Grocery

Store. There were three large concrete steps leading to the front entrance. Almost every evening, rain, sunshine, or snow, about six of us would congregate on the steps. We would buy Twinkies, Hostess Cupcakes, and Mallow Cups, along with soda. As each purchaser would exit the store, everyone would holler, "Dibbies!" for a share of their food.

Each evening, Franny Vokel—a heavyset, big-boned woman—would open the store door and scream as loud as possible, "I want you goddamn kids off my steps. Now! If you don't get off, I'll get the broom and beat your asses!"

Franny Vokel was Earl's aunt. She was one of the most colorful women in Braddock Heights. In addition to the grocery store, Franny and her husband, Chuck, owned a tavern, which was attached to the grocery store.

Along with her duties as store owner, she was also the tavern's bouncer. Some evenings we would watch in amazement as a body or two would fly out the tavern door and fall down the steps. Franny would be standing at the door entrance, swearing at the top of her lungs at the person she just ejected.

We would usually hang around the store steps for about an hour. Within that time, hopefully, we could determine which of the girls was baby-sitting. Baby-sitting nights were usually on weekends and great fun.

Normally, the boys would be paired up by the girls depending on who had the hots for whom. If you got tipped off in advance that your pairing had a face only a mother could love, you found a substitute or conveniently got sick.

A "no show" was the same as being expelled from the baby-sitting circuit for a few weeks. Unfortunately, some of the cutest girls in the Heights had ugly girlfriends.

If you wanted your chance at the pot of gold, you sometimes had to squeeze a bit of fat first. Baby-sitting nights were strictly sex education. Some of the girls had restrictions while others were accommodating.

The Barend family, although poor, always had food for guests. Ray and Harold were separated at mealtime. Rose Pauline is at the head of the table. Ray has his mouth open. Bernard Harold is to Ray's right, and Harold is looking into the camera. The girls are Alberta's friends.

Chapter Twenty-eight

Newspaper Boy

I am no Horatio Alger hero. Although I did start out in prescribed style as a newsboy.

—Eric Johnston, *America Unlimited*

Ronnie always had more spending money than any of us. At first, I thought it was because his parents were wealthy. He would exit Vokel's Grocery Store with two Hostess Cupcake packs and two Mallow Cups almost every night. Ann Marie, Liz, Nancy, Jim (the Chief), Bill "Willie" Boothby, and I would decorate the large cement steps at the entrance to the grocery store and welcome him so we could share his goodies.

One evening, I said to Ronnie, "It must be nice to have wealthy parents."

"Don't be stupid!" he replied. "I work hard for my money. Where do you think I go when we get home from school? I'm working while you guys are playing. I've had my newspaper route for a year."

What a great idea, I thought, *a newspaper route.* It would give me spending money, and I would have plenty of time to play. I asked if there were any openings for newspaper boys, and he told me he would ask Sam, his route manager.

It was the summer prior to the start of sixth grade. I was twelve. A few days after I inquired about the position, Ronnie told me the morning route would be available in September. If I wanted it, Sam would stop by my house to interview me and explain the responsibilities.

About the second last week of August 1950, Sam came to my house. He was the district manager for Gannett Newspapers in Rochester. Braddock Heights had a morning newspaper—the *Rochester Democrat & Chronicle*—and an evening newspaper, the *Times Union*. I would be responsible for the delivery of the morning newspaper.

Sam was a short balding man who kept his left arm against his side to control its shaking. The rumor was Sam had Parkinson's disease. It became apparent the longer you knew Sam that his handicap would not control his life. He had built up his right arm to be so strong that he could lift a large bundle of newspapers with only his right arm.

He told me, "The morning newspaper must be delivered to the homes no later than 6:00 a.m. That is the time for the last newspaper, not the first.

"There are a lot of people who leave for work early, and they want to read the newspaper before they leave. If you do a good job, your customers will reward you at Christmas when you take them the *Democrat & Chronicle* calendar. That is when the people show their appreciation for your getting the newspaper to their homes early.

"There are 187 newspapers that must be delivered no matter what the weather. Each weekend you will collect money from your customers, and the following Monday morning you must pay me for the newspapers whether you collect the money or not."

Just before he left, Sam handed me a white canvas bag with the newspaper's name emblazoned on the side. I didn't see him again until 4:30 a.m. on the Monday preceding Labor Day weekend.

My mother got me out of bed ten minutes before he arrived. She was so anxious she couldn't sleep. I didn't think people were actually awake at that time of the morning. The newspaper route was a mixture of joy and hardships. It thoroughly tested my resolve to work. It was a seven-day-a-week job with no holidays or vacations.

After the newspapers were delivered this early morning, Harold visits with his mother, Rose, before school.

Ronnie and I would often discuss strategies for customers who were difficult. We agreed that if anyone called in a complaint to the newspaper about either of us, we would cease delivery of their newspapers for a week—no evening newspaper, no morning newspaper.

After the third time we did this, Sam was so upset his whole body was shaking. He realized we were conspiring to get even with customers, and he threatened to fire both of us.

He had a major problem, and we knew it. He could not find anyone willing to take our routes. We knew everyone who lived in the hamlet, and no one wanted or was willing to take our jobs.

That summer prior to my entering the seventh grade, Ray purchased a blue Cushman motor scooter. He kept it parked in our garage. He replaced the regulation muffler system with dual straight pipes to let everyone know he was coming.

Ray forbade me to take the scooter for rides on the public road because I was too young and did not have a license. In ten minutes I learned to operate the scooter by just going up and down the driveway.

Ray left high school early to help our parents. He received his high school diploma years later but never made it to college. He found employment on the night shift at E. I. du Pont in Rochester. This meant he was gone from midnight until about 9:00 a.m. It also meant I got to sleep in the bed by myself.

He never went to sleep before work—he would be with a girlfriend until it was time for work. His work schedule not only enhanced my sleeping space, but it also allowed for a little chicanery.

For three weeks, in the spring of my thirteenth year, my newspapers were delivered via the Cushman scooter. I saw more lights go on throughout the hamlet between 4:30 and 5:00 a.m. during this period than ever before or after.

Each time I took Ray's scooter, I gambled my parents would not awaken until after I completed my route. I would walk the scooter out of the driveway and then kick-start it after I was a good distance from our house. When I finished delivering the newspapers, I always shut it off a distance from the house and pushed it up the driveway and into the garage.

After my second week with the motor scooter, the Greece police had been alerted to my adventures. It then became a game of chess. The beginning of the third week, the police were sending patrol cars to Braddock Heights at 5:00 a.m. I surmised the police were determined to get me.

One morning the police stationed a car at 5:00 a.m. on Edgemere Drive. They waited for the sound of the scooter.

As I drove toward Edgemere Drive delivering my newspapers, I head a siren coming toward me. I immediately shut off the scooter and pushed it behind a house. I left it and walked out with my white bag filled with newspapers and nonchalantly continued delivering my papers. This was the third time in three days I had to leave Ray's scooter behind a house and return for it later.

About four houses away from where I had left the scooter, the police pulled their car alongside me and asked, "Where is the motor scooter you were riding?" I kept walking toward another house with a newspaper in my hand and replied, "I don't know anything about a scooter. I don't know what you are talking about."

They were very annoyed. The officer riding on the passenger side had his head sticking out the window, and he was motioning for me to walk over to the police car. "I want to talk to you!" he said. "We can take you in for questioning, you know."

I just kept walking from house to house, and they continued slowly driving alongside me. "I have to get my papers delivered, or my people will be angry," I said to the officer leaning out the window. I continued, "I do not want to be late for school."

The officer who was driving the car asked me, "Kid, you wouldn't happen to have an extra newspaper, would you?"

"It'll be 15¢," I replied.

He handed me the money. I gave him the newspaper and they left. I knew he didn't think I would charge for the newspaper. When I told him 15¢, there was a slight pause, and then he dug in his pocket for a few minutes. It was very gratifying.

Driving the scooter had become quite risky. In addition to being concerned about my father, mother, brother, and the neighbors, I now had to worry about the Greece police. After my encounter with the police, I decided against ever again taking the scooter on my route.

The next morning, I filled my newspaper bag with papers and walked to the end of our driveway. As I proceeded to the right, I could see a Greece police car sitting at the end of Third Avenue. I turned to look in the opposite direction and saw another police car waiting in someone's driveway about five houses from ours at the other end of Third Avenue. I smiled and knew I had made the right decision even though my motor scooter days were over.

I kept the newspaper route until January of my freshman year of high school. Two weeks prior to delivering the Christmas calendars, I informed my customers I would be giving up the newspaper route in January. I received more than $1,000 for the Christmas calendars. I'm not sure if it was because they were happy to know I was leaving or my unfailing efforts to get the newspapers delivered by 6:00 a.m. no matter if it was shining, raining, or snowing.

One of the gifts—$50 and a big smile—was from a very attractive lady who was about thirty. Each time, for almost a year, when I went to her house to collect my weekly payment, this lady would drop something and then place her hand on my groin area as she bent to pick it up. When I told Ronnie, he went to her home and offered her a free two-week trial subscription for the *Times Union*. She told him the morning newspaper filled her needs.

Chapter Twenty-Nine

MAKING MONEY

Work is prayer.
Work is also stink.
Therefore stink is prayer.

—Aldous Huxley, *Jesting Pilate*

Ray, Earl, Ronnie, and I increased our incomes by working evenings. After a rain or a lawn watering, we would go from lawn to lawn with our metal buckets and flashlights looking for night crawlers, which are large slimy worms.

We searched on our knees five and sometimes ten lawns, carefully looking for big fat worms. We had to be quick of hand and not squeamish; sometimes the worms broke in half as we pulled them out of their holes or off the wet grass.

The owner of the Braddock Bay Boathouse and Livery would purchase the night crawlers from us for a penny each. Some nights we would collect five hundred or one thousand each.

After spending two or three hours collecting worms, our hands and clothes smelled. The worms dispensed scummy, foul-scented mucus, which tended to coat our hands. We knew enough to avoid contact with everyone.

After collecting the worms, the owner of the bait shop required us to individually count them at the bait shop. After doing this twice, I suggested the owner install a scale and he purchase the worms from us by the pound. Because he sold each worm individually and received the same price for the big ones as the small ones, he resisted my suggestion.

A week later, I asked if he would allow us to count the worms when we placed them in the bucket. I promised we would separate every one hundred with a piece of newspaper. The owner was a little reluctant to trust our count, but he quickly realized this made sense, and we could be trusted.

Now we only smelled when gathering them. It was my first business experience where honesty and trust were an integral part of each transaction.

From finding night crawlers to trapping muskrat, fox, and beaver, Ray, Earl, Ronnie, and I were constantly busy. Each of us saved our money and purchased a number of traps. We had learned the value of reinvesting our money to increase our earnings.

Every morning while delivering the newspapers, I would check our line of traps. Earl and Ronnie had first choice for placing their traps because they had been setting their traps before Ray and me.

Consequently, they took the prime trapping areas in Braddock Bay for muskrat.

Every day after school, I would pull on a pair of hip boots and wade into the cold reed-filled, marshy waters to inspect the traps. If there was a catch, it was probably dead, or sometimes we had to kill it.

For three years, we trapped, collected our catch in a big bag (a converted canvas newspaper bag), and then took them home to be skinned in our backyard. Once we had accumulated ten or more pelts, we called a man from Rochester who purchased them. My great-grandfather on my father's side, Phillppe Bazinet, a French trapper, would have been proud of us.

Even though we set our traps for muskrat, we occasionally trapped a fox and once got a skunk. We skinned the skunk in our backyard. After we accomplished the skinning, my mother would not permit us into the house until we took off all our clothes and buried them.

Despite the temperature being about forty degrees, she showed little mercy. She did throw towels out the window, so we would not be standing outside naked while we cleaned our bodies with a very strong scented soap. She would not come near us or allow us into the house until we washed and perfumed our bodies.

That was our last experience with a skunk. Despite all our work and grief, no one bought the skunk pelt.

Chapter Thirty

CHILDREN OF REVENGE

*Tell me who your friends are and
I will tell you what you are.*

—Favorite Quote of Rose Suhl Barend

In September 1951, I was thirteen. I had just entered seventh grade. When I arrived for my first day of class, I was placed in a room that included seventh—and eighth-grade students. Because of retirement and budget constraints, Sister Agnes Cecilia taught both grades. She was my worst nightmare.

The Sisters of St. Joseph wore black gowns with what appeared to be a starched-white covering, which engulfed their faces. I always thought Sister Agnes Cecilia was so mean partially because she was so uncomfortable in her required habit.

During the first week of school, I brought with me a rubber squirt gun, which was designed to look like a cigar. If you squeezed the center, water would squirt out one end—I planned to have a little fun with it at lunch. I took it out to show the girl sitting in front of me and forgot to put it away.

It was sitting on my desk when Sister Cecilia began touring the room. When she saw the rubber cigar, she did a double-take and went ballistic. She grabbed it, thinking it was a cigar.

Unfortunately for her, it was loaded with water. The water squirted in her face and dripped from the white-starched habit surrounding her face.

She threw the cigar across the room and then screamed and whacked me. I knew it was coming, so I had put my hands over my head and tried to crouch down on my seat. When she was finished, I had gauges and cuts across both hands. I had a feeling this would not be a good year.

A few months later, Tommy got his revenge. He waited for the right day when Sister Cecilia was patrolling the halls to inform her that Joe, Rob, and I were in the boys' room playing nickel pitch.

In her bombastic, uninhibited style, Sister Cecilia pushed open the door to the boys' room and found us in bent-knee position pitching nickels against the wall. She ordered us to surrender to her all our nickels. After we had handed over our money, she lined us against the bathroom wall and searched our pockets to make sure she had all our money.

I was the last in line and had the good fortune of watching my two peers be searched, struck across the head with her keyed hand, and then told to return to class. Each time the hand struck, I knew my turn was coming.

When she stuck her hand in my right pocket, she let out a scream. There was just a big hole in my pocket. I delayed urinating before she entered because I was winning nickels and consequently an erection developed. Her hand touched my penis and then moved like lightning and struck me across the face.

She screamed, "Get out of here! You filthy thing! You are going to stay after school and write the Our Father five hundred times."

When I returned to the classroom, I asked Joe, Tom, and Nancy Bauman if they would quickly scribble a page or two of Our Fathers for me before their buses came.

When the buses arrived, they handed me three hundred Our Fathers. I prayed Sister Cecilia would look only at the first few pages that I wrote. Ten minutes after the buses left, I was done.

Sister Cecilia didn't stay around to check my work. She asked Ms. McShea (who by now wore glasses that made your eyes water when you looked at her) if she would check my work. Ms. McShea counted the number of pages with me. She knew I needed about thirteen pages.

After she finished, she smiled at me and said, "You had better get moving if you want to catch your bus." She was unaware the buses had left ten minutes ago. I grabbed my books and was out the door in a flash. I got lucky hitchhiking. I arrived home about the same time as the bus; my parents did not know the difference.

When the weather was pleasant, Joe and I would often make our way home from school without the help of the bus. It was fun meeting people when we hitchhiked and much more adventurous than the school bus. Part of my punishment, Sister Cecilia thought, would be for me to walk home. She never realized I hitchhiked.

Joe opted not to take the bus that day and waited for me just past the entrance for the school building. I hurried to Latta Road, and we began the journey home.

About a mile from school, there was an orchard with the best red delicious apples. We hustled to the orchard, checked the road to see if anyone was coming, and then scurried in. The trees were loaded with apples. After filling our pockets, we quickly returned to the road.

Getting in and out of the orchard was no easy matter. There was a ditch four feet wide by three feet deep between the road and the apple trees.

On one occasion, the owner unleashed his dog on us from about five hundred yards away. He must have realized we were stealing his apples. The large Collie began barking and then ran full speed at us. With our pockets full of apples, we quickly ran toward the road. We tumbled into the ditch and lost a few apples but managed to get to the safety of the road. The dog stopped on the orchard side of the ditch—barking and growling at us. We quickly hurried down the road and hoped the farmer was not coming behind the dog.

After running a good distance away from the orchard, we continued our walk toward home while munching on red delicious apples. Periodically, we turned to face an approaching car with our thumbs pointing in the direction of home. I had my book bag slung over my shoulder and an apple in my mouth. Joe very seldom brought books home.

When I asked him why he never studied at home, he said, "Smart people don't have to study."

"Maybe so," I replied, "but if you're so smart, why wouldn't you want to be even smarter?" He didn't have an answer.

Then I asked him, "If you're so smart, why did you convince me to steal that watch with you?"

He looked at me very mad and said, "No one would have ever known the difference if you didn't get caught. Why did you tell your dad? My father was really mad when your dad asked that we accompany you to Schaffer's Store to return the watches. My dad believed me when I told him I did not steal a watch. Why did your dad want me to tell Mr. Schaffer I stole a watch? My father said it was to make you look better."

"Joe, I'm sorry about the watch," I replied. "I should have never taken it, and I'm glad I gave it back to Mr. Schaffer. What you do with the watch you stole is your business. My dad asked me where I got the new watch, and I told him I found it. When he said, 'You never lied to me before—now tell me the truth,' I told him the truth. I'm glad I told him."

That was the beginning of my seventh grade. The intensity of that year was like Beethoven's "Eroica" or maybe Mozart's "Requiem": the movement kept increasing in its intensity. In my case, it wasn't good.

A year after the police attempted to trap me on the motor scooter, Joe bet me $5 I would not drive the motor scooter to school. I knew this adventure would be dangerous and tricky, but I was tempted by the challenge and the $5. Being an eighth grader and soon to graduate and get money and presents from my aunts and uncles made me consider his offer cautiously—I did not want to get caught and jeopardize my graduation.

Once a week, my parents left for Rochester before I boarded the school bus. When the right day arrived, I pulled the scooter out of the garage and kick-started it. Then, I headed for Joe's house. His parents gave him anything he wanted. It was fun being with someone who had everything when I had so little.

When I got to his house, I revved the motor, which made a loud popping and banging sound because of the dual straight pipes. They were loud enough to annoy people, which gave me a strange pleasure.

Joe came running out of his house with his mother in tow. She was hollering at him not to go with me. He just waved her off and jumped on the back of the scooter.

I immediately asked, "You got the $5?"

Joe replied, "When I heard you, I grabbed it off my dad's dresser. Here, take it before I lose it."

He handed me the money, and I took it with one hand while steering the motor scooter with the other. I felt funny about taking the money when he told me he took it from his father's dresser. I asked him, "Did you steal this money from your dad?"

"Of course not," he replied.

We arrived at Our Mother of Sorrows about ten minutes before the school buses. I hid the motor scooter behind the church wall adjacent to Latta Road where there was an indentation in the building. Leaving the scooter there allowed us to enter and exit without being seen. Within an hour of our arrival, most of the seventh and eighth graders were in awe of our adventure. When I showed them the $5, I became their hero.

That afternoon, just before dismissal, one of the girls told Joe that Sister Cecilia heard I had driven the motor scooter to school. She sent some students to search for the motor scooter. Once they located the whereabouts of the scooter, Sister Cecilia was planning to keep me at school until the Greece police arrived.

We immediately left school and ran to where I left the scooter. I kick-started the scooter, and Joe jumped on the back. As we were pulling out of the parking lot, Joe said, "Don't look back because Novena Punch is running up the road in our direction, and she is screaming."

I turned the hand throttle wide open and let the exhaust pipes blast as loud as possible. Then, I screeched the tires onto the road. We left Sister Cecilia in a cloud of dust. We didn't stop for apples that day.

Except for running the scooter at maximum speed, the ride back was uneventful until about fifty feet from Joe's house. The scooter became difficult to steer. When I pulled it to the side of the road, I realized the front tire was almost flat. We pushed the scooter to Joe's house and left it parked against the chain-link fence, which encircled his house. I hitchhiked the additional mile home.

God has a funny way of working—while I was hitchhiking, two Greece police cars passed me. The officers did a double-take when they realized it was me. They never stopped to offer me a ride.

When I arrived home, I told my dad what happened. I offered to buy a new tire for the scooter before Ray attempted to pulverize me. My dad agreed to put the scooter in his truck and bring it home, providing Ray and I accompanied him to Joe's house.

When we arrived at Joe's house and began loading the scooter, Joe's mother came out of the house and told my father I was a very bad influence on her son. My father replied, "I will make sure Harold does not chum around with your son anymore. I agree with you; they are not good together. I know my son is honest, and he tries to be good, but sometimes his goodness has a hard time shining through. I can't speak for your son."

Ever since the watch incident, my dad never trusted Joe. Prior to our last outing together, my dad asked me how I could like someone you can't trust, "If he'll steal from Mr. Shaffer, he'll eventually steal from you or anyone else he believes is a convenient target," he told me. Time may have proven my dad right.

Seven years after being booted out of Our Mother of Sorrows School and serving in the U.S. Army, I received a newspaper clipping from my mom: it was of a murder trial in Rochester.

A prostitute and a young man lured a businessman into a motel room where they supposedly robbed and killed him. The businessman was wearing a diamond ring. When the robbers couldn't get the ring off his finger, they cut the man's finger off. The prostitute turned state's evidence and testified against Joe.

Joe swore under oath he was innocent. He was acquitted of the crime. His father eventually had to sell his department store to pay his son's legal fees.

Unlike me, Joe was allowed to graduate from Our Mother of Sorrows. Our names appear as part of the class of 1953 as posted on the Internet.

In high school Joe's dad showered him with everything a young man could desire, including a new Corvette convertible. Joe would periodically cruise through Braddock Heights with gorgeous girls beside him. He and I seldom spoke other than to say hello. At that time I envied him.

Dancing with the Devils

After we arrived home with the motor scooter, my parents received a call from Father O'Rourke. He informed them I was no longer welcome at Our Mother of Sorrows. They should immediately make arrangements for my transfer to another school. He told them to call Sister Agnes Cecilia in the morning and she would make preparations to have my records forwarded.

He ended by saying, "I do not want to see him in this school again."

"Father," my dad replied, "no matter how little you think of my son and my family, we are members of your parish." In that brief reply, my dad told Father O'Rourke exactly how he felt. He did not care much for the Catholic school system or Father O'Rourke, but he felt empathy for my mother, and he truly believed I was being unjustly punished.

My mother was devastated. She believed it was a prerequisite of life for every person to have a Catholic education. According to her belief, I would now be with the devils.

Unlike my dad, she felt the punishment fit the person. I didn't feel sad, relieved, or overjoyed. I was very disappointed only because I would miss receiving all the money and gifts my brother received when he completed eighth grade and graduated from Our Mother of Sorrows. In public school, there would be no graduation ceremony for students moving from eighth to ninth grade.

When my records were transferred from Our Mother of Sorrows, somehow my IQ test scores had been changed from 130 to 115. My mother didn't object. She thought it was good that they lowered my score because the public school administration would not expect as much from me.

It never occurred to me that Our Mother of Sorrows lowered my IQ score to ensure this transferee would not reflect ill on the teaching staff at Our Mother of Sorrows. Based upon my subsequent high school habits, Sister Agnes Cecilia, SJ, did me a big favor.

Chapter Thirty-One

HILTON CENTRAL SCHOOL

Anyone who has been to a public school will always feel comparatively at home in prison.

—Evelyn Waugh

After a week of being in limbo, a secretary from Hilton Central School called my parents, informing them I could begin school the following Monday. The secretary mentioned it was customary for at least one parent to accompany a new student on their first day. My mother gave me a definite no—she would not go into a public school. She was ashamed and disappointed because of my being asked to leave Our Mother of Sorrows.

I was the first son or daughter of Bernard and Rose Barend not to graduate from a Catholic elementary school. That morning, my dad would have driven me, but I knew he would miss an opportunity to work. I volunteered to take the school bus. It was the least painful course for both of my parents.

My transition from parochial to public school was more welcomed by me than the school administrators at Hilton Central School. Unlike Our Mother of Sorrows, which only emphasized religion and academics, the public schools were more complete and included the mind and the body.

That Monday morning, I walked to the Braddock Fire House, which was located directly across from Vokel's Grocery. I boarded the school bus along with Ronnie Lupo and a number of girls. Most of the kids who lived in Braddock and Grandview Heights had already heard about my forced transfer.

In 1952, Hilton Central School was a one-story modern brick building with lots of windows. It was located on the Main Street about a mile west of the Village of Hilton. There was a large circular drive in front of the school and a parking lot to the right.

The first day I was told to immediately report to the principal's office. Joe Lester, the junior high administrator, welcomed me to the school. He wore a big name tag just to ensure his name was embedded in your brain. I stood at a counter in the principal's office while he flipped through the file that Sister Cecilia had forwarded.

He said, "We received a five-page letter from Sister Agnes Cecilia explaining how you are capable of succeeding academically, but she mentions you lack maturity and discipline. You terrorized fellow students, broke one boy's nose, and were part of a gang that sprayed one of her best students with a fire extinguisher. What do you have to say for yourself?"

I was bit annoyed. Even before my first day at Hilton, Sister Cecilia had left her mark. I had a very bad feeling about this tall dark-haired man who was my new interrogator.

"I don't know what she means by lacking in maturity and discipline," I said. "I always did my homework and never made a disturbance in class."

"Don't be a smart-ass with me," he responded. "When you break someone's nose, you have a problem, and I am sure you knew what you were doing. There is more to school than learning from books. You must be able to get along with other students. If you broke one boy's nose and tried to attack another boy with a fire extinguisher, you're not getting along very well with others."

I didn't think it would help if I explained the boy was not attacked with a fire extinguisher—he was only foamed, and the other kid started the problem. I decided not to say anything. It was a smart decision.

A few months later, I learned Joe Lester's hand was every bit as quick as Sister Cecilia's, and his words were sharp and cutting. Joe Lester did not accept any wise answers or lip.

When he decided to attack verbally, it was always in front of other students. He knew how to use his tongue and positioned himself to intimidate and punish. In addition, he wore a large ring, which, not unlike Sister Agnes Cecilia, SJ, would find its way to your head.

Transferring to Hilton was a breeze academically. The Catholic schools had prepared me well for the rigors of the classroom but nothing else.

In gym class, I was lost. The only athletic training I received was from the baseball and football games we played after school or on weekends. During baseball season, my fielding skills were terrible, but my batting was good. When I hit the ball, I could send it a mile.

After school, during September and October, the Braddock Heights kids gathered on the ball field and played coed football. I had great hands for catching the ball, and I could usually make a reception even if the ball was thrown a foot or two above my head. I could jump higher and run faster than the other boys. I hated to get tackled because it hurt. Our football games consisted of about eight boys and four or five girls, all playing without protective gear.

The first couple of weeks, when I attempted to tackle the older boys, they usually dragged me ten or fifteen yards, and my body would be aching for days. After a few bruises, I decided to hurtle my body at their legs to upend them—it usually worked. But my body took a beating.

As for the rest of the athletic calendar: track—the only running experience I ever had was running from my mother or the police. Soccer, tennis, badminton, archery, dodgeball, and basketball were all foreign. The first time I played basketball was in a gym class at Hilton. I went the wrong way and made a basket. I was the goat of our gym class for a few weeks.

During one month of each year, the physical education classes had coed dancing. The teacher would pair each boy with a girl. The boys laughed and the girls giggled at how stupid we looked. Every boy held his breath, hoping he would not get stuck with someone who would be a catalyst for peer commentary.

Prior to summer dismissal, the Hilton eighth-grade class held elections for class officers for the coming year. There were about sixty students in our class. Tommy Harradine and I were nominated for class president.

I attempted to decline the nomination, but the class refused to accept my withdrawal, and my name was placed as a candidate. Immediately after I attempted to decline, Joe Lester, who was overseeing the nominations, walked to the front of the class and said, "It is a great honor when a person wins the respect of his or her peers to be nominated for a student office. Anyone who attempts to decline this honor by his fellow students is admitting his own inability to serve in that position. I think you should take this into consideration when you vote."

I lost the election by a 2:1 margin. In retrospect, Joe Lester was right: I lacked confidence in myself to be a leader, and I had never learned to be comfortable speaking to a group. My early years of stuttering had left an emotional mark.

Academically, the eighth grade was a cake walk. My grades were all 90 or above, and I never took a book home.

Chapter Thirty-Two

HIGH SCHOOL

To spend too much time in studies is sloth; to use them too much for ornament is affection; to make judgment wholly by their rules is the humor of a scholar.

—Francis Bacon, *Of Studies*

Having completed one year of public school education, I was about to be elevated to the freshman class. The elevation was in my eyes only—upper-class students looked upon the freshmen as lower than whale shit. This, of course, increased interclass rivalry and an occasional tussle over a girl, sports team, or some inconsequential subject.

While the clubhouse was a laboratory for learning, high school for me was a field house for play. I have a very difficult time relating to someone who has experienced a high school journey without pleasure.

Throughout my four years of high school, I continued my efforts to satisfy my sexual capacity while restraining my mental cultivation. Unlike grammar school, I passed through high school without ever taking a book home or studying except in a study hall. I forgot the reasons I asked Joe why he never brought a book home.

I knew college was an unreachable dream for me financially. Consequently, my plan was to do what I had to do academically in order to maintain my eligibility to play sports. I wanted to graduate from high school, but I refused to expend any unnecessary effort.

During my freshman year of high school, while passing time in the hall, Hazel Jenkins, the guidance counselor at Hilton High and one of the finest people I have ever known, pulled me into her office and asked me to tell her my future plans. I told her I would buy a car and then get a job and make some money.

She responded, "You are going to waste your life. Why aren't you preparing for college? You have very good grades and the potential to do well in college. Why aren't you taking a foreign language? I want you in a Regents program—I am changing your courses. You will have to study harder, but it will be worth it."

I thought, *Oh shit! My vacation is about to end.*

I really didn't mind taking the more challenging classes, but my near-sightedness made it difficult for me to clearly see the blackboard. I was too vain to wear glasses, and I was not about to tell anyone I needed glasses. I saw some of the glasses the kids wore whose parents were poor, and I wanted to avoid that look.

Consequently, in algebra I began to get lower grades. I couldn't see the teacher's homework assignments, which he put on the chalkboard at the front of the class. I knew I wasn't going to college because it cost money and my parents did not have the money to send me. Nor did they have the money to get me the glasses I needed to see the blackboard.

I was not about to tell anyone my problem: what most students saw clearly, I saw with a big blur. I would squint and squint and then make a guess at what I should have been seeing clearly.

If I sat in the front of the class and squinted, I could see about 50 percent of what was being put on the board. Unfortunately, when I entered class late, I would take the only seat available, which would usually be toward the back of the class. In algebra much of the teaching was done on the blackboard, and my grades continued to drop.

Wrestling

I opted to join the wrestling team during my freshman year partially because I never played organized sports before enrolling at Hilton.

My cousin Johnny Barend was a popular professional wrestler from Rochester, and most students expected me to wrestle. My near-sightedness made it difficult for me to play basketball or baseball without wearing glasses.

I was big and very muscular. I opted to wrestle in the "Unlimited Weight Class," which was 190 pounds and over even though I did not weigh 190 pounds in my freshman year. My first year, I made the sectionals. Just when I thought I was invincible, I was soundly beaten and lost two teeth thanks to an undefeated senior from Brighton, New York.

In June of my freshman year, the annual Hilton High interclass track-and-field competition took place. The purpose was to determine which class would reign as track-and-field champions for the year. Historically, a junior or senior team always won the event, and the freshmen team always came in last.

I knew if I had some support, the freshmen could put a scare into the upperclassmen. Unlike most track events, this interclass rivalry was conducted only one event at a time, and any student could participate in as many events as they desired.

Even though I had never competed in them, I registered for the high jump, shot put, discus, long jump, and the 440-yard dash. The first event was the discus. I had never thrown a discus before stepping into the chalk-lined circle. Because of the traditional procedure of permitting the upperclassmen to go first, I had an opportunity to observe a number of throws before stepping into the circle.

After a foul on my first attempt, I proceeded to hurl the discus farther than anyone. The juniors and seniors were stunned.

The freshmen were in first place after the first event. I followed by coming in second in the high jump and long jump and winning the shot put. The freshmen class came five points short of winning the event, but it was the first time in the history of the school that a freshmen team had placed second. We won respect.

At the track meet, the junior varsity basketball coach asked me if I had ever played basketball or ran track. I told him no. He told me I could really help his team, and he asked me to practice basketball over the summer.

I quickly learned, at Hilton High, basketball and soccer were the sports that attracted the most spectators. Any other sport was second class.

That summer, I convinced my dad to have the Braddock's Volunteer Fire Department install a basketball hoop on top of the backstop at the softball field. I practiced shooting hoops for hours. I learned to cope with a hazy rim and practiced sometimes in the dark to better develop my touch.

When November arrived, I was ready to try out for the basketball team. In addition to playing on the dirt field, I had honed my basketball skills with the rich kids who lived along Edgemere Drive. They had basketball courts at their homes, and I became a regular visitor.

That July, while playing at Dr. Iuppa's home on Edgemere Drive, I jumped for a rebound and came down on another player's foot. Consequently, I broke my left ankle and tore some ligaments. I was on crutches for a month. Fortunately, when school began, I shed my crutches and made the basketball team.

During my sophomore and junior years, I became friends with Don Jackson. Don was a Canadian Indian from Val Dor, Quebec. His parents owned a resort called Jackson's Landing. Don was given a rare opportunity to attend high school in the United States. The Rice family, residents of Hilton, took their summer vacations at Jackson's Landing. When Don was sixteen years old, Mr. Rice extended an invitation for him to live at their home in Hilton and attend high school.

Don completed high school in three years and played basketball with me for two of the three years. Don and I would sneak into the gymnasium of the church he attended and shoot baskets for hours.

After he graduated from high school, rumors abounded that the family he stayed with had wished for him to marry their daughter. Don returned to his family and married an Indian girl from Canada. Although I never visited the resort in Quebec, he promised if I did, he would guarantee me the best fishing I ever experienced. At my fiftieth class reunion, I learned Don had died a few years ago.

To See or Not to See

During my junior year, I was asked to report to the nurse's office for a series of eye examinations. Prior to this, I managed to be absent whenever the eye testing was scheduled. I knew wearing glasses would destroy my image. It would be much worse than seeing fuzzy objects.

After the examination, I knew I was in trouble. The nurse kept asking me, "How do you see to play basketball? How do you see the blackboard in class?"

She just kept asking me one question after another. She was shocked. Within hours she had contacted all my teachers and coaches.

My math and English teachers were the first to make adjustments. In both classes, I was assigned a seat in the first row.

My basketball coach, Ron Eckler, never said a thing to me about wearing glasses. He probably figured it would do more harm than good to force me to wear glasses. Hours and hours of practice looking at a fuzzy rim helped me to hone my touch so I could shoot very well despite my handicap.

In my senior year, I was voted to the All Monroe County Basketball First Team. I was second in the county in scoring and first in rebounding despite the fact I probably had the worst vision of anyone on the court.

In my senior year, a few days after the last Hilton High basketball game of the season, I received a call from Freddie Holbrook. He was an outstanding basketball player at Spencerport High School. Freddie called to congratulate me on having a good season. He was grateful I only scored fifteen points against Brockport—it gave him the scoring title for the county.

Brockport, which won the league, beat Hilton the last game of the season. Ron Eckler, the Hilton coach, decided to play each senior only half the game in order to give everyone an opportunity to play. Some of the guys sat on the bench most of the year with little opportunity to play. In retrospect, it was the right thing to do.

During the three years I played basketball at Hilton High, my parents attended one game.

Chapter Thirty-Three

TRASHING THE NEIGHBORHOOD

Early to bed, early to rise
Work like hell and advertise.

—Ted Turner

Upon entering my sophomore year of high school, my dad was just beginning to make a living with his stake-body truck. Then, someone offered him an opportunity to purchase their small trash collection business. He borrowed the money to purchase the business and launched himself into the garbage hauling business with about two hundred weekend customers.

My father could not lift the trash cans, but he had a son who could—and his son had friends. My father arranged with his customers to have their trash collected every Saturday morning rain, snow, sleet, or shine.

Most of his customers were located about five miles from Braddock Heights. Having retired from my newspaper route, now I would have to drag myself out of bed at 4:30 a.m. every Saturday to assist my dad with the trash collection.

Within three months of his purchase, my dad doubled his customers. He promised all his customers his employees would carry their trash cans from house to curb and return them after they were emptied. No other trash collector in our area offered this service. Via word of mouth, new customers were being added every week.

My dad could afford to have the cans brought to the curb and returned because he had cheap labor. He convinced my friends the pay was good; it was cash and immediate. Bill Boothby, Jerry Barker, and Ken Asmuth became steady employees. Ronnie Lupo and Jim Elkins worked for our competition: Jim Powers Trash Collection.

In the fall, when someone came across a discarded basket of tomatoes, we would have tomato fights—in the winter, snowball fights. My father would holler at us, but we just kept slinging tomatoes or snowballs, whatever was in season.

My dad would drive the truck while two of us would go house to house, placing the cans at curbside. Another two employees threw the trash into the truck.

Unfortunately, Saturday mornings always came too early. Hilton High School scheduled most of its basketball games on Friday evenings. This meant getting home after a game at a reasonable hour—if we had a good game, our fun could last until 2:00 or 3:00 a.m.

I was very good friends with Barb Van Dorn, a cheerleader. After basketball games, Kenny Asmuth, Nancy Buell, Barb, and I would take my car for hamburgers or ice cream. Then I would drive Barb home.

She always invited me into her home when we were about to say good-bye. On cold nights, we would stand by a heat register and hug and kiss for an hour while Kenny and Nancy were in my car with their motors running and their heaters on.

Double dating at the Hilton High School Ball. (L-R) Harold Barend, Barb Van Dorn, Nancy Buell, and Ken Asmuth.

I thought for sure we would get married and have the best athletes in town. The only time our hugs would be cut short was when her mother's voice cut through the quiet, asking, "Barb, is that you?" I would be out the door in five seconds.

My dad knew I would be moving on eventually. During the latter part of my senior year, he was approached by two brothers named Dugan. The Dugan brothers were interested in purchasing my father's trash business, and my dad was interested in selling.

There was a new law pending in Albany that would require all trash collection businesses to use compactor trucks. A compactor was very expensive, and my dad's small business could not justify the expense. His only option was to sell the business.

He came to terms with the Dugan brothers. His sale price was to be paid in cash. The Dugan brothers came to our home in Braddock Heights with a certified check. My dad refused the check. He told them, "I will only accept cash."

The next day, they returned with the cash. My dad, the two Dugan brothers, and I sat at the kitchen. I watched as the three of them conducted their business. After the transaction was completed, I asked one of the brothers how they had got their money. They responded, "We played the stock market while attending Dayton University. We made quite a bit of money."

I asked if they had a good tip. The younger brother responded, "Spooner Mines and Oil. A friend of ours recommended the company. We researched the company and believe it will be a winner. He has never been wrong"

The next morning, I drove to Rochester and withdrew a thousand dollars from my savings account.

Without any effort on my part or my parents, I had been awarded the money by the company that insured the auto that hit me after I jumped off the milk truck. It had to remain in the bank until my eighteenth birthday. During that twelve-year period that the bank had the thousand, I received a total of about $30 in interest.

The next morning, I drove to the bank in Rochester and withdrew all my money.

With my money in hand, I went to Merrill Lynch and met with a stockbroker to inquire about the purchase of Spooner Mines and Oil. The broker could not find the listing on the New York Stock Exchange and the American Stock Exchange. He referred me to Sage Ruddy, an over-the-counter stock brokerage firm in Rochester, New York, that specialized in low-priced stocks.

The broker at Sage-Ruddy found the company listed on the pink sheets. It was a Canadian company listed on the Toronto Stock Exchange.

When the broker informed me the stock was selling for 4¢ a share, I did not hesitate. I told him I wanted to purchase $900 worth of the stock.

It was the first time I had ever bought stock. The broker looked at me in shock. He kept asking if I was sure I wanted to invest that much money in a stock selling for 4¢ a share.

It never dawned on me how risky this investment was. I had faith in the two men that just bought my dad's business, and I believed their tip would eventually be a winner.

Chapter Thirty-four

SUMMERTIME

It's a sure sign of summer if the chair gets up when you do.

—Walter Winchell

I was always busy during my summer vacations. Unlike many of my friends, my parents did not have the money to send me to a summer camp. Braddock Heights was a very good place to be during the summer. It hosted many summer residents.

If we wanted to go swimming, we could swim in the bay, pond, or lake depending on the water temperature. All three were clean and posed little danger of disease. Sometimes we would water-ski or just relax in a rowboat with a fishing rod.

I often worked with my father doing odd jobs—some attic cleaning, masonry, cleaning walls in houses, repairing driveways. There was no job too small for my dad.

During the first month of summer after completing the eighth grade, Charley King, one of my newspaper customers and a friend of my dad's asked if I would like to work for him. He was a retired engineer who planned to construct a retaining wall at his home, which fronted on Lake Ontario. He told me it would be very hard work; then in the same breath, he asked if he could get his newspaper a little earlier in the morning. I had been delivering his paper at 5:30 a.m. I changed my delivery route and set my alarm a half hour earlier to accommodate him.

Each summer, I always looked forward to returning to bed after delivering the newspapers at 5:00 a.m. Now, my life changed—my commitment to work for Mr. King required me to be at his house at 7:00 a.m. He and I worked five hours a day, six days a week.

That summer, he showed me how to move three-thousand-pound blocks of concrete fifty to sixty feet and maneuver them into position. I received much more than money from working with Charley King.

He helped me to better understand the laws of physics and made clear some very simple rules of life. His favorite saying was "If it doesn't fit, don't force it. If something doesn't go, there is a reason for it. Find the reason, and the problem will be solved. Always use your head before brute strength."

He made that comment after a concrete block we were positioning got stuck. I placed my back against the huge block and attempted to jump-start it. He watched and laughed. "Where are you going?" he asked, knowing the answer was nowhere. "Let's find the problem before you kill yourself."

He checked the wheels and found a stone had jammed between the metal plates that covered our path and the rollers that the concrete block was sitting on. He placed a long metal bar under the concrete block, moved it back about an inch, and then had me knock the stone out of the way. After he did his magic, the block was rolling again.

I gained about twenty pounds of muscle that summer.

During my nonworking hours, I purchased a single-shot twelve-gauge shotgun. It was a must. When fall came, I wanted to hunt ducks and pheasants like my friends.

Three or four times each month, Earl, Ronnie, and I borrowed a clay pigeon machine. On Saturday afternoons, we carried the machine with its long bending metal arms into the field where the clubhouse once stood.

When the arms of the clay pigeon machine were pulled into a cocked position, a heavy spring was stretched to its maximum; the force thus propelled a clay disc high into the air. A good shot destroyed the circular clay disc before it descended. We spent a lot of money that summer learning how to shoot clay objects. I was a pretty good shot, but I had to learn to adjust to the blur because of my poor vision.

The summer following my second year of high school, Ronnie purchased a hydroplane racing boat with a sixty-horsepower Mercury motor. We were crazy on water.

His boat was powerful enough to pull a surfboard; we surfed and surfed for hours. The surfboard was attached to his boat with two ropes, each about seventy-five feet long. The ropes were joined like a Y about twenty feet from the boat. The Y was reversed from a single rope to another, branched rope where it was attached to the board. The board was about four foot in length and about thirty inches wide. There were two rubber foot pads in the center of the board.

Normally, three or four of us would take turns board-surfing behind Ronnie's boat. The first time Ronnie took me surfing, I was in the water waist high lying stomach down on the board with a piece of rope in my hands that was fastened to both sides of the top portion of the board. Before my attempt started, Ronnie positioned his boat about forty feet in front of me.

Unlike water skiing, the boat did not accelerate rapidly. It gradually increased speed, allowing me sufficient time to move from lying flat on my stomach—to bended knees—to standing. It was a maneuver that required timing, balance, strength, and initially caused me to experience a considerable number of thrills.

The first two summers of high school consisted of a bit of work and a lot of fun. I began to seek out new challenges and loftier goals. I was determined to swim the channel that divided Manitou Beach and Braddock Bay. It was a distance of only about three miles, but it was normally choppy water with a strong undercurrent. The depth of the channel varied from ten feet to about sixty feet.

When I mentioned my plans to Ronnie, he thought I was crazy and wanted no part of my drowning. Jim Elkins, Jerry Barker, and Bill Boothby, on the other hand, readily agreed to accompany me in a rowboat.

My first attempt was successful but exhausting. When I reached the sandy beaches of Manitou, I attempted to stand but fell backward because of dizziness. My friends pulled me to shore and proceeded to stuff my mouth with chocolate bars. That was the beginning of a series of marathon swims, which helped me build my body.

Having tired of surfboarding and water skiing, we decided our new summer thrill would be a water-ski jump. Not unlike for the clubhouse, we scavenged lumber and metal supports from neighbors and junkyards until we accumulated all the necessary pieces.

When the jump was completed, we tied a number of large floatation containers and old truck inner tubes to the bottom of the jump and then pulled it to a spot in front of Ronnie's house, which faced Lake Ontario. The jump rested in about eight or ten feet of water. The portion of the jump that reached out of the water was about six feet high, but with enough speed, one could soar into the air eight or ten feet.

Ronnie was the first to go over. He was smart enough to ensure the driver was not one of us. He asked a neighbor, who was a dentist and owned a large inboard, to pull him over the jump. Before going, Ronnie appeared cocky as hell, but I knew he was scared. I knew because my turn would be next, and I was already scared.

We watched in awe as he flew off the top of the boards. He came down on his skis, continued for a few feet trying to regain his balance, and then plowed into the water with a huge splash.

Within twenty minutes of his initial jump, I was sitting on the edge of a wooden dock waiting to be pulled onto the skis. I was so nervous I had forgotten about my last dock departure on water skis—a huge sliver stuck in my rear when the boat pulled me off the edge of the dock. At that moment, all I could think of was keeping the ski tips up and what it was going to be like when I became airborne.

There were about twenty neighbors and peers who had gathered along the break wall of Ronnie's house. It wasn't every day when the community hooligans build a ski jump and are about to kill themselves. No one wanted to miss the action.

The dentist slowly moved his boat away from the dock until the pull line was taut, and then he gunned the motor. I was up and moving away from the dock. The boat pulled me in a huge semi-circle. When we were directly in line with the jump and about three hundred yards away from the jump, the boat was traveling at full speed; I leaned on my skis and swung to the side of the boat heading directly for the jump.

My heart was pounding, and I was scared. In a matter of seconds, I was airborne. When I hit the water, I thought I had broken every bone in my body. The crowd watching the spectacle let out a big cheer when I surfaced.

One of my friends told me later, "We thought you would be crippled after that fall." I never attempted to jump again. I knew God had intervened on behalf of the fool, and I had no intention of testing his patience.

Toward the end of that summer, Ronnie and I were cruising Lake Ontario in his hydroplane race boat when we spotted two girls sunbathing on shore. I was lying on the bow of the boat, and he was operating the throttle. He sped past then, and we waved—when they waved back, we knew it was an invitation to get closer.

Ronnie circled the boat at full speed and headed toward them. He planned to shut the engine about fifty yards from shore and coast in. As we approached full speed, the girls were frantically waving—our egos were large enough to believe they couldn't wait for us to arrive. Suddenly, my body was hurtling through the air, unattached to the boat. The bottom of the boat hit a huge rock. The boat was ruined.

The girls rescued us and brought us to shore in a rowboat. One of their fathers was a doctor. He constructed a sling for my broken arm and bandaged Ronnie's cuts and badly bruised body.

I called my dad, and within a short time, he arrived to take us home. He returned that night with Ronnie's father to salvage the boat. My dad brought the boat back to Ronnie's home, where it was displayed for all the neighbors to see. Ronnie and I had once again become the talk of Braddock Heights. All the neighbors questioned how two boys could get into so much trouble in such a small quiet community as Braddock Heights.

The boat remained adjacent to the Lupo residence for a couple of months. During this time, the stories of our incident spread throughout the whole area.

Every customer on my newspaper route had heard about the accident, along with our friends in Grandview, Hilton and even parts of Rochester. Each time the story was retold, it became a bit more embellished.

The pinnacle was a call from a reporter from the *Rochester Democrat & Chronicle* asking if it was true that in our attempt to save two girls who were drowning, we destroyed a speed boat and injured ourselves. For a second, I thought how much fun it would be to agree with his story but quickly decided in favor of the truth.

Beautiful Upper Saranac Lake—my next stop for the summer at the Wawbeek Hotel.

Chapter Thirty-Five

The Wawbeek Hotel

Life should begin with age and its privileges and accumulations, and end with youth and its capacity to splendidly enjoy such advantages.

—Mark Twain

The summer following the completion of my first year of high school, I was approached by Digger O'Dell, a porky red-haired, freckled-face boy of sixteen.

He asked, "Would you be interested in working this summer at a hotel in the Adirondack Mountains? It will be fun, and you will make money."

The thought of making money and having fun always appealed to me. When something sounded too good, I had learned from my dad: be careful. Seldom is the proposition as good as you think. He would say, "You are looking at the situation from the eyes of the taker. The giver has a much different motive."

When I began work for Mr. King, I had him detail the work arrangements—what time were we to start and finish, would I have a lunch break, etc. I asked Digger, "Why are you asking me to work for this hotel? Are you related to the owner? What are you going to be doing there?"

Digger, with his belly overlapping his belt, answered, "The people who own the Wawbeek Hotel are Harry and Terry Purchase. My mother knows them from the country club. They asked her if she knew two high school or college boys who would like to work as assistant chef and lifeguard. I thought you could be the lifeguard, and I would be the assistant chef."

I immediately had visions of sitting in a tall white wooden chair on a sandy beach with lots of girls to make friends with. "Digger," I asked, "what exactly does a lifeguard do at a resort hotel? Are there duties other than watching the guests swim?"

"That's all you'll be doing," he replied. "I wish I could swim like you. I'd take your job in a second."

I questioned him further about the job and what I had to do to get it, and he replied, "I'll just tell the Purchases about your marathon swims. They'll know you can swim, and you'll have the job. By the way, we'll have to share a cabin. The food and lodging are all included in our pay."

I discussed the proposition with my parents, and they were overjoyed to have one less mouth to feed for the coming summer. I had become a pretty big eater and, for starters, usually drank a half-gallon of milk at lunch and another at dinner.

Three days after the beginning of our summer vacation, I received a call from Digger, informing me his mother would pick me up tomorrow morning. "Be ready," he said. "She doesn't like to wait." Alberta loaned me her suitcase; otherwise, I would have had nothing to carry my clothes in. In ten minutes, I had packed all my clothes.

Mrs. O'Dell had just purchased a new Oldsmobile convertible and agreed to drive us the six hours to Upper Saranac Lake. Digger sat in the front with his mother while I was consigned to the back with Digger's thirteen-year-old sister who had a crush on me. She was insistent on having the top down so her long red hair could blow in the wind like Scarlett O'Hara's in *Gone with the Wind*.

The Wawbeek Hotel was situated on upper Saranac Lake. The hotel had a main lodge and about twenty cabins. Each of the smaller cabins was built in the same motif. The main lodge had about twenty guestrooms, dining room with a huge fireplace, a bar area with another fireplace, and a recreation room with Ping-Pong tables and a pool table. Outside the main lodge, there were clay tennis courts, a boathouse with a docking facility, and a small beach area. The hotel closed during the winter months and reopened for the summer.

The hotel catered to a wealthy clientele from New England and New York City.

Digger and I were the only staff personnel who were not college students. The chambermaids, busboys, waitresses, and maintenance personnel were almost all from either the Eastman School of Music or the University of Rochester.

After our welcome by the owners, Harry and Terry Purchase, we were shown to a cabin that was to be our home for the next two months. The cabin was quite Spartan. We each had a dresser and a level of the bunk bed. Digger immediately informed me he had to sleep on the top because of his claustrophobia. My sleeping conditions could not have been worse in a concentration camp. If Digger was in bed before me, I had to squeeze under the bulging springs. If he jumped into his bed when I was asleep, the springs would be tested to within inches of my body. On a normal night, there was about six inches between the bulging springs and me. Sleeping under Digger was a stressful situation.

Toward the end of the first week, Digger and I were asked to go with a driver into the Village of Tupper Lake. A doctor was to examine us to ensure we were physically fit to work. It seemed a bit strange to have a physical to determine if you were healthy enough to work *after* being hired.

I asked Digger, "What if I don't pass the physical?" He replied, "You'll have to go home. Your parents will have to drive to the Wawbeek Hotel and get you." I was getting a bit nervous. My parents would have an attack if they had to travel to Tupper Lake to get me. I knew the answer already—if

Digger failed, he would simply return with his mother and leave me to find my way.

The middle-aged female doctor called Digger and me into her office. While I sat watching, she asked Digger to strip to his shorts and then lie on his back on a padded table. She walked over to him and placed her hand on his penis to move it away and then asked him to cough. As he was attempting to cough, he had an erection, which she immediately erased by taking her finger and whacking his penis. He let out a scream. She never said a word. When it came my turn, I closed my eyes and held my breath when she examined me for a hernia.

Despite my efforts to extract from Digger the method of compensation, I never learned until my first pay day how much compensation I would earn—$50 per week in cash plus tips. It didn't seem possible a lifeguard could earn tips, but I received some very big tips.

Upon arrival, I learned my responsibilities included getting up early in the morning and rolling the clay tennis courts with a large metal roller that was pushed by hand. After rolling the courts, I could join the other employees for breakfast.

After breakfast, I would have to clean the guests' personal boats and then assume my duties as lifeguard. The tall wooden chair was missing, along with the hordes of girls. The majority of the guests were members of AARP.

The few families with teenage daughters received my special care. I was happy to accommodate the young ladies on canoe trips and picnics at a neighboring estate where No Trespassing signs were posted.

Every Friday or Saturday evening, the Wawbeek employees were allowed to take Harry Purchase's station wagon and drive into the main shopping area of Tupper Lake. The drinking age was eighteen. I was big for my age and obnoxiously smart.

After a couple of weeks, Mary, one of the waitresses, asked Digger and me to join her and a number of other Eastman students on their twenty-minute ride into town. Mary was a third-year Eastman School of Music student. She was blonde, about medium height, and had large blue eyes.

Every evening after dinner, she would return to her room, change into her bathing suit, and then walk to the boathouse. I would usually be there, cleaning the boats and picking up. Mary would lie on the dock until I came out. Sometimes one or two people would be there besides her, but most of the time, it was just her and me.

The first time, she asked me to watch her because she did not want to swim in the dark without someone observing. I stayed while she flopped around for about ten minutes. When she swam back to the dock, she jokingly accused me of not watching her. After a few times, I became comfortable talking and being with her, but I was still concerned because she was twenty-one or twenty-two, and I was just sixteen.

One evening while she was swimming, she swam to the dock and asked me to come to the edge of the dock. She wanted to hand me something. She placed her bathing suit in my hand. I was shocked, and she was smiling. "Why don't you come in and swim with me? The water is beautiful, and no one will be coming. Take off your bathing suit and come in."

I didn't know what to do. I was afraid if we were caught, we would lose our jobs. *Oh, hell,* I thought, *the owners never come down here at night.* I walked into the boathouse and then slipped out of my swim trunks.

On another occasion, I was lying on the wooden dock adjacent to the boathouse. An attorney and his very corpulent wife, both in bathing suits, asked if they could use a rowboat. I prepared the boat for them and assisted them into the boat so they could row on Tupper Lake.

I returned to the dock and watched as the husband rowed and his wife sat in the back of the boat. When the boat was about twenty feet from the dock, I watched her climb out of the boat but never release her hold on the boat. The water was about twenty feet deep.

After she entered the water, she moved herself hand over hand to the back of the boat. She had her hands on the boat and was kicking with her feet while her husband rowed. He was just lazily putting the oars in the water and pulling.

I then heard her say, "I am going to let go of the boat and try to swim. Don't row away." When she released her grip on the boat and attempted to swim on her own, the lawyer pulled hard on the oars and swiftly rowed away from her. I watched in amazement as she went down and came up screaming. He was still rowing away as if in a race.

I ran into the boathouse and grabbed the large round life preserver that hung on the wall. The preserver had a long rope attached to it. I scaled the preserver perfectly to the woman. I knew my only hope was to get her on the large preserver and pull her to the dock. If I had jumped in the water to save her, she would have pushed me underwater.

Her husband was one of the few people who never left me a tip when he and his wife departed the Wawbeek.

When Sally and I got married, we spent our honeymoon at the Wawbeek Resort Hotel. I wanted to expose her to paradise on earth. When we were checking out of the hotel, Harry and Terry Purchase came to met us. They refused to take any money for our stay.

I recently had lunch with Digger, who is a successful businessman and splits his time between Florida and Rochester, New York. He sent me an e-mail, "Purchase, Henry J. 'Harry,' died July 9, 2011, in Fort Lauderdale, Florida. Survived by his wife, Theresa 'Terry.'" He and Terry owned and operated the Wawbeek Resort Hotel on beautiful Upper Saranac Lake, New York.

Chapter Thirty-Six

THE FORTUNES OF LIFE

Enjoy yourself, drink, call the life you live today/your own, but only that, the rest belongs to chance.

—Euripides, *Alcestis*

The time between my sophomore and senior years in high school was an experience few people could ever understand or appreciate. My life was flowing according to plan. I was dating almost every week. My only interests were athletic and social.

College was a no brainer—my high school grades made it appear I had no brains. I knew my parents' pockets were empty—no money for college. Consequently, I would forgo academics for a life more tailored to my needs. From my sophomore to my senior year, the only time I ever took home a book was during my regents exams of my senior year.

Hilton Central Junior and Senior High School in the 1950s. During the Halloween season, the outhouse was placed above the main entrance with the words "Seat of Education" painted on the outhouse.

Every year during the Halloween period, which lasted for a week, the teen population of Braddock Heights would congregate to plan a strategy of havoc. During my four years in high school, we literally raised hell at Halloween.

Two days before Halloween, we convinced Ernie, one of our classmates, to get his dad's farm truck. We conducted our surveillance and located an old outhouse just north of Hilton. Our plan was to meet Ernie at the Hilton ice cream parlor around 8:00 p.m.

When he arrived, four of us jumped into his truck and pointed him in the direction of the outhouse. The old wooden outhouse was sitting in an open field about five hundred yards from the farm owner's home. When we approached the farm where the outhouse was located, it appeared no one was home at the main residence. The house was dark.

Ernie stayed in his dad's truck while four of us slipped through the cornstalks to the location of the outhouse. We quietly pushed the wooden-framed toilet onto its side. Then we slowly lifted the outhouse. As we were lifting, we were surprised—the outhouse was still in use.

Undaunted by the leaking feces and the smell, we started carrying it toward the truck. Fortunately, it was dark, and we couldn't comprehend the mess we were making. As we moved the old wooden structure, a trail of bent cornstalks followed us along with a foul odor.

When we approached the truck, we slowly moved it to an upright position and then pushed it onto the flatbed truck. The truck had been waiting at the roadside in silence. Ernie refused to allow us to ride in the cab of the truck because we smelled. The four of us were relegated to accompany the outhouse in the back of the truck.

When we arrived at Hilton High, Ernie backed the truck onto the wide cement walk leading to the main entrance and continued in reverse until the truck was a few feet from the main entrance. En route to the school, we spray-painted in red the words "The Seat of Education."

When the truck stopped, we jumped off and quickly placed an old wooden ladder against the roof overhang at the main entrance of the high school. Four of us climbed the ladder onto the roof. Ropes were attached to the wooden outhouse and then tossed onto the roof. Two of us got onto the roof and began pulling on the ropes that were attached to the outhouse. The other two pushed on the sides while trying to avoid the seepage from the bottom. It slowly went up the ladder while leaving a messy trail. As we were pulling, fecal matter ran down the front of the building and spotted the front sidewalk.

About ten kids had gathered on the sidewalk in front of the school to watch the project. I was anxious to leave.

The next morning, when I exited the school bus, Wayne Furness, the high school principal, was waiting. He was handpicking students as they exited the buses. He motioned a select few of us to follow him.

When we entered his office, I saw three other students who were part of our construction project. I was amazed at how quickly the principal had learned our identities.

We soon realized he didn't have any knowledge of the culprits. He started with those most likely to have been involved. When we realized his strategy, no one admitted guilt.

Annoyed and frustrated, the principal pulled out his book. In the book was a listing of each of our names. Under each name was a list of infractions. He glared at us for a few seconds and then pulled a pen out of his shirt pocket and, with it, scratched a heavy line under each name. His last comment was "This is it. I am drawing the line here and now. Barend, I don't care how many baskets you score. This is it. No more chances."

Cow Dung

The day before Halloween we gathered cow dung (they were like flying saucers) from a farmer's pasture and placed the dung in a paper bag. That evening we took the paper bag with the cow dung to one of the homes in Braddock Heights. The person who lived there would always chase us during our Halloween ventures. He vowed he would catch us and turn us over to the police. He was deemed to be the meanest man in Braddock Heights.

We crouched low and moved slowly to the man's front steps. I was holding the bag, and Ronnie had a box of matches and fire starter. While Ronnie ignited the bag, I rang the doorbell. We quickly hid behind some bushes. We watched as the man opened the door and stomped on the bag—mission accomplished.

Roadblocks

Throughout the Halloween period, we built roadblocks on Edgemere Drive but always under streetlights. We were not trying to provoke accidents—only the people. Lawn furniture, trash cans, and whatever else we could quietly move from someone's yard were part of our roadblocks. Placing the collectibles in the center of the two-lane street constituted our roadblock. The blockade would force drivers to get out of their cars to remove some of the items to pass.

We searched out locations where yard fences were close enough to the road and a garden hose was available. We placed the garden hose in the fence and proceeded to turn the water on when the motorist attempted to remove the blockade. Certain people were exempt from getting soaked: parents, big tippers, and people we liked. The unlucky person would normally run at the spraying hose in a fury. The hose would always be stuck in a fence, and we would be a good distance away.

One evening, Franny Vokel was driving into Braddock Heights when she encountered our roadblock. When she stepped from her car, she began cursing and screaming, "You son-of-a-bitching kids! I'll make sure every one of you is put in jail; I know it's Lupo and Barend."

When I heard my name, I couldn't resist: I turned the water on full force. She just stood there with water pouring down, screaming and yelling. Good to her word, she contacted the Greece police and requested they patrol the hamlet of Braddock Heights during Halloween.

Vokel's Grocery Store.

Franny Vokel was the uninhibited and colorful owner of Vokel's Grocery Store in Braddock Heights. In the 1950s, it was the gathering spot for local teenagers. We would adorn the concrete steps at the front entrance much to Franny's displeasure.

A Lesson for Life

One of our Halloween traditions, and the last act of vandalism each year, was to crown the champion who could knock out the most streetlights throughout Braddock Heights. In my sophomore year of high school, our goal was to eliminate all the streetlights in the hamlet.

Knocking out a streetlight was an incredible experience. At the instant of impact, a bright light would flash for a few seconds, lighting up the whole block. To avoid being seen, we would run as fast as possible away from the bright flashing light.

The previous summer, while walking on the beach, I found a large very light sandstone. I saved it for this very event. After I threw the sandstone at a light, I planned to retrieve it.

Thanks to Franny Vokel and a number of other people who experienced our Halloween pranks, this year, the Greece police had extra cars patrolling Braddock Heights and Grandview Heights.

After we knocked out 90 percent of the streetlights in the hamlet, the police finally realized what we were attempting to accomplish. We knew the last few lights would be difficult to remove because each evening at six, a patrol car would appear and continue patrolling the areas that were lit.

I devised a strategy to split into two groups. One group would attempt to bait the police while the other would knock out a light or two. The plan would have worked perfectly, except unbeknown to us the Greece police had a second car in hiding.

Jerry, Ronnie, Anne, and I volunteered to knock out two lights at the opposite end of the street from where the rest of the pack was going. I was leading the contest with nine kills—my sandstone would eliminate the whole globe.

We walked to our destination from behind houses and remained in the dark until the group at the opposite end of the street emerged. It was a cold dark October night.

When the police noticed the group at the other end of the street moving in the direction of a streetlight, a police car began to slowly move in their direction. At that instant, we ran from the yard and began throwing at the light. I hit it with my sandstone. The bulb and globe shattered, and the whole block became daylight.

When the light flashed, the patrol car in hiding put on its siren and flashers and came screeching in our direction.

The four of us immediately ran for the cover of darkness behind the houses. Two policemen jumped from their car and began chasing us on foot. We had about a five-hundred-yard lead on the policemen.

It was so black while we were running we could not see five feet in front of us. I was running as fast as possible and was ahead of Bill, Ronnie, and Annie.

In an instant, my life changed. One of the residents whose backyard we were running through had strung a wire clothesline. I hit the clothesline going full speed. It caught me in the mouth. The wire found the open space where I lost two of my back teeth wrestling. The clothesline proceeded to shear eighteen of my teeth off. I fell to the ground and lost consciousness.

The threesome behind me quickly dragged me to a ditch and threw leaves over me then continued to run. The police never caught my friends or me.

About thirty minutes after I encountered the clothesline, Bill, Ronnie, and Annie returned to find me bloody and half conscious. "Oh my god!

Harold, what happened to you? Your whole face is full of blood!" Annie screamed.

I tried to stand. My feet were shaking, and my face was in excoriating pain. I put my right hand to my face. When I pulled it away, it was completely wet. My hand was covered with blood. My mouth felt as if someone had run a truck through it.

Jerry and Ronnie put their arms around me and carried me to the back door of Fifty-ninth Third Avenue; ten of our friends were walking behind us. The lights were on in my house. Ronnie just opened the door and helped me into the back porch. He kept saying, "You'll be OK. You'll be OK. Your mother will take care of you."

The group made a quick exit when they heard my mother coming. I was holding onto the wall when my mother saw me. She screamed.

My dad ran to her not knowing I was the cause of her grief. When he saw me, he started to cry. My dad never cried.

My mother looked at me and said, "Why can't you be like the other boys? Why must you always be in trouble?" Then she raised her face to the heavens and said, "Why, Lord, why have you done this to me? I can't take it any longer."

My dad took my mother by the arm and slowly walked her to their bedroom. She was starting to have an epileptic seizure. Alberta stayed with me and cleaned the blood from my face and mouth. Piece by piece, she and my father removed my broken teeth and proceeded to clean the three large cuts inside my mouth caused by the wire clothesline. I was in a lot of pain.

The following morning, Alberta called Dr. Goldstein, DDS, and explained what had happened to me. He agreed to take me the next morning. We had to be in his office by 8:00 a.m. He canceled all of his other appointments for that day. Dr. Goldstein's office was on Alexander Street in Rochester.

It was a painful forty-five-minute drive from Braddock Heights to inner-city Rochester. The only painkiller my parents had in the house was aspirin. My mouth was still bleeding, and small pieces of my teeth kept falling onto my tongue.

Dr. Goldstein had been my dentist for many years. He knew we did not have dental insurance and always gave us a reduction in his fees. In the past he had taken great pride in my teeth, almost like an artist bringing a canvas to life. His work had enhanced my smile.

Alberta walked behind me as I climbed the twelve steps to Dr. Goldstein's office. When I opened the door, Dr. Goldstein was standing there. When he saw me, he just shook his head and said, "We will make you well again." Dr. Goldstein knew I had lost something irreplaceable and very precious: my smile.

I sat in the dentist's chair for seven hours that day. He had given me about eight shots of Novocain. My whole face felt numb. Fourteen of my teeth had been sheared off at the gum by the wire clothesline while four others had pieces broken off.

He had to split my gums to extract many of my teeth. He worked and worked and only took one break until he was finished. He was the most patient and forgiving dentist I have ever known.

Before the accident, he thought I was a nice boy. He once told me if I had been Jewish, he would have made arrangements to introduce me to his daughter. Her picture was on a stand in his operating room; she was very attractive. After the accident, he never mentioned his daughter again. He must have thought I was a schmuck.

It was a lesson that has followed me through life. I was now in the same class as those old people who soaked their teeth in a glass of water. I hated what I did to myself. In a split second, my life had totally changed. I would have to find a way to kiss a girl without her knowing I had falsies. If there was a positive derived from this event, it marked the finale of our Halloween escapades.

Alberta had recently graduated from St. Joseph's Academy in Rochester and was working full-time. She made the arrangements to pay Dr. Goldstein for my dental work. Her unselfishness reminds me of the story behind Dürer's praying hands.

The story behind the creation of the *Praying Hands* has been told and retold thousands of times. Albrecht Dürer, the creator of the *Praying Hands*, has become famous as an artist. His brother, Albert, also a gifted artist, paid the price for his brother's success (some argue the story is fiction while others claim it to be true). The sources of this widely circulated story are unknown.

In the fifteenth century, a family with eighteen children lived in a small village near Nuremberg, Germany. Albrecht Dürer, the father, worked very long days as a goldsmith in order to feed and clothe his family. Two of Dürer's sons had dreams of pursuing their talent as artists. Unfortunately, because of the family's financial situation, there was not enough money to send either boy to the art academy in Nuremberg. Consequently, the two boys agreed to toss a coin to determine who would work in the mines and support his brother, who would attend the academy. Four years later, the winner who attended the academy would pay the expenses for the one who worked.

Albrecht Dürer II won the toss and attended art school. His brother, Albert, went into the mines to finance Albrecht's education. Upon graduation, Albrecht had won considerable acclaim. His etchings, woodcuts, and oil paintings were considered far superior to his peers and instructors. He began to earn considerable fees for his works.

Upon return to his village, the Dürer family had a dinner in his honor. After the meal, Albrecht gave a toast in honor of his brother who had worked to pay his expenses. At the end of his toast, he said, "Now, brother, it is your turn. Now you go to Nurenberg to pursue your dreams of being an artist, and I will take care of you."

Albert sat with tears in his eyes. He shook his head and softly said, "No, no, no." He rose and wiped the tears and slowly unfolded his hands and said, "I cannot go to the academy. These are no longer hands of an artist. Look what four years in the mines have done to my hands. The bones in each hand have been smashed at least once. I have been suffering from arthritis so badly in my right hand I cannot even hold a glass to return your toast, much less make delicate lines on a canvas with a brush. Brother, for me it is too late."

To pay homage to Albert for all he had sacrificed, Albrecht Durer drew his brother's abused hands with palm together as if praying. Albrecht Dürer has numerous portraits, charcoals, watercolors, and copper engravings hanging in museums throughout the world; but the one almost everyone is familiar with is the hands of his brother—the praying hands.

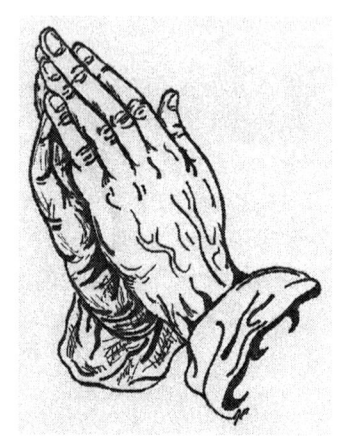

Albrecht Dürer's the Praying Hands.

A week after my extractions, I was still home. My mouth was still a mess, and I was in a lot of pain. My appearance could have qualified me for *Mad Magazine*. My face was swollen and bruised, and my eyes were black.

I refused to see any of my friends. When they came to the house, I never ventured out of my bedroom. My mother was hostess to about eight girls and boys who stopped by on a regular basis to check on my condition and enjoyed my mother's homemade chocolate chip cookies and milk.

About ten days after my visit to Dr. Goldstein, Alberta arranged for me to have an upper plate. Dr. Sansone was a very good dentist and an even better psychologist. He understood my fears. He told me it would be possible to construct the plate so the inside of it would simulate the roof of my mouth.

He said, "If a girl puts her tongue in your mouth, she will never be able to tell you have a plate. I will make ridges on the roof of your plate just like the roof of your mouth." In an instant, he made me feel whole again.

I did not return to school for three weeks. When I did, it was with a new set of teeth. Fortunately, I was physically stronger than most of my peers. They knew this was a subject not open for discussion.

The Barend family together on April 16, 1955—Ray and Elane's marriage. Harold was the best man, and Alberta was a bridesmaid.

Chapter Thirty-Seven

CRIME AND PUNISHMENT

If you want crime to pay, become an attorney.

—Will Rogers

The year following my Halloween tragedy, Ronnie and I were returning from a Saturday evening party with Earl Vokel. Earl was driving his car. It was an old Chevy that would have never passed today's inspection.

While driving on the portion of Edgemere Drive that was still under construction, Earl's headlights started flickering, and subsequently his car battery went dead. It was a cold fall night, and we were about one mile from home. There were no streetlights on this portion of Edgemere Drive—it was dark.

The company hired to widen and pave Edgemere Drive had left their trucks parked on the side of the roadway. The three of us quickly realized there would be a battery in one of the trucks.

Fortunately, Earl had a flashlight. We took tools and the flashlight and walked about two hundred yards to one of the dump trucks parked on the side of the road. After we managed to open the hood, within minutes we extracted the battery and carried it back to Earl's car. The truck battery did not fit into Earl's battery holder, so we fastened it with rope.

We made no pretense at being quiet. Earl promised us he would return the battery the next day. We assumed people would understand that it was a temporary loan. Unfortunately, everyone did not think like us.

After we closed the hood, a man came running out of his house screaming at us. We jumped into the car and prayed it would start—it did. The man was about fifty feet from us when Earl managed to start the car and speed onto the road. Our pursuant ran back to his house and got into his car. He chased us. Although Earl had a quarter mile head start, Earl's car was no match for the man's new Buick. It began to close fast.

Instead of heading in the direction of our homes, Earl swung his car onto Cranberry Pond Road and headed for the large open field behind the homes on Third Avenue. The pursuit car was about fifty yards from us when the road ended. The minute the pavement ended and the grassy field began, Earl turned his car lights off.

There were wagon trails stretching across the field, and Earl knew everyone by heart. He knew the person chasing us would not venture into the field with a new car. As expected, the car lights giving chase suddenly disappeared. We were scared but relieved.

We waited in the field for about twenty minutes, hoping the concerned citizen would decide to leave. After many tense moments of waiting, Earl drove out of the field and onto East Manitou Road. He immediately drove to my house, dropped off Ronnie and me, and thanked us for helping him get the battery. He promised he would return it sometime tomorrow.

The next morning, while I was still in bed, the Greece Police arrived at my house. Earl and Ronnie were sitting in the back of the police car. Unfortunately, the man chasing us got a good description of Earl's car. The Greece police were at Earl's house at 7:00 a.m. before he could get his battery charged and the borrowed one returned. They were there to arrest us for stealing the battery.

My mother was livid, and my dad was trying to make some sense out of the situation. Once we were stuffed in the backseat of the police car, they drove directly to the Greece police station. A different policeman was assigned to each of us. We were put in separate rooms. For five hours the police interrogated us and had us scared shitless.

Without any of us knowing, Carl Lupo, Ronnie's dad, who was now the Monroe County coroner, contacted the Greece police and explained what had happened. He told them to keep us there and scare us so another incident like this would never happen again. They did exactly that.

After five hours of being questioned separately and then together, the police said they were taking us to the Town of Greece Justice of the Peace for sentencing. I knew if a bond had to be posted, the next time my parents would see me would be in jail.

When we were in front of the Justice of the Peace, he admonished us for our crime. He then read us the maximum sentence he could give us. He asked if we had anything to say. We pleaded for mercy and explained we had no intention of stealing the battery. He stared at us for about three minutes without saying a word and then told us we would be on probation for sixty days. We would be released into the custody of our parents.

He said he was not going to have this incident entered as a crime against us because the construction company did not want to press charges. Fortunately for us, Carl Lupo knew some of the people who owned the construction company, and they preferred not to have any bad publicity.

The Truth Always Works

Beginning the summer following my junior year in high school, Tommy Brennan called and said he had a couple of hot dates. At the time, I was eighteen years old and Tommy was seventeen. The two seventeen-year-old girls lived in a subdivision in Greece. Their homes were within a hundred yards of each other. Tommy knew one of the girls—Beverly. He had never met the other girl.

Tommy jumped in the backseat with Bev, and the other girl got in the front with me. I proceeded to drive toward Hamlin Beach on the Parkway.

While driving on the Parkway, all of a sudden a flock of sparrows filled the road in front of me. Instead of slamming on my brakes, I gunned the car, thinking it would scare the birds and they would fly off. Unfortunately, a couple of the birds hit my car.

The girl who was sitting in the front seat with me screamed and hollered for me to stop the car. She wanted out of the car. I pulled the car to the side of the road and tried to convince her it was an unfortunate accident, but she was adamant about not getting back into the car. After about fifteen minutes of trying to convince her to get back into the car, I drove off and left her standing on the Hamlin Parkway.

I pointed my car toward the Village of Hilton. I planned to find a pay phone in Hilton and have Bev call the girl's parents and explain what happened. Hopefully, they would arrange to get her home.

Before we arrived in Hilton, Bev asked Tommy if he would drive my car, so I could get in the back with her. Tommy agreed. He continued driving in the direction of the Village of Hilton. While Bev and I were making love in the backseat, Tommy drove the car through the Main Street of Hilton beeping the horn all the way. That eliminated our phone call from Hilton.

We returned to the Hamlin Parkway but found no sign of the other girl. We then headed toward Beverly's home. After we dropped Bev off, I convinced Tommy we should go to the home of the girl we left on the Parkway and tell her parents what happened. He wanted no part of it. I told him we had no choice. I was concerned about her safety. Tommy sat in the car while I knocked on the front door. The father answered the door. I introduced myself and explained why I was there. He looked at me with a serious surprised look. He asked me to step inside the house. I was scared. I thought he was going to beat the hell out of me. After he closed the door behind me, he asked me to start from the beginning and tell him the whole story. I explained everything, including hitting the birds.

He asked if I touched his daughter. I told him no. I said I never even put my arm around her—I did not even have time. He smiled when I said I did not have time. It was my first indication I might leave with my limbs intact. After I finished telling him the whole story, he said, "I was just on my way to the Greece police station to have a warrant sworn out for your arrest for attempting to rape my daughter. I don't think you would be here if my daughter's story was true."

He then called his daughter to come into the room and asked her to tell him the truth. All she said was "He killed those birds." He thanked me for having the courage to come forward and said it saved both of us a lot of grief.

When I returned to the car, my whole body was shaking. If I hadn't returned to do the right thing, I probably would have been on my way to jail, and she would have had to carry a lie for the rest of her life.

Chapter Thirty-eight

HAVE WHEELS, WILL GO

*Carriages without horses shall go,
And accidents fill the world with woe.*

—Martha Shipton

During the beginning of my junior year of high school, I used some of my savings to purchase a 1947 stick-shift pink Ford convertible for $150. The car cost me less than my insurance. Because of my age, I was placed in a risk pool, and the insurance premium was about $200 every six months. Consequently, if I wanted to keep the car on the road, I had to earn money for my automobile expenses.

Memories were etched in my mind of the many evenings after basketball practice when Bill Boothby and I made the six-mile journey from Hilton High to Braddock Heights in the middle of the winter. Many evenings, when we arrived home, our faces would be frozen from the wind and ice, and our clothes would be wet from walking through snowdrifts. I am not sure if our parents felt it built character to make us endure that trip or if they were apathetic to our plight. I promised myself I would not repeat the same arduous journey in my senior year.

After I purchased the car, I didn't change the color or fix the convertible top, which sometimes permitted water to drip on the person in the backseat. I had only one concern—to make it go faster. Two of my friends and I installed a truck motor and a special clutch in the '47 Ford. When we were finished, it could fly. My intent was to have the fastest drag racing vehicle in the area.

Bob Rabjohn, a member of the senior class at Hilton High and a basketball player, had just purchased a new Chevrolet convertible. He made it a point on numerous occasions to challenge me in front of other students to a drag race. I finally agreed to his terms: the winner gets the keys to the loser's car.

It was a June day, just before completion of the school year. The word about our race had spread throughout the school. The day of the race, I left school a little early. Even though I traveled the road almost every day, I wanted to drive the strip we would be racing before our competition. When I arrived, there were about a hundred students from Hilton High School who were waiting anxiously for the excitement to begin. They also left school a little early.

We agreed the race would take place on a half-mile section of East Manitou Road that went straight for about a mile. East Manitou Road was a two-lane macadam road with deep ditches along each side. As the crowd began to mushroom, many of the spectators got into their cars and drove toward the finish line. Some kids jumped on running boards while others begged for seats inside.

Only a few residents used this section of East Manitou Road, which was the back door into Braddock Heights. It was an old farm road, which connected Braddock Heights to the west. No cars other than those of the spectators and racers were on the road. To ensure there would be no accidents, prior to the race some of the kids blocked a section of the road beyond the finish line. This prevented oncoming cars from entering the race path.

Thirty minutes before the start of the race, the road was lined with kids. One of the girls volunteered to start the race. She was handed a three-foot stick of wood and told the race would start when she lowered the stick. Her instructions were to lower the stick fast and don't move until the cars were past her. She positioned herself between our cars and held the piece of wood over her head. I remember thinking it was just like the movies—but she had to be crazy standing about ten feet in front of our cars.

I positioned my Ford convertible to the right of the new Chevrolet convertible. We were both revving our engines. My top was up, and my competitor's was down. My friends who were versed in auto racing advised me to put the top up to reduce drag. I took their advice.

Jerry Barker asked if he could ride with me during the race. I was nervous, and Jerry was always good company. Someone had taken chalk from school and used it to draw the starting and finishing lines. After we pulled our cars to the starting line, the girl with the wooden stick walked closer to our cars. She stood there holding the piece of wood upright. It gave the event a bit of drama. Then, she quickly lowered the stick.

Our cars lurched forward with wheels screaming. It was like a scene out of *Grease*. At the quarter-mile mark, I was half-a-car-length ahead of the Chevy. Then Rabjohn's car began moving into my lane almost as if he wanted to squeeze me off the road. I moved my car to the right with one tire on the edge of the ditch. Jerry hollered, "You're going to go off the road! Get over!" When I pulled my wheels back onto the road, there wasn't an inch between the two cars.

One person at the finish line claimed the Chevy had won while four claimed I won. The majority of the spectators said it was too close to call. It was a photo finish without a camera. No keys changed hands, but my love life was embellished.

The following September, Rabjohn and his buddies spread Limburger Cheese on the tailpipe of my Ford. That was the only way they could beat me.

No Panties on the Antenna

Shortly thereafter, I was driving my Ford convertible on a country road near Hilton. Jerry Barker, Jim Elkins, and Bill Boothby were with me. A New York State Trooper passed us going in the opposite direction. He quickly made a U-turn and pulled us over. He asked to see my driver's license. He glanced at it and then handed it back to me.

With a smile, he asked if we were proud of our conquests. He said, "Take those woman's underpants off your antenna before I find something wrong with the car." I jumped out of the car and removed my trophy. Humility has never been one of my best traits.

A Life-changing Motorcycle Accident

The following two summers during my junior and senior years of high school, two other accidents occurred that had a major impact on my life. Michael Pozzangera, a good friend of mine and classmate at Hilton High, purchased a motorcycle.

It was big, and it could fly. He was speeding when he lost control and flipped the motorcycle. He flew off the motorcycle, and his body landed in a roadside ditch.

Michael would have survived in good condition if the motorcycle had not come down on him or if he had been wearing a helmet. At that time New York State did not require motorcyclists to wear helmets.

The impact of the cycle coming down on his face split his optic nerve. At seventeen, he was blinded for life.

I recently saw Michael at our fiftieth high school reunion. Although still blind, he works at staying in good physical condition; he looks great. He is married and has children.

Death before Graduation

The other accident resulted in the death of one of our friends and classmates.

Ronnie and I had gone to a party and returned home about twelve on a Saturday night. It was three weeks before the Hilton High School graduation. Ronnie's father, Carl Lupo, was still the Monroe County coroner.

An hour after we got home, Ronnie's dad called and told him to get out of bed and bring Harold with him to the Monroe County coroner's office in Rochester. He said it was very important, and he wanted both of us to come as soon as possible.

Carl stood about five feet ten inches and weighed about 240 pounds. He was solid muscle. A retired professional boxer who still believed in physical fitness, Carl was every bit a first-sergeant type of guy. If he said you do it, you did it.

When we arrived at the coroner's office, Ronnie's dad met us in the lobby. He explained how a good friend of ours was killed a few hours ago because of driving fast. He wanted us to see the results of a car going too fast.

Mr. Lupo said, "I asked both of you to come because I do not want to see either of you here again. I hope what you see will convince you reckless and fast driving will get you injured or killed, and that will cause a lot of heartache and suffering. Don't be stupid, and don't be selfish. Think about all the people you will hurt. That boy lying in there could easily be either of you. I know how you two screw around. I know all the police in Rochester and Greece, and they keep me informed. I don't care if you screw all the girls in the world, but don't kill yourselves by doing something stupid. Now go in and see him."

It was a sight I will never forget. Carl Lupo must have known the sight of Wayne Pinkney lying on a stainless steel table would be etched in our minds forever.

While we stood there looking at a body covered with a white cloth, Carl walked to the end of the table and pulled the cloth. I gasped. It was a sight I just wasn't ready for.

Yesterday, at school, we had been having a good time with Wayne—today he was lying motionless in front of us on a steel table. He was no more. His body had ballooned. There were large chunks of flesh torn away from his chest, arms, and head.

On our way home, Ronnie and I discussed how lucky we were because we did not go to the party that night. Jerry Barker and some of the guys from Grandview Heights were at the party with Wayne but left in a different car.

Wayne Pinkney was an integral part of our group at Hilton High School. He was well liked and a good friend. After he left the party that evening, Wayne was driving a borrowed car. On a sharp curve, he lost control of the car and hit a large tree. The convertible top was down. Wayne was thrown from the car, and his body sheared off a number of the tree limbs. Tommy Davidson, a passenger in the front seat not wearing a seatbelt, was also thrown out of the car and into a field. He was injured but not seriously.

While I was in the army, Ronnie Lupo got married. Ronnie and his bride, Elaine Quinn, are on the far right. The wedding party (l-r) front row: Pattie A. Lupo, JoAnn Quinn, Pattie Ellen Rap; back row (l-r) Jim (Chief) Elkins, Jerry Barker, and Ron Pauley.

Chapter Thirty-Nine

WORKING THE GRAVEYARD SHIFT

*There is nothing more debasing
Than the work of those who do well
What is not worth doing at all.*

—Gore Vidal

After high school graduation, having neither the money nor the academic achievements to afford a college entrance, my options were limited. My brother Ray assisted me in getting a job at E. I. du Pont in Rochester, New York. DuPont hired a number of college students and young people who were in transition. It was employment illegal immigrants would have scorned.

The college students were there for the summer. The rest of us were there until we got fired or found something better. We were hired to work on alternate shifts: 4:00 p.m. until midnight and midnight to 8:00 a.m. Those who worked these hours called it the graveyard shift for a good reason.

I worked in a dark room where film emulsions were made. When you entered the darkroom from the outside, it took about ten minutes for your eyes to adjust. It was so dark throughout the building that "cat eyes" were installed along the walkways.

The room where I worked, an area ten feet by twelve feet, and the restrooms were the exceptions to darkness. DuPont wanted to ensure its pots were properly cleaned. Consequently, the room was so well lit you could clearly see the cockroaches in every corner.

My job was to clean the emulsion out of stainless steel pots. At the beginning of my shift, I always hoped the person who worked before me did not leave a stack of dirty tubs for me when I arrived. If so, I would be working hard all night. It was common courtesy to finish your work before the end of your shift.

Most evenings, I alternated shifts with a fellow by the name of Marv Brundridge. Marv was a good friend who usually left me with fewer pots than I left him.

Marv was an outstanding basketball player at Madison High School in Rochester, New York. He and I comprised 80 percent of the scoring for the DuPont industrial team, which played in a league at the YMCA. My ability to play basketball helped to ensure a few extra months of employment at DuPont.

Because of the environment where we worked and the nature of the people there, incidents took place that instilled a bit of adventure to an otherwise dull job, making for interesting stories. There were about seven middle-aged women, eight young men, and a couple of supervisors who worked in the darkroom on the night shift. It was not uncommon to be walking down an aisle and have a woman's hand reach out and grab your behind or groin. When you turned to see who did it, the person would be gone.

If your body required a bowel movement, it was best to hold it as long as possible. There was one bathroom for the women and one for the guys. A guy sitting on a toilet in a stall was a sitting duck for all kinds of abuse. Rolls of toilet paper would fly over the stall wall or buckets of cold water would rain down on you.

One evening about three hours into my shift, I had to use the bathroom. I quietly entered the room and checked carefully to ensure no one saw me enter the room. After a few minutes of finding my comfort zone on the toilet, I heard a noise above me. I looked up to see a fire hose coming over the side of the stall. Before I could get off the toilet, water poured down on me. I was soaked.

I had three more hours of work, and my clothes were clinging to my body soaked with cold water. When I exited the stall, the fire hose had been shut off and no one was in the area.

I was hell bent on getting revenge. I returned soaking wet to my work area and filled a stainless steel container with the coldest water I could get. I took the container and walked to a recess in the walkway. I stood there motionless for about five minutes in total darkness, holding the stainless steel container filled with water and shivering in my wet clothes. I knew it was about time for one of the fellows responsible for my soaking to take a break.

When I heard someone approach my position, I stepped out and flung the water at him. I quickly moved to make my departure. The person I had just drenched with freezing cold water was quick enough to grab me. Unfortunately, it was not the person I expected. It was the night supervisor.

The next morning there was plenty of discussion as to my future with DuPont. It was decided to allow me to continue working until the basketball season was completed. It was made perfectly clear to me that my career with DuPont was about to end. When the season ended, I was abruptly discharged for lack of work.

PAL Basketball

Prior to working at DuPont, I had played basketball with Marv on a Police Athletic League team and at the Baden Street Settlement House in Rochester, New York. The coach of the PAL team would invite the best players from Monroe County to play on his team.

Consequently, my teammates were excellent basketball players; the competition was good and the exposure high. We played a number of exhibition games at places like the Rochester War Memorial Arena.

Charlie McKay, an outstanding athlete at Edison High, and Al Butler, an all-American from East High, were also on the team. Charlie McKay became one of my good friends. During the eighteen-month period prior to entering the service, Charlie "Duckets" McKay and I were together almost every evening—playing basketball and picking up girls.

One of the more memorable exhibition games I played with the PAL team was at Elmira Reformatory in Elmira, New York. It is a high-security prison for young criminals. Our coach wanted to make sure everyone who played on his team knew firsthand what it would be like to be in jail. He would always schedule a game with the prisoners at Elmira Reformatory.

Prior to our game, the warden took us on a tour of the prison. It was not the place to go for rest and recuperation. It left its mark on my memory.

While we were warming up for the game, the prisoners were brought in and seated to watch the game. Guards were standing in the aisles and throughout the gym with machine guns. The atmosphere was not conducive for playing your best basketball. We won the game.

Baden Street Settlement House

Sometimes we played basketball at the gym in the Baden Street Settlement House. The gym was located in the middle of a low-income, mostly black settlement project in inner-city Rochester. The basketball court was comparable to one found in a new high school. It had a hardwood floor and bleachers for spectators.

When we played pickup games, the bleachers would be filled with young blacks hoping to see Marv Brundridge or Al Butler dunk—doing their magic.

Charlie and I were anomalies; we were almost always the only white guys in the building. I was so visible the black players called me the Milk Bottle.

On one occasion, Charlie invited another white basketball player to join us. He was from East High School. During a game, he elbowed one of the black players in the face and proceeded to have words with him. Marv Brundridge walked over to me and said, "Harold, get your buddies and get the hell out of here quick before someone gets hurt."

I dropped the ball and walked to Charlie McKay and said, "Marv said we had better get out of here right now." I looked up at the bleachers, and the kids were standing up and starting to move toward the players on the floor.

We ran for the exit and jumped into to my car. As we screeched out of the parking lot, bottles and stones flew in our direction. Neither Charlie nor I ever played again at the Baden Street gym.

Puppy Love

Prior to my employment with DuPont, I met Carol Rankin. Carol and I dated for more than a year—if there was ever a song indicative of our relationship, it was "Puppy Love." Carol's parent's never appreciated my dating their daughter. When I would pick her up at home, her parents were polite but cold. They did not appreciate her dating someone destined for (as they saw it) Elmira Reformatory or Sing-Sing.

According to Carol, her parents learned where I lived and one evening drove her past my house to show her how poor my family lived. They wanted her to understand that poor people breed poor people and a life with me would be difficult and disastrous.

Carol didn't care; she was attractive, bright, and a rebel. To make matters worse, her father was a supervisor at DuPont. He was somewhat pleased when I got a job on the night shift. It meant I would spend less time with his daughter. After the water incident, he was assured I would someday be in jail.

With the forces of society against me and parents who preferred their daughter be with a well-groomed, college-educated young man instead of a wild kid who just barely made it out of high school, our relationship was doomed.

Chapter Forty

THE U.S. ARMY

An army is a nation within a nation:
It is one of the vices of our age.

—Alfred de Vigny

Having failed miserably in my first full-time employment, I decided to make some fast career decisions. I was a prime prospect for the military draft (the draft was not eliminated until after the Vietnam conflict), and I was not looking forward to serving time as a foot soldier.

After a couple of days with an army recruiter, he convinced me my name would surface within six months, and I would be receiving my marching orders.

When the United States Army recruiter asked what, other than a high school diploma, were my attributes, I mentioned that I had written some articles for a weekly newspaper. He latched onto this information quickly.

After I completed a few tests, the army guaranteed me enrollment in their prestigious U.S. Army Information School. I agreed to enlist for three years. The U.S. Army agreed in writing to send me to the U.S. Army Information School in New Rochelle, New York, and subsequently to Germany.

When my date of departure arrived, January 16, 1959, my dad drove me to the recruiting station in Rochester. We were told to bring with us toiletries, basic essentials, and a few clothes.

A group of about thirty men, including myself, boarded a bus and were driven to Buffalo, New York, for our physicals. A number of guys who had been drafted were devising various schemes to fail their physicals. It seldom mattered what you told the doctor regarding your physical or mental condition. Upon completion of the physical, if you could crawl, you passed.

After an overnight stay in Buffalo, we were sent by train to Fort Dix, New Jersey, for eight weeks of hell. It was our welcome into the U.S. Army—basic training. When we arrived in New Jersey, a military bus was waiting at the train depot to take us to Fort Dix. On this cold wind-whipped day, a sergeant was standing by the bus door shouting profanities at the group because we were moving with caution across the frozen, snow-covered walkway.

The bus entered Fort Dix and made its first stop at the barber shop. I was quite proud of my full head of hair, which showcased a ducktail. Within seconds my hair was history. The soldier administering the damage moved the buzz cutter across my head until there was nothing but a skull with a few hairs protruding.

As we exited the barber chair, we were directed to return to the bus—again, with a few profanities.

When mission "crosshairs" was complete, we were moved to a large wooden building, which would be our home for the next eight weeks. The room temperature was about fifty degrees. It had ten bunk beds on each side and an open center aisle about eight feet wide by about seventy feet long. The bathroom was at the end of the room; it was a big room with eight toilets. The toilets sat in the open adjacent to one another—no partitions, no sense of dignity.

In single file, we entered the building. As we exited the bus, there was a staff sergeant directing each man to a bunk bed. We were told to stand in pairs of twos facing the aisle at the end of the beds we would occupy. We stood in front of metal bunk beds with two green foot lockers at the end of the bed and a tall wood locker at the head of the bed. This procedure continued until the bus was emptied.

While standing at attention, a black first sergeant with a chiseled body entered the room and walked down the middle of the aisle. When he got to the opposite end of the room, he turned and looked at the assembled group still standing at attention and said, "What a sad, sorry bunch of rejects and reprobates we have here. It is my responsibility to make soldiers out of you in eight weeks. I can guarantee these will be the worst eight weeks of your life. If anyone wants to leave now, they can. We'll issue you a dishonorable discharge. Does anyone have anything to say?"

One of the recruits responded, "No, sir." The first sergeant walked up to the young man and put his face inches from his and proceeded to explain the difference between and officer and a sergeant. He began by saying, "Ignorance has a way of surfacing very early in boot camp, and, mister, *you* are ignorant. Get down and give me twenty-five pushups. I am not 'sir,' you dumb bastard. I am First Sergeant Bates. Don't you ever forget my name."

The young man standing adjacent to him made the mistake of looking down to see how the push-ups were being administered. First Sergeant Bates immediately noticed the young recruit's head move. He quickly moved to within inches of the new recruit. His toes were almost touching the recruit's, and his face was so close to the recruit's that their noses almost touched.

Sergeant Bates hollered in his face, "Do you know how to stand at attention? You are a disgrace. This could be the worst bunch of recruits I have ever trained. Because you are so interested in knowing how to do a push-up, get down and give me thirty push-ups. I don't want to see any part of your body touch the floor other than your hands and toes. Do you understand me, asshole?"

Before the recruit who was being chastised had an opportunity to answer, one of the fellows standing across from me started to grin. The first sergeant spun around, saw him, and screamed, "Asshole! Do you think this is funny? I'll tell you what is funny. You have KP tomorrow. Be in the kitchen ready to work at 3:00 a.m. tomorrow. If for any reason you are not there, I will make an example out of you."

After that, you could hear a pin drop. There were no movement of bodies, no smirks or smiles, no sneezing or coughing—every face was looking straight ahead. We were scared. I thought someone would wet his pants.

First Sergeant Bates then proceeded to announce, "Five more men will be needed for KP tomorrow morning. The last five to leave the barracks and enter the formation tomorrow morning will be assigned KP. Every morning thereafter those at the two ends of the formation will be so honored with KP. It is our way of implementing God's words: 'The last shall come first.'"

The soldier who grinned and was given KP would be awakened at 2:30 a.m. Those picked for KP at reveille would not have to report until 4:00 a.m. The extra hour and half of sleep was like gold.

Following his introduction, First Sergeant Bates read our names and asked us to come forward and get our metal name tags. We were instructed the tags should never leave our bodies— not when we sleep, shit, or shower. The name tags always stayed on us.

After dispensing the name tags, First Sergeant Bates lined us in single file, and we marched to a quartermaster building. Here we were issued our shoes, boots, shoe polish, duffel bag, dress uniform (coat, pants, hat, shirt and ties), socks, underwear, jacket, pants, shirts, helmet, M1 rifle, canteen, military belt, sheets, blankets, pillow, and press-on name tags.

Once we had received all our military issue, we then had to carry it through snow and ice back to the barracks. We made about four trips from the quartermaster building to our barracks, carrying load after load of military issue. Like most of the other men, I placed my issue on my bed. I was assigned a bottom bunk.

First Sergeant Bates introduced a staff sergeant who would instruct us in the proper way of storing our equipment, hanging our clothes, and making our beds. He was the man responsible for our daily chores and ensuring the cleanliness of the barracks. He was a Korean War vet and a guy you could easily come to hate.

His educational segment lasted until 2:00 a.m. We could not go to bed until everyone was able to make their beds to the approval of the sergeant. The test was this: a quarter had to bounce at least an inch above the bed when flipped onto the bed. If the quarter did not rise an inch, the sergeant would tear down the bed and you had to begin again.

The first two weeks were tough. We had to endure pull-ups before breakfast and marching in the freezing cold. We had to stand at attention sometimes for forty-five minutes to an hour in freezing cold. Every exercise you could possibly conceive of for an aerobics class, we did on frozen ground with temperatures sometimes zero or below. We sat for hours on the freezing ground while someone instructed us in the use of a gas mask, M1, or other military gear.

My break came one morning during the third week of training. The post commander sent a request to each battalion commander asking for basketball players interested in trying out for the post team.

While everyone was standing at attention, First Sergeant Bates announced, "The post basketball team is seeking experienced basketball players. If anyone here thinks they are good enough to make the team, step forward. But understand before you step forward, if you do not make the team, you will make up all the time you lost."

Only two of us stepped forward. The first sergeant motioned for us to come forward and introduced us to the battalion and said, "These are either two very good basketball players or two very big fools. We will know very soon."

We were told to be at the post gym that afternoon for a tryout. While the team that was practicing wore basketball shoes, the other fellow and I had only our combat boots. We both made the team. Five players had been rotated out of Fort Dix on new assignments, and the team was desperate for good basketball players.

The practices began every day at noon. The other fellow, who was in a different barracks than me, and I requested from the coach an additional two hours of practice each day. He was more than pleased to send a note to our first sergeants asking that we be released from duty at 10:00 a.m. and reassigned every day to the gym until practice was completed.

My first sergeant was furious. He vowed in front of my roommates that he would find a way to have me make up the time I was missing in basic training. He was blowing smoke, and the guys in my barracks realized it.

Everything was going fine up until the last week of basic training. This was the week before graduation. Hopefully, we would be leaving Fort Dix and moving onto another assignment. The post basketball team was tied for first place, and I was a happy camper. I was in great shape mentally and physically.

At this stage, I really didn't need the extra two hours of practice my coach had originally agreed to, but I continued to leave at 10:00 a.m. and slept for two hours on the mats before the team came for practice.

Vigilante Justice

In the bunk bed above me was a young man from Rochester, New York. He ran afoul with the guys he lived with. One evening I was approached by one of the team leaders from our barracks. He asked if I had anything missing. I mentioned I was missing a few dollars, but it was no big thing. He proceeded to tell me they had evidence that my bunk mate was stealing from a number of guys. They had gone through his personal items and found things belonging to other people. They said they were going to beat the shit out of him.

I was told to pretend I did not hear a thing. Five guys came that evening, gagged him, and proceeded to beat him while he was under the blankets. I closed my eyes and said a prayer for the little bastard.

The beating lasted for about ten minutes. After they beat him, they dragged him into the shower and wire brushed him. When they threw him back on the bed, his body was covered with blood.

Before graduation, in lieu of being court-martialed for stealing, he was given a dishonorable discharge. No charges were placed against the soldiers who administered the beating.

Twenty-mile Forced March with Full Gear

Every soldier, no matter if they played basketball, played in the band, or served the chaplain, had to complete a forced march of about twenty miles with full military pack—including helmet and M1 rifle. This was a prerequisite before completion of basic training. I was in good physical condition for playing basketball but not for marching twenty miles with a full-military pack.

The company commander led the march. The only equipment he carried was a swagger stick. He maintained a brisk pace. Each company's first sergeant marched alongside their respective group. About seventeen miles into the march, I was really feeling exhausted, and so were the fellows around me. I hollered, "Slow down! We are exhausted."

Shortly thereafter, a number of other soldiers began to complain and asked that the pace be slowed. All of a sudden, the whole procession came to a halt. The first sergeants were brought forward to meet with the commanding officer. After a short meeting, they returned to their respective companies.

First Sergeant Bates looked at his company standing at attention before him and said, "I want the man who first hollered 'Slow down' to step forward. If he does not step forward, everyone will be up all night and tomorrow cleaning their M1 rifles, and instead of being trucked back to your barracks, you will march back. Do you hear me?"

I knew I was a dead man. If I stepped forward, Bates would delight in his sadistic torture of me. On the other hand, if I did not step forward, it would be hell living with the guys in this company—many of whom had become my friends.

I said a quick prayer, closed my eyes, and then pushed the guy in front of me aside to step out of formation. The first sergeant's eyes grew about twice their size when he saw me. He stared at me with a shitty grin and then hollered, "The jockstrap! You've been playing too much basketball and not doing enough soldiering. Maybe we should keep you another eight weeks. In the meantime, you can entertain us by doing fifty push-ups."

I thought, *This isn't as bad as I thought.* I got down to begin doing the push-ups, but then he said, "No, no! Not here—over there."

The first sergeant pointed to a large mud puddle. He ordered me to get into the middle of the puddle to do the push-up in my full gear. It was the beginning of March, and it was cold.

When I completed the push-ups, I was full of mud, and my clothes were soaked. Upon completion of the last three miles, I sat on the cold ground with my company. My clothes were wet, and water was still in my boots. We had to wait about twenty minutes for the military transport to pick us up.

After we were loaded onto the truck, one of the drivers recognized me. He played basketball with me on the post team. He brought me a blanket and asked, "How the hell are you going to play basketball this weekend?" He continued, "I was really looking forward to this game. For you, I don't think it will happen. Get to the dispensary as soon as you get back. I'll inform the coach as to your condition. Take off your shoes and check your feet—you probably have blisters."

That evening when we got back, First Sergeant Bates refused me permission to go to the dispensary. After his staff sergeant took him aside and explained how he overheard one of the truck drivers talking with me, the staff sergeant told Bates the guy played basketball with me on the post team and planned to make a report to the basketball coach.

Within ten minutes, a jeep pulled up to the barracks, and the driver called my name.

He was to take me to the post hospital. The hospital kept me overnight. I had four huge blisters and a bad cold in the making. I did not play basketball that last game. The coach filed a complaint with the post commander who subsequently court-martialed the first sergeant.

During the last week of basic training, I was given my next assignment—U.S. Army Information School at Fort Slocum, New York. I was given travel money to return to Rochester, New York, and a two-week leave before I had to report to Fort Slocum.

Prior to departure, we paraded in dress greens and M1 rifles before the review stand, which featured the post commander, a number of dignitaries, and parents. My parents did not attend. Once the parade was over, we tossed our hats in the air.

After farewells, I slung my bag onto my shoulder and walked to the main entrance of Fort Dix. I showed the military police at the gate my leave papers and then continued walking away from the military base—hoping never to see Fort Dix again.

Hitchhiking during the fifties and sixties was relatively safe. Today, there are too many perverts and nutcases more than willing to pick up hitchhikers. I hitchhiked home, thus saving the travel money I received from the U.S. Army.

When I arrived at the New York State Thruway exit for Rochester, I called my father. He drove to the thruway exit with his truck and returned me to Braddock Heights. I had two weeks before my next assignment, and I planned on having fun.

Chapter Forty-One

FORT SLOCUM, NY

Military intelligence is a contradiction in terms.

—Groucho Marx

Fort Slocum is also referred to as David's Island. It was named for Major General Henry Slocum, who was a Civil War hero. During the Civil War, the eighty-acre island was used as a medical facility to house and treat 1,800 Confederate prisoners of war. In June 1949, it was designated "Slocum AFB." In 1950, it was returned as an army base and closed fifteen years later.

The island, accessible only by ferry, is off the coast of the city of New Rochelle, New York. For many years, the U.S. Army used the facility as a training school for personnel programmed to work in the information branch of the army. After 1965, it was used as a training school for personnel who participated in the Up with People program. A number of years ago, ownership of the island was returned to the City of New Rochelle. In 2007, the City of New Rochelle voted not to preserve any of the buildings. The city is presently in the design stages for the development of the island.

When my leave ended, I took a Greyhound bus to New Rochelle and then hitched a ride to the ferry. The ferry, which was the only means of access to and from the island, could only be boarded at the dock in New Rochelle or at Fort Slocum going to New Rochelle.

Two military police were positioned at both docks to check ID, passes, and orders. No vehicles other than military were allowed on the island.

Dressed in civilian clothes, I showed my orders to the MP and then slung my duffel bag over my shoulder to board the ferry. Little did I know how much that ferry would govern our lives for the next eight weeks. The ferry made the crossing every hour, but it stopped at 10:00p.m. Consequently, if you were not on that last ferry and there was a roll call that evening, you were AWOL.

When the ferry completed its twenty-minute ride across the bay, the passengers disembarked at Fort Slocum. I showed my travel orders to the MP at the dock then asked for directions. The MP pointed me in the direction of a grouping of ivy-covered buildings.

With my duffel bag over my shoulder, I walked toward the brick buildings. They reminded me more of a college campus than a military base. All of the buildings were constructed of a dull red brick. Ivy had begun its climb on all the exteriors. It had the feel of privileged military. The barracks were situated in a cluster.

I walked directly to the building where the officer of the day was located. He glanced at my orders and then rifled through some papers. After a few minutes, he told me what building and room I was assigned. He suggested I grab some sheets, a pillow, and blankets from his building before I left. He informed me reveille would be in front of our barracks at 7:00 a.m.

It was a welcome relief from 5:00 a.m. during basic training. Unlike basic training, my hair was starting to grow back, and I no longer shocked myself every time I looked in the mirror.

With my duffel bag slung over my right shoulder and my left arm filled with bedding, I walked to the second floor of the barracks where I would be housed for the next ten weeks. When I located my room, I opened the door and walked in.

To my surprise, I had a roommate: Gino Dietrich. Gino was Puerto Rican. He had been drafted. His fondness for the army paralleled mine. We shook hands. I proceeded to get a quick verbal tour of the island. Gino was also enrolled in the Information Specialist program. Being bilingual and with an excellent voice for broadcasting, he was a prime candidate for the program.

Each morning there would be a roll call. The first sergeant would make an appearance at reveille, and then we would never see him again until the next morning. He would usually make the announcements for the day and then give us an outline of our day. Most days were filled with classes: creative writing, radio broadcasting, newspaper layout, military etiquette, etc. At the end of the Army Information School program, we were expected to pass an examination. Passing the exam was required before graduation and being sent to our next assignment.

Every Saturday evening, the girls from the College of New Rochelle would take the ferry to the island and participate in a dance sponsored by Fort Slocum. The girls were always chaperoned by nuns from the Catholic college. On a number of occasions, I had a nun tap me on the shoulder and tell me not to dance so close. She would give the girl I was dancing with a stern look to let her know she meant business.

One of the soldiers stationed at Fort Slocum developed a fondness for one of the coeds. They made plans for a date only to learn the college had strict rules about dating. Only double dates were permitted. Consequently, they needed another couple to have their date. I agreed to a blind date with his friend's roommate.

Unbeknown to the roommate, I was white; unbeknown to me, she was black. Despite our difference in color, we had an enjoyable evening. She told me her father would kill her if he ever knew she was on a date with a white boy. I told her my friends would think I was nuts if I told them I dated a black girl.

It always occurred to me as strange that we would discriminate because of skin color, but we never think twice about wearing black clothes, driving black cars, sitting in black chairs, or decorating our homes with black marble.

When my eight weeks at Fort Slocum were completed and I received my certificate of completion, I was given another two-week leave before I had to report for my next assignment: Fort Hood, Texas. I was somewhat shocked, having been promised a tour of duty in Germany.

After graduation ceremonies at Fort Slocum, I grabbed my duffel bag, put my travel money in my pocket, and took the ferry to New Rochelle. I walked to an interstate entrance and then proceeded to show my sign to the approaching cars, which read, Rochester, NY. Within five hours, I was being dropped off at the thruway entrance at Henrietta—just on the outskirts of Rochester. Once again, I called my father, and he came to pick me up.

It surprised me how he always made the effort to give me a ride home now that I was in the army. In high school, on the other hand, I had to walk home every night after practice—winter, spring, or fall. If I played a sport at Hilton, there was no school bus to transport me the six miles to Braddock Heights.

Neither my father nor Bill Boothby's father ever offered to give us a ride home after practicing for a sport. Some nights we would trudge through snow knee-deep and confront subzero winds.

Two Weeks of Leave

My two-week leave before reporting for duty at Fort Hood was a whirlwind of fun. I didn't have a car at Fifty-ninth Third Avenue, Braddock Heights, so I had to count on friends and relatives to either transport me or allow me to use their vehicles.

I spent most every evening at Tiny's Bar on Irondequoit Bay with Bill Hargarther, Jerry Barker, and Jerry Malibar. The owner of the bar, Tiny, was anything but tiny.

It was a small bar that filled to overcapacity with college kids every night during the summer. Beers were a dollar, the sixties music was blaring, and the dance floor was packed body to body—everyone loved it. It was the perfect spot for young people to meet.

Chubby Checkers was a hot item at the time, and we twisted and twisted until we could convince our dancing partner to take the short walk from Tiny's front door to the sandy beach, which enveloped the bar. My friends always had plenty of blankets in their cars reserved for the right situation. I had a number of opportunities to take a blanket and spread it on the beach and then proceed to do what young people do in a situation like that.

One evening on the beach, when I was heavily involved in the passion of life, the girl I was with cried, "Oh, my finger! My finger is cut."

When I looked up, her finger was stuck in the opening of a beer can. It was impossible to extract the finger without taking her to the emergency room.

She and I were both embarrassed by the situation. After that evening, whenever I saw her at Tiny's, I said hello but never again asked her to dance.

Chapter Forty-Two

FORT HOOD, TEXAS

A military operation involves deception. Even though you are competent, appear to be incompetent. Though effective, appear to be ineffective.

—Sun Tzu, *Art of War*

With part of my travel money, I purchased a plane ticket from Rochester, New York, to the Dallas-Fort Worth, Texas.

I arrived in Killeen, Texas, in the summer of 1959. It was so hot that you could fry an egg on the sidewalks. The City of Killeen had a population of about twenty-two thousand and bordered the military base. Fort Hood is located a little to the east of the center of Texas.

When I arrived at the military base, many of the infantry and armored divisions were being returned to Fort Hood. There was plenty of activity. Elvis Presley had been stationed at Fort Hood prior to being sent to Germany. He was always a few months ahead of me. Presley arrived at Fort Hood before me and left for Germany about the time I arrived at Fort Hood.

I was assigned as an information specialist to an infantry division—which is not the place an information specialist would want to be for any length of time. My first sergeant was a short chubby man about fifty years old who was cunning and diabolical. He had reviewed my records before my arrival.

He informed me the battalion had a basketball team and I would be expected to participate. The battalion did not have a place for an information specialist. Consequently, I would be expected to perform other duties.

For the time being, he informed me, I could familiarize myself with the base. I really didn't mind not having anything to do for the first few months. It gave me an opportunity to spend a lot of time at the post's gym and make some new friends.

At the gym, I met a local businessman named Earl. He was friends with the base commander and had a free pass to use the facilities whenever he pleased. Earl and I became good friends.

He convinced me to coach a basketball team comprised of teenage boys who were children of military personnel stationed at Fort Hood. Earl had been coaching a basketball team in the base teen league for years. His teams always won the league and the state tournament. I agreed to coach providing he would assist me in selecting a group of players that might pose a challenge to his team. When it came time for the lottery picks, he told me which players to select.

Everything was going fine until the end of the season. We won the championship and a subsequent tournament in Waco, Texas. While in Waco, I experienced some good Texas hospitality. After completing the tournament, I took the team to a local diner. When we entered the restaurant, the man behind the counter hollered in my direction,

In 1960, the Sharks basketball team (consisting of teenage boys who were sons of military personnel stationed at Fort Hood, Texas) played in a Waco Basketball Tournament. While in Waco, we tasted true Texas hospitality. We were chased out of a restaurant by a man wielding a baseball bat because we had two black players. I was the coach and wanted our team to eat together.

"You aren't coming in here with those niggers." I was startled. I said, "We're a basketball team, and we just completed a tournament in Waco. Can't we get something to eat?"

He reached under the counter, pulled out a baseball bat, and said, "I don't give a shit what you are. You got five seconds to get those niggers out of my restaurant."

The two black players who were with us began to get scared and begged me not to start a problem. I quickly ushered the team out the door, and we gathered on the sidewalk in front of the restaurant to discuss the situation.

The boys told me it would be that way no matter which restaurant we went to in Waco. At that time, blacks were restricted to certain areas in many restaurants in Texas. I asked why no one had told me this would happen, and the boys looked at me in disbelief. One boy said, "Coach, we thought you knew. Everybody knows this is the way it is in Texas."

I suggested we all eat together in the back room reserved for blacks; the boys reminded me it would cause a disturbance. They told me that is not what the U.S. Army or their parents would want. It was the worst-tasting hamburger I ever had.

Fort Hood Newman Center

In addition to coaching the teenagers, I joined the Newman Center. Some friends of mine encouraged me to join the Catholic Center because it was the best place to meet local girls.

Many of the girls from Mary Hardin Baylor College (a woman's Baptist college) in Belton, Texas, (Belton was within a few miles of Killeen) would come every weekend to the social activities sponsored by the Newman Center. The priest who administered the Fort Hood Newman Center was very gregarious and scholarly; he helped to make the activities fun and educational.

Although Mary Hardin Baylor College was primarily a Southern Baptist college, it didn't inhibit the young ladies who attended the Newman House functions from socializing with young Catholic men. At one of the Newman functions, I met a charming young lady named Mary Lou. If I had been a Texan and a Southern Baptist, I would have easily fallen in love with her.

One Sunday afternoon, I made a date with her. I borrowed a friend's car and drove to her campus. When I entered the dormitory where she was staying, I asked the receptionist, a rather heavyset lady who was sitting behind a counter, if she would call Mary Lou and inform her I had arrived.

The woman made the call then asked me to fill out an information card. At first glance the card appeared to be asking for standard personal information until I reached the lower portion of the card. There were a number of questions about my religious beliefs and what, if any, religion did I practice. I felt violated and filled in adjacent to the question regarding my religion: agnostic.

When Mary Lou came down, I turned to the lady and handed her the card. I took Mary Lou's hand, and we proceeded walking across the lawn toward my parked car. When we were about twenty feet from the car, the corpulent watchdog came barking and running out the front door, hollering, "Mary Lou! Mary Lou, stop! You can't go out with him. He is an aggoonositic!"

Mary Lou looked at me and asked what I did. I said, "Come on, let's get out of here." We jumped in the car and pretended to ignore the massive shape moving in our direction. Without looking back, we had a wonderful day.

Senator Keating Intervenes

Shortly after my arrival at Fort Hood, I called my parents to say hello. My mother told me they had never received any money from the government. My recruiting sergeant told me I would be able to claim my parents because I helped to support them prior to enlisting. He said my parents would start receiving the checks after I finished basic training.

I told my mother to write a letter to Senator Kenneth Keating's office and explain the whole situation. At the time, Senator Keating was our elected senator in Washington DC. Once Keating's office received my parents' letter, everything began to move. An inquiry was requested by the senator's office.

Neither my battalion captain nor my first sergeant was happy they had to answer to a senator's inquiry. After consulting with the captain, the first sergeant indicated to me that things would no longer be comfortable for me at Fort Hood. He said I would learn the U.S. Army was a team and the Washington scumbags were not a part of our team.

Like Fort Dix, Fort Hood had a post basketball team. Earl encouraged me to try out for the team; he knew it would be much better for me to be assigned to the gym than the battalion. Earl knew the army officer who coached the post basketball team, and he considered it a slam dunk for me to be on the team. I attended the tryouts and thought I had done well. When the names of those selected for the team were posted, my name was not on the list.

I later learned from Earl that the coach had wanted me on the team but received word I should not be considered. Someone with a considerable amount of influence was miffed because of Senator Keating's intervention on my parents' behalf; my battalion captain decided I would play on *his* team.

A week later, I was asked to report to the first sergeant's office. He had prepared two sets of papers that had me requesting a change of my military operating status from information specialist to infantry. He told me to sign the papers. I told him I had to read them first. He slammed his fist on his desk and hollered in my face, "Sign the goddamn papers now!"

I was scared. I knew I did not want to sign those papers. I said I would not sign the papers unless I could read them first. He said, "Read them now and sign them."

After I read the papers, I realized they wanted to put me in the infantry and keep me from going to Germany. I set the papers on the first sergeant's desk and said, "I am not signing them." He jumped out of his chair and grabbed me by the shirt and said, "You are about to realize the fury of a pissed-off first sergeant. Do you want that, soldier? You are disobeying a direct order, and I will have you court-martialed." A few days later, I was demoted from private first class to private.

Shortly after my demotion, I was assigned to the finance department as a private, the lowest-ranking person in the department. While working there, the payroll folders for my battalion captain and first sergeant were placed on my desk for review. I reviewed them and then asked the soldier who was working next to me where the wooden boxes adjacent to his desk were going. The boxes contained about fifty payroll records. He responded: South Korea.

I thanked him and then took the two payroll folders for the captain and first sergeant and placed them in one of the wooden boxes. The soldier sitting next to me saw me do it and gave me a big smile. For three months the first sergeant and captain received no pay. After that, they received advances until their payroll records could be located or reconstructed.

I knew the first sergeant and the captain would not stop making life miserable for me. That evening I called my parents and asked them if they would write another letter to Senator Keating and explain what this captain and first sergeant were doing to me in retaliation for us contacting the senator's office.

I practiced basketball at the gym almost every evening except when the battalion had games scheduled. I loved the game of basketball, but I had no intention of letting our battalion captain relish any victory on my behalf or jeopardize what little chance I had of getting to Germany. In most of battalion games, I played poorly. I made a number of bad passes and shot the ball poorly. I was subsequently relegated to the bench.

Insurance for Soldiers

One evening, while walking back to my barracks from the post gym, a black Cadillac approached me very slowly. I was walking on the side of the road. The car slowed to my pace and continued moving alongside of me for about a hundred yards. I looked to my left to try to determine who was in the car. The windows were tinted. I thought it was a high-ranking officer or a VIP.

I knew it was impossible to get onto the base without permission and clearance. The person on the passenger side lowered his window. A big head emerged with black hair. He looked very Italian. He asked me if I was stationed on the base. I responded yes. He asked what I did, and I responded that I worked in the finance department updating personnel files. He asked if I ever had an opportunity to come across mailing lists.

At this point, I became cautious; I asked why he wanted to know this information. He said he owned an insurance company, and he was trying to sell insurance to the soldiers stationed at Fort Hood. The hitch—he was only allowed on the base if he had an invitation.

He was hoping to send a mass mailing for free pen and pencil sets to soldiers stationed at Fort Hood. In order for soldiers to get the pen and pencil sets, they had to meet with him to discuss their insurance needs. The man handed me a Parker pen and pencil set, at that time worth about $20. He said that this was what their free gifts looked like. He told me to keep the pen and pencil set. He placed his business card in the box and said if I decided to provide him with any names, I could give him a call, and we would make arrangements to meet.

The next morning, I asked the soldier sitting at the desk adjacent to me what the army did with the reams and reams of the used computer paper that listed the soldiers and their addresses. He told me they just throw them in the garbage. I asked if it was classified information, and he looked at me and laughed and said, "Of course not." He motioned for me to follow him. We walked outside and went to the back of the building where all the trash cans were sitting. There were about six large uncovered trash cans full of used computer paper.

"Everything goes to a big dump in Killeen," he said. All six of the cans were filled with stacks and stacks of old computer paper. It was the kind of computer paper with holes on each side so the wheels on the printer could advance the paper. Every sheet was filled with names and addresses of personnel stationed at Fort Hood.

That evening on my return from the gym, I stopped by the trash cans at the finance office. I dug through one of the cans and found two large computer lists. I placed them in my gym bag. The next morning I called the insurance salesman and offered to meet him that evening at the gym. Subsequently, I met with him about four times.

One afternoon when I stopped by the mailroom to pick up my mail, I heard the mail clerk say to one of the soldiers how his mailroom has been flooded with offers for free pens. He was going nuts trying to sort them. It appeared he had about two hundred postcards waiting to be sorted. I took my mail with a very straight face, thanked him, and left. In my heart I was giving a little payback for the shit the army subjected me to.

Just prior to my departure from Fort Hood, I hitchhiked to Houston, Texas, where I stayed for the weekend with Cliff and Helen Loisey and their cute young daughter Judy.

Cliff was my cousin via my dad's sister Marie. They were wonderful hosts.

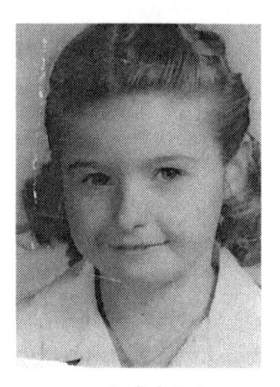

Judith Loisey   *Cliff Loisey*

After I spoke with my mother, she told me she again contacted Senator Keating's office. Within a few days of my mother's call, the senator's office made a direct call to the Fort Hood post commander. They explained the seriousness of the accusation against the captain and his first sergeant. Within two weeks of the call, new orders were issued for me to be transferred to Ludwigsburg, Germany. The captain and the first sergeant couldn't get rid of me fast enough.

When my day of departure arrived, I avoided seeing the first sergeant. All my military equipment was checked in, and I was cleared to go. I packed all my possessions into one suitcase and a duffel bag. With suitcase in hand, the duffel bag slung over my shoulder and an envelope full of addresses in my other hand, I walked to the gym.

I knew I would find Earl shooting baskets. When he saw me, he waved, tossed the ball to the side, and jogged to where I was standing. We shook hands, and I thanked him for all his help and especially his friendship.

Earl asked if I needed a ride anywhere, and I told him I had to make a stop in Killeen before getting onto I-95 and hitchhiking to Rochester, New York. He looked at me kind of strange then asked if I was serious about hitchhiking. I smiled and said, "Of course." I told him the address of the insurance agent, and he drove me there and waited while I conducted my last business.

My insurance agent's business associates were not too happy to see me. The last mailing list, unbeknown to me, was a duplicate of a previous list. They wanted their money back—and fast. There were three of them in the office, and they were big.

I explained it was a mistake, and to show my good faith, I would give them another list to replace the duplicate at no additional charge—and it had more names. They took the list and walked into the back room. They examined it for about five minutes. When they returned, everything was fine.

I told them I had another list with me if they were interested in buying it. They asked to see it. After another ten minutes of examination, they returned with a fistful of money. I stuck the money in my pocket and started for the door. As I was opening the door, one of the men asked when they could expect to see me again. I responded, "In a few weeks."

I slowly walked to Earl's Cadillac and breathed a sigh of relief as he drove me to the entrance ramp for I-95. I pulled my suitcase and duffel bag from his car, shook hands again, and said good-bye to a really good friend.

While standing at the side of the road, I pulled from my suitcase a handmade cardboard sign that read ROCHESTER, NY. When cars approached, I flashed the sign. It was fun to watch the expressions on the people when they saw my sign. A number of cars slowed, looked at the sign, and the drivers would laugh or smile at me. I got the impression I would never get to Rochester.

After about twenty minutes, a couple stopped. They drove me to an exit north of Waco. I stood there for about ten minutes when a young girl stopped and offered me a ride. She drove me almost to the Texas border. When we arrived at her exit, it was dark—almost 2:00 a.m. She offered to let me sleep in her apartment for the evening but prefaced it by saying she was a minister's daughter and I would have to find my own ride back to the interstate because she was a teacher and had to be at school early.

It was tempting, but I decided against it. I was carrying a lot of cash. The army had given me cash for my travel expenses home and to New York City to board the boat for Germany. In addition, I had my last monthly payment and the money from the insurance people. I had most of the money hidden in my duffel bag and suitcase. I only kept about $80 in my pocket.

After the teacher dropped me off, I sat on my suitcase under a traffic light and waited for about two hours. A large tractor trailer stopped. The driver rolled down the passenger's side window and said, "If you can stay awake and keep talking to me, I'll take you to the New York State Thruway exit for Rochester." I told him he had a deal—as soon as I fell asleep, he could kick me out.

Everything was fine until we got to Dayton, Ohio. The tractor trailer was filled with bags of onions, and the dock workers in Dayton had just gone on strike. When the driver backed the truck to the loading dock, there were no dock workers to assist him. A dock foreman mentioned it could be a week before the strike was settled.

Neither the driver nor I had slept in almost two days. The driver said he had to remain there until the strike was settled unless he could find someone to unload the onions. He told me he normally paid the union workers $150 to unload his truck. I asked if he would be willing to pay me if I unloaded the truck. He smiled and said sure.

The driver spoke to the dock foreman and arranged for me to use a hand truck. The foreman showed me where the wooden pallets were stacked. The dock foreman said if I loaded the bags onto the pallets, he would use his motorized lift truck to move them. After five hours, the truck was emptied, and all the onions were stacked on pallets. I was exhausted, and I stunk of onions.

The positive—I was $150 richer and assured of a ride to Rochester. I slept almost the whole way from Dayton, Ohio, to Rochester. The driver didn't mind because he slept while I was unloading the onions. After he dropped me off at the Henrietta exit of the New York State Thruway, I found a pay phone and called my father, who once again came to pick me up.

Nothing much had changed at Fifty-ninth Third Avenue. The house needed painting. There was still no shower or bathtub, and the garage continued to lean like it was drunk. The constants that I appreciated when I got home were my mother's chocolate chip cookies, juice cakes, and my parents' warm welcome.

My dad was quite proud of me. I had not only graduated from high school—which they never thought possible—but I was now also representing my country, and they were getting financial assistance.

Chapter Forty-Three

BREMERHAVEN, GERMANY

So long as blood shall warm our veins,
While for the sword one hand remains,
One arm to bear a gun—no more
Shall foot of foeman tread thy shore!
Dear Fatherland, no fear be thine,
Firm stand thy guard along the Rhine.

—Max Schneckenburger, *The Watch on the Rhine*

After an extended vacation at home, my dad drove me to the Greyhound bus station in Rochester. From there, I took the bus to New York City and then a cab to the docks in New York. There was a military ship awaiting my arrival and about eight hundred other military personnel. With my duffel bag slung on my shoulder and suitcase in hand, I walked up the plank to the ship.

As soon as my feet landed on the steel deck of the massive military ship, I was greeted by a sailor. He looked at my orders and then told me to follow the signs and go down two flights of stairs. There, he said, I would find my suite.

When I completed my descent to the second floor, I looked straight ahead and saw a large room with hundreds of hammocks hanging. I was told to find an empty spot and pretend it was home for the next five or six days. I slid my duffel bag and suitcase under the hanging piece of canvas. That constituted my storage space.

I was forewarned not to leave any valuables in my duffel bag or suitcase. The cash I brought with me, I kept on my person all the time—even while I slept.

Our only responsibility while on the ship was our personal well-being: don't fall over the side of the ship and don't get hurt when the ship encounters rough waters. During the day, I often walked through the sleeping areas trying to find a familiar face or looking in on a poker game.

On one occasion, I stopped at a poker game. There were eight players and a pot of about $1,000. I was shocked that these men were willing to gamble their pay. If they lost, they would have to wait a month before their next pay.

When the cards were shown, one of the Puerto Rican players accused a black player of cheating. The black player had won the pot. The Puerto Rican pulled a knife and said he wanted his money back. He said he was cheated.

The Puerto Rican had two of his friends sitting beside him who were also playing in the game. The black player also had a few of his friends in the game. I could see nothing but big problems about to happen. I quickly made my exit and never learned the result of the game. On future walks, I avoided that section of the ship.

Our destination was Bremerhaven, Germany. Bremerhaven is large port city almost directly west of Hamburg. When we arrived in Bremerhaven, an American band was playing, and a large group of people had gathered to watch the ship dock.

There were about forty military trucks and cars waiting to take the military passengers to their final destination. Prior to leaving the ship, we were given the number of our transportation vehicle.

Once off the ship, it was a matter of finding the truck with the right number. The cars were reserved for the officers. When I located the truck, I asked the driver if he was going to Ludwigsburg, and he confirmed he would be stopping only at Seventh Army installations, and the Second Quartermaster Division was in the Seventh Army.

I threw my duffel bag and suitcase into the back of the truck then, with the help of an outstretched arm from one of the soldiers who was already in the truck, climbed on. It was a long ride from Bremerhaven to Ludwigsburg in the vintage World War II troop carrier. The seats consisted of long pieces of wood on each side of the truck. I sat directly across from another soldier the whole trip. It was difficult to exchange pleasantries with someone chewing gum and staring you in the eyeballs.

It was an ominous beginning to what I hoped would be a happy ending to my military enlistment.

Chapter Forty-four

Coffey Barracks

*The most important single influence in the life of
a person is another person who is worthy of emulation.*

—Paul D. Shaffer

It was early afternoon when we arrived at Coffey Barracks. The truck stopped at the main entrance. The driver hollered, "Whoever is going to the Second Quartermaster Group, unload your things now!" I tossed my duffel bag onto the roadway in front of the guardhouse, jumped down, and then lifted my suitcase off of the truck. The truck immediately roared off, leaving me standing in the middle of the road facing the entrance to Coffey Barracks.

I walked to the guardhouse and showed the MP my orders. He gave me directions to the building where I would be housed. He suggested it would be a good idea to check in, clean up, put my personal items away, and then walk to the administrative building to meet my superior officers.

I did as he suggested. Like Fort Slocum, I had one roommate. His name was Palka. He was a couple of years younger than me and assigned to the quartermaster field operation. During my stay at Coffey Barracks, I never really became friends with Palka.

After unloading my personal items, I walked in military dress to the administrative building to meet my superior officer, Captain Robert V. Reynolds. The captain was waiting for retirement and placed himself in a comfortable position as the public relations voice for Coffey Barracks. He stood about six feet and was very lean.

The captain showed me my office, which was adjacent to his. He informed me I was there to generate goodwill between the German community and the American soldiers stationed at Coffey Barracks, and as an information conduit for the American service personnel.

Captain Reynolds was responsible for the dissemination of all information to the U.S. and German media. In addition, he was responsible for helping to foster goodwill between the German residents of Ludwigsburg and the military personnel stationed at Coffey Barracks.

Captain Robert V. Reynolds.

Captain Reynolds was a survivor of the Bataan Death March. Of the thirty-eight thousand soldiers taken prisoner by the Japanese, only one out of every ten survived. He survived the infamous death march and three and a half years of captivity in a POW camp. He tells his story in a book entitled *Of Rice and Men*.

Captain Reynolds was an easygoing officer who had suffered much. He appreciated and enjoyed life. He was my immediate supervisor at Ludwigsburg, Germany.

The commanding officer for the Second Quartermaster Group at Coffey Barracks was Colonel Robert Stegmaier. Colonel Stegmaier was a graduate of the class of 1937 at West Point Military Academy. He died at the age of ninety-two. He was a true soldier and a gentleman. I am proud to have served under him. I was very fortunate to have served under two officers who cared about their men and their country with a passion.

The morning after my arrival at Coffey Barracks, I was standing at attention in formation in front of the barracks I was assigned. There were about fifty men in our barracks and an additional two hundred quartered in other buildings on post or living off post with their wives. For most of the soldiers stationed at Coffey Barracks, this was a job—8:00 a.m. to 5:00 p.m. During military exercises, unfortunately, there was no clock.

U.S. Army information specialist Harold Barend at Coffey Barracks, Ludwigsburg, Germany.

On the first day, within an hour of my arrival, the captain walked into my office with Colonel Stegmaier. I jumped up to salute the colonel. He smiled and told me to refrain from the normal military protocol while working in the office. We would be seeing each other on a regular basis, and he wanted to make it a workable situation.

The colonel almost immediately indicated Coffey Barracks had a basketball and a football team, and he would appreciate me trying out for the teams if I felt I could play at that level of competition. I later learned the colonel had a connection state side who directed athletes to his unit. He knew my background before I even arrived.

The days at Coffey Barracks were anything but routine. Shortly after arriving, I found my way to the post gym where I soon learned the colonel had high expectations for a very successful basketball season. During my normal working hours, I coordinated news media events, made dispatches to the *Stars and Stripes*, and assisted in German—American social events.

Captain Reynolds and Colonel Stegmaier both took an interest in my education. After a considerable amount of fishing on their parts to determine the depth of my academia, I admitted having had little use for books. They were both shocked.

Within a month of my arrival at Coffey Barracks, I received a list of books they both thought I should begin reading: *Crime and Punishment*, *Huck Finn*, *The Fountainhead*, *All the King's Men*, *Tale of Two Cities*, and *Don Quixote*. When I finally finished the first six books, they asked me to read *War and Peace*.

It was a struggle reading the first couple of books. My head just wasn't into reading, and my concentration was nil. Once I finished *Crime and Punishment* and *Huck Finn*, it became easy and enjoyable. They had encouraged me to reach out and see the world.

Christmas in Germany

One of the most rewarding events I formulated was a Christmas party for handicapped children. The German children were living at an orphanage in Ludwigsburg. I used some of the petty cash money to purchase gifts for the children. I arranged for each child to be escorted throughout the party by an American soldier. Each child received a Christmas present from his/her escort.

The event generated a considerable amount of goodwill between the local community and the U.S. military. The military newspapers and the local German news media reported about the event. The colonel received a letter of thanks from the Oberbürgermeister (lord mayor) of Ludwigsburg.

German Families Invite Americans Soldiers for Christmas Dinner

Every year, German residents from Ludwigsburg and the surrounding areas extended invitations to American soldiers to share Christmas dinner with them. It was my responsibility to sort through the invitations and select U.S. Army personnel to be guests at German families.

I reserved for myself the invitation, which read, "Our family would like to extend an invitation to an American soldier for Christmas dinner. We have a daughter, eighteen years old, and a son, twelve years old. My son and daughter both speak English."

After a wonderful Christmas dinner, I joined the family for a walk. The father and son walked in front of Heidi, her mother, and me. After about five minutes, the father said to me, "Walk with us in the front. The women walk behind." Not wanting to disrupt custom, I immediately bid farewell to the ladies and joined the men. I made a number of return visits to Heidi and her family. She and I both enjoyed a love of life and many wonderful moments together.

No Dogs or American GIs

"Goodwill be dammed!" This seemed to be the attitude of many American soldiers upon their return to their army posts after participating in a two-week military exercise in subzero temperatures. The weekends after their return from the field, all hell would break loose.

American soldiers would flock into beer taverns and attempt to eject any and all German army soldiers who might be there. Brawls would erupt, and some bodies would go through the doors while others left via the windows. Eventually, the tavern owners would learn in advance of an arriving group of U.S. soldiers and place signs in big black letters on the plywood, which replaced the broken windows: No Dogs or American GIs.

Within days after these incidents, I would be asked by the colonel to meet with the local business owners and attempt to resolve the damage caused by our army personnel. I soon realized this was a recurring problem and not isolated to a few individuals. I arranged a meeting with the German army officers in charge of the soldiers stationed in the Ludwigsburg area and Colonel Stegmaier.

The outgrowth of these meetings was the creation of a Soldier-to-Soldier Exchange Program. Personnel from the German army would live with the U.S. soldiers and U.S. Army personnel would stay a week or two with soldiers from the German army. Initially it was tenuous at best.

The first German and American soldiers who were asked to participate in the exchange feared retaliation for the many brawls. Eventually, the program was a huge success. It helped to create a better relationship between both armies. Everyone benefited, especially the tavern owners.

Oberammergau Passion Play

During the summer of 1960, Colonel Stegmaier and his wife obtained three tickets to the passion play at Oberammergau. They invited me to join them for the enactment of the story of Jesus of Nazareth.

The play begins with Jesus entering Jerusalem and continues until his crucifixion and resurrection. All of the cast members—approximately two thousand—are residents of Oberammergau. The play, which originated in the 1600s, is performed from May to October on the tenth year of each decade. The most recent performance was in 2010.

Stunning in its magnitude, magnificent in its beauty, and captivating in its presentation, the play is five hours long with a three-hour break. It begins about 2:30 p.m. and ends at 10:30 p.m. There is a two—or three-hour dinner break.

When I attended, the seats were cement. After the first hour, vendors would begin selling cushions to the audience. As the play progressed, the cushion sales increased. It was a very clever way to capitalize on a hard surface. After the play, most people left their cushions, and the vendors would reclaim them for another performance. Today, more comfortable seating has been installed.

The person playing Jesus is Anton Preisinger.
Photo copyright: "Passion Play Oberammergau, 1960."

In 1960, I attended the Oberammergau passion play as a guest of Colonel and Mrs. Stegmaier. I purchased about twenty slides from vendors at the Oberammergau passion play.

Twelve years later, Hurricane Agnes flooded the basement of my home in Vestal, New York. During the flooding, all of the passion play memorabilia, photos and slides that I saved, were destroyed. In 2011 I was replacing part of a bookshelf in my basement and found a slide tucked in the corner of the floor. It had been there for thirty-eight years; it survived the flood. A miracle? You decide.

Tuebingen University

While stationed at Coffey Barracks, my journalistic efforts included feature articles about local festivals and stories, such as a feature article comparing life at a German university to an American university. For three days, I followed two students around Tuebingen University, eating and drinking with them.

Harold Barend joins Elizabeth Hartmann, then a twenty-three-year-old law student at Tuebingen University, and two of her classmates for a learning experience, coupled with a few beers.

A Masterpiece for 1,200 Marks

One afternoon while in Tuebingen, I saw a young man standing on the street attempting to sell five oil paintings. I walked to the man and looked at what I thought were his paintings. He informed me he was a student at the university and he was attempting to sell the paintings to get money for his tuition. I asked if he painted them, and he said no; they were painted by his uncle.

All but one of the paintings were impressionist. The painting that attracted me had three old sailing vessels engulfed with vibrant colors.

I inquired as to the cost of the painting, and the student said the one I was looking at was 1,200 marks or about $300 American money (at the time a German mark was worth about 25¢).

I had never bought a painting before. I had just gotten paid, and I still had money with me from an aborted leave—about $350 in cash.

The man proceeded to tell me the painting I liked was not worth as much as the other paintings. It was created by his uncle when he was a student living in Chicago and attending the Art Institute of Chicago. The other paintings were priced much higher. I wasn't influenced by the value. I told him that didn't matter; I liked the painting with the three ships.

Having no education in art, I could not relate to the other paintings. The paintings I did not like were considerably more expensive and, as history has proven, much more valuable.

After I bought the painting, the young man said, "You are an American; you must know my uncle. He painted these." I asked who his uncle was, and he answered, "William Wendt." After I told him I had never heard of his uncle, he looked at me with a strange look as if I was the dumbest guy on the block.

He went on to explain how his uncle, who died in 1946, was a famous American artist who lived in California. He said he left Germany when he was a young boy. Before he died, he returned to Germany a number of times to visit his sister who was this young man's grandmother. He left her about thirty paintings. They were to be used to help her family. This young man was given five of the paintings to help pay for his education.

When I returned to my office at Coffey Barracks, I showed the painting I had purchased to Captain Reynolds. He examined it closely for about ten minutes then said, "Take me to where you bought the painting."

Within twenty minutes, we were at the site where the man had set up shop, but no one was there. I walked over to a lady who was standing at a nearby corner and asked if she might know where the young man went who was selling the paintings. She replied, "An American dressed in a suit and carrying a small briefcase came by and bought all of the paintings." She continued, "He asked the student who was selling the paintings to help him carry the paintings to his car."

I returned to the captain's car and told him what I had learned. He responded by saying, "I will give you twice what you paid for that painting right now if you would like to sell it." I did not say anything for about thirty seconds. I thought, if he wants to pay me $600, it had to be worth more than that. I told him no. I explained it was the first painting I had ever bought, and I really liked it.

Just before I left for another assignment, Captain Reynolds told me to take good care of the painting and not to sell it until I find out how much it is really worth. Prior to my discharge, I shipped the painting home from Germany and insured it for $1,000. I figured it had to be worth about $1,000 if the captain offered $600.

Twenty-five years ago, I hosted a party at my home. One of my guests was a doctor who collects art. He advised me to get the Wendt appraised ASAP. The appraisal was between $30,000 and $40,000.

William Wendt—a student's work.

I purchased this painting in Germany more than fifty years ago. It was done by William Wendt when he was a student at the Art Institute of Chicago. Wendt was born in Bentzen, Germany, in 1865 and immigrated to the United States when he was fifteen years old. He is known for his vibrant, colorful impressionist landscapes. In 1911 Wendt founded the California Art Club. He became known as the dean of California artists. He died in 1946.

Chapter Forty-Five

BASKETBALL AND TRACK AT COFFEY

To win without risk is to triumph without glory.

—Corneille, *Le Cid*

The colonel was delighted when our basketball team won the championship. The basketball games played at Coffey Barracks were to standing-room-only crowds. There was no charge for American military personnel or German citizens. Many of the spectators were local residents and German VIPs who had been invited by the colonel and Mrs. Stegmaier to watch the American game of basketball.

Upon completion of our undefeated season, I was asked by members of the team to try to extend our season by arranging some exhibition games. I made up a list of potential games and then asked the colonel if we could have two weeks of temporary duty (TDY) to play the games.

The game locations were from Stuttgart to Munich, to Berchtesgaden to Nuremberg and Wiesbaden. After getting the colonel's blessing, I began calling the teams I had listed, but only one agreed to play: a U.S. Air Force base in Wiesbaden, Germany. I never brought this fact to the attention of the colonel.

Prior to our leaving, I had informed Lieutenant Wilcox, who played on our team, of the game schedule and asked what he wanted to do. He threw the question back to me and said, "What do you want to do?"

I replied, "Let's go. It will be a great opportunity for the guys to see Germany, and maybe we can pick up a game or two on the road."

Lieutenant Wilcox was in charge of the motor pool; he arranged for us to have a pea green military bus and petrol coupons. Ten of us were given two weeks TDY to play basketball and a bus to take us.

Just prior to our departure, the colonel asked me to call in periodically to let him know how we were doing. He said he and his wife might like to attend one or two of the games. I almost shit.

As the bus was exiting Coffey Barracks, the lieutenant, who I originally briefed regarding our shortened schedule, said to me, "Don't worry, they can't do any more than court-martial us and throw us in the brig." He then paused and continued, "Fortunately for us, the colonel likes to win, and I don't think he will upset his team's chemistry."

We traveled from Ludwigsburg to Stuttgart to Munich. In Munich, after touring the city, we decided to visit the University of Munich. In groups of four, we walked through the university buildings.

As we approached one classroom door, there was a black drape over the door window. Someone in our group decided to open the door. At that moment we saw a nude model posing in front of an art class. The students in the class started screaming at us, and the model immediately covered herself. As we hurried to exit the building, about ten students were in hot pursuit.

From Munich, we went to Berchtesgaden—where Adolf Hitler had his hideaway. After traveling to the Austrian border, we turned north toward Wiesbaden.

We won it all. The Second QM Group Basketball team poses with their trophies after winning the championship. Colonel Robert Stegmaier is on the far right. To his right is Lieutenant Wilcox. Harold is in the front row kneeling, second from the left.

The Wiesbaden Air Force base had an excellent undefeated basketball team; they were looking forward to playing us. The evening we played, the gymnasium was filled to capacity with air force personnel. It was loud, and the fans were not cheering for us. They were stunned when we beat their team; it was a close game. Fortunately for us, the commanding officer at the Wiesbaden Air Force base sent Colonel Stegmaier a letter telling him we were a fine group of soldiers who represented his unit well.

The Second Quartermaster Group Track Team.

After basketball season, I ran track. The major event for the season was a meet against the German Army at Soldier's Field in Nuremberg. I had originally planned to attend the meet, take a few photographs, and then write a story about the track meet.

When I arrived at Soldier's Field, I was told to find a pair of track shoes that fit me and get some shorts and a top from one of the assistants. I ran the 440 only because I was forced into it. I was not in shape to run. My time was fifty-five seconds while the winning German time was fifty-three seconds. It wasn't even close.

We competed at Nurnberg's Soldiers Field in a track meet against the Germany Army. Soldier's Field had been a favorite place for Nazi party rallies. This drawing was made from a 1937 rally. The swastika was the prehistoric sign that Hitler made his emblem. The Nurnberg arena was built to Hitler's specifications for mass rallies. After the war, the arena was converted into a sports facility.

The German community hosted the American track team for the meet at Soldier's Field. Families from the Nuremberg area provided room and board for the weekend. During my stay with a host family, I heard a strange noise each time I used the toilet, like something was dropping and going *plunk, plunk*. When I asked the husband what made the sound, he began laughing. He then took me outside and showed me a wheel barrel sitting under what appeared to be a downspout—except the downspout was attached to the toilet.

It was a common practice in the sixties in Germany to recycle human fecal matter for fertilizer. Because of this, the U.S. government would not permit the purchase of crops grown in Germany for U.S. military consumption.

Chapter Forty-six

SEVENTH ARMY HEADQUARTERS

*It is only when I am doing my work that I feel truly alive.
It is like having sex.*

—Federico Fellini

Shortly after our bus trip, Seventh Army headquarters requested that I be transferred to Stuttgart, Germany, to coordinate news dissemination and assist in public relations. I served one year, eight months, and fifteen days in Germany. My last eight months and fifteen days in the army were at Seventh Army headquarters.

I reported directly to a warrant officer whose name I cannot remember. Perhaps it is a Freudian response to the man's moral character. He was married and had three children. His mistress was a very attractive forty-year-old German secretary who needed job security. At work, she assisted the warrant officer and me. Without any sexual overtones, she and I became close friends.

After my arrival in Stuttgart, the warrant office gave her two tickets to the *West Side Story* for her and her mother. The Broadway cast was making a European tour, and the play was in English. One of their stops was Stuttgart, Germany.

She asked if I would be interested in attending the play with her because her mother did not understand English. It was my first introduction to a musical. It excited me and brought me a step closer to the good life. The secretary asked me not to mention to her boss that we attended the play. That was my first indication that all was not right in paradise.

On another occasion, she asked me if I would accompany her to the mineral baths near Stuttgart. After we changed into our bathing suits, we entered a very large pool area. Everyone was walking in a circle in a very disciplined manner. Before entering the pool, I stood on the side, watching the people methodically walk step by step. No splashes—just the movement of a mass of bodies in a circle. As my friend approached, I dove into the water.

Whistles began blowing, and the guards were shouting at me in German. I quickly took my place adjacent to my companion, who was laughing and walking in a circular motion with a throng of Germans. A good number of people gave me very strange looks. It was an opportunity for me to practice my German language skills and hide my American identity.

While working in Stuttgart, I had a considerable amount of freedom. The warrant officer, who was my immediate superior, was elated whenever I suggested time away from the office to write a feature article or attend a function. He was suspicious and did not want any interference with his mistress. Therefore, I scheduled as much time out of the office as possible.

Leica School

The Leica School offered to the general public and American military personnel a free three-day seminar in the fundamentals of photography. The course, sponsored by Leitz Corporation, was conducted in English and attracted approximately two hundred American military personnel each year.

A U.S. Army photographer and I enrolled in the course. I thought it would make a good story for our military newspapers and present our service personnel with an opportunity to learn photography from one of the best camera manufacturers in the world.

Of the eight students in the Leica three-day photography course, three were U.S. military personnel. The course instructor and Harold Barend are in the center.

My feature story entitled "Soldiers Perfect Photography Technique" was published in U.S. Army newspapers throughout Europe. Private First-class Daby accompanied me during the course, and four of his photos were used with the article. The article told about the free three-day course offered by Leitz Corporation, Wetzler, Germany.

The article explained how U.S. military personnel could enroll in the course and what they could expect to learn. Prior to the article, about two hundred U.S. military personnel attended the course each year. After the article was published, American enrollment more than doubled.

Idar-Oberstein

A few weeks after I wrote the Leica story, my supervisor's secretary informed me of a small city in Germany that was the gem-cutting center for West Germany. I thought it might make an interesting story for American military personnel who wanted to purchase diamonds or precious gems for their loved ones.

I arranged transportation, requested a photographer, packed my gear, and traveled to Idar-Oberstein. While there, I interviewed a number of gem cutters and merchants.

We took pictures of men grinding gems on large stone wheels driven by water and of other men at their desks polishing gems. After I completed the Idar-Oberstein article, I returned to Idar-Oberstein and gave the gem cutters copies of the story along with the photos we had taken of them.

One man was so thrilled that he gave me a large polished emerald. I had no idea what the emerald was worth or if it was synthetic or real. It was a wonderful gift of friendship and appreciation.

Hitchhiking Across Europe

While at Fort Hood, Texas, and Coffey Barracks in Germany, I took very little leave; I had accrued so much leave that it was going to be impossible to use it all before my discharge. Therefore, I set a plan in motion. There was a window of opportunity between June and November to see as much of Europe as possible.

Two weeks of my accrued leave in July 1961 was approved. I planned to combine the leave with an assignment: a story on how military personnel could see Europe on the cheap. My leave was quickly approved with the understanding that I carry my military leave papers and my dog tags at all times. My first two weeks would be temporary duty, and the second two weeks would be personal leave time if I needed it. I had thirty days to see as much of Europe as possible.

On July 12, 1961, I began my journey in civilian clothes with my dog tags on my neck and a suitcase in my hand and sneakers on my feet. I carried no military clothing with me. In addition to my toiletries, I packed a few polo shirts, shorts, a few pants, socks, underwear, and a windbreaker. I was traveling light. I had about $300 with me. Most of the money was hidden in my socks.

From Stuttgart, I caught a free ride with the military courier to the Rhein-Maine Air Force base just outside of Frankfurt, Germany. That afternoon, when I arrived at the entrance to the air base, I informed the military police of my intentions to take a free military air transport flight to Lyon, France. (At that time, the free flights were a courtesy provided by the U.S. Air Force to military personnel on leave. If a flight was leaving and there was room, a U.S. serviceman or woman could fly free.)

The MP directed me to a building where the courier dropped me. Within a short time, I was cleared for takeoff.

It was a bumpy ride. I had to sit in a metal seat designed for paratroopers. After we arrived at the U.S. Air Force base in Lyon, France, late that afternoon, I reported to the transit barracks and was given a free meal and bunk for the night. That evening I went into Lyon and visited the magnificent cathedral.

Prior to my flight departing for Lyon, I was told there were a number of flights every day from Lyon to Paris. The next morning, I caught a ride with a U.S. Air Force pilot who was flying a small plane into Paris. He told me about an inexpensive hotel not far from the Champs-Elysées. From the airport, I took a bus into Paris and found the hotel. I planned to spend three or four nights in Paris.

On July 13, I took the elevator to the top of the Eiffel Tower and then walked to the Arch of Triumph. The following day, July 14, was Bastille Day. I planned to see the parade on the Champs-Elysées.

The morning of the fourteenth, I walked to the Champs-Elysées and found a place in the crowd. I had checked out of my hotel and was carrying my suitcase. After the parade, I planned to visit the Cathedral of Notre Dame and then begin hitchhiking toward Lourdes.

While standing in the crowd and watching the parade, I noticed a very attractive young lady standing beside me. She kept looking down at my suitcase, which was parked on the pavement at my feet. The suitcase had a shiny brown hard shell. On both sides of the suitcase were a number of decals from places I had visited. She looked at me and then spoke to me in French. I replied, "I do not speak French; I am an American."

The nineteen-year-old French woman began speaking to me in English. We talked for more than an hour. She asked about Hollywood and the movie stars and if I knew any of them. She was fascinated with America and the American way of life.

After the parade, she asked if I would like to join her for coffee and a pastry. With my suitcase in hand, I walked with her to a small French pastry shop. We sat and talked for another hour. She was interested in learning as much as possible about the United States and how the French people were perceived in America.

She was a dancer at the world-famous Folies Bergere, which was located in the Pig Alley area of Paris. She asked if I was familiar with the Folies Bergere. I acknowledged my ignorance. I later learned the Folies Bergere featured exquisite floor shows. The dancers at the Folies were clothed in elaborate costumes, which often disappeared by the end of the show, leaving the performers naked.

After I explained my plan to hitchhike to Lourdes, she started to laugh. She said, "It will be almost impossible to hitchhike out of Paris. I will take you to a train station and put you on a train going south. Take it to the end, which will be the outskirts of Paris. From there you can get a ride to Lourdes."

When we got up to leave, I began getting dizzy, and I was feeling nauseous. I had eaten a cream-filled pastry that made me sick. She felt terrible because she had taken me to the pastry shop.

She knew I had checked out of my room and had nowhere to go. She grabbed my hand and said, "Come with me." She took me to a pharmacy where she knew the pharmacist. She explained to him what happened. He gave me an antibiotic for food poisoning.

From there we walked to her apartment. She gave me her bed and nursed me for two days. I was a mess—vomiting and diarrhea. The medication made me drowsy. I stayed in her apartment and slept while she danced. When I recovered, I was anxious to continue my journey, but she insisted I stay one more night. I will always remember the Folies Bergere and that night in Paris.

Viva la France.

Next Stop: Lourdes, France

An American soldier hitchhiking in France is not an ideal situation. Once again, I constructed a cardboard sign with my destination in large black letters. When cars approached, I would flash the sign.

After leaving Paris, a young couple gave me a ride to their castle in Bordeaux. When they invited me to join them for dinner, I graciously refused. I was hoping to arrive in Lourdes before dark. The husband then proceeded to walk to a large glass wall. He pushed a button, and the wall moved revealing about one hundred bottles of champagne and wine. After toasting with champagne to our health, to a safe journey, and to love, the couple drove me to a highway that would take me to Lourdes. As I was leaving their car, they wished me a happy journey.

While flashing another piece of cardboard that announced LOURDES, a car stopped, and the driver spoke to me in French. I replied that I did not speak French. He screamed at me, "American bastard!" He then spit in my direction and quickly drove off.

Within the hour I was able to get a ride to the outskirts of Lourdes. On my way from Paris to Lourdes, I noticed many remnants of bombed-out buildings still left from World War II. While the French real estate took a beating during World War II, the German cities and countryside were bombed and bombed and bombed. Yet all the while I was stationed in Germany, the only reminders of the devastation from World War II were those purposely left as a reminder of the war. For example, in Stuttgart, the debris from the bombing of the city was formed into a mountain, and a cross was placed at the top.

My ride left me about a half mile outside of Lourdes. With suitcase in hand, I walked into the City of Lourdes. As I approached Lourdes, there were many signs directing me to the grotto. On the way, I saw new homes and homes that had been completely refurbished. It was an indication of a much higher living standard than most other parts of France.

I walked past merchants lining both sides of the street hocking everything from Bibles to relics to holy water. The sight of them turned my stomach. It was a testament to man's ability to capitalize on the Virgin Mary. The living standard of Lourdes had certainly been helped by the visit of the Blessed Virgin.

Lourdes is famous for the grotto constructed at the site, where it is believed in 1858, the Blessed Virgin appeared to Bernadette Soubirous, a peasant girl. A large beautiful cathedral and a statue of Mary are at the site where the vision occurred. More than 2.5 million people visit the grotto annually. Catholics from throughout the world make pilgrimages to the grotto, many in hope of a miracle.

When I arrived at the cathedral, I was told a large procession was about to unfold. Everyone was welcome to participate in the procession, and merchants were there hocking their candles. I opted not to participate in the procession and instead climbed onto the upper levels of the church to watch as thousands of people walked in a candle-lit procession.

After the procession passed, I walked to the grotto and knelt at the railing to thank God for all He had given me and to ask for a safe journey.

Surrounding me were empty wheelchairs and crutches that had been left by people who came to Lourdes with the hope of a miracle and left with a new life via the waters of Lourdes.

Despite my sickness while in Paris, I was still on schedule and had spent very little of my money. Lourdes is in the southwestern part of France near the Pyrenees foothills. I hoped I could get a ride to a guesthouse or hotel in the Pyrenees Mountains where I would spend the evening before entering Spain. After walking about two miles beyond Lourdes, I took my cardboard sign that read LOURDES on one side, flipped it, and wrote with my heavy black pen: ZARAGOZA. Hopefully, I would get to Zaragoza, Spain, within a day or two. There was a large air force base at Zaragoza, and I was hoping to fly from there to Madrid on a free military air transport flight (MATS).

Chapter Forty-seven

PYRENEES

Men trip not on mountains; they stumble on stones.

—Hindustani proverb

Within an hour of leaving Lourdes, I received a ride from a man who took me to the base of the Pyrenees Mountains. He drove a very small car at a very high rate of speed. I was thankful when he stopped to let me out for fear of getting killed. Whenever he approached an intersection, he never slowed his vehicle. He just started blowing his horn about two hundred yards before the intersection and continued going about sixty miles per hour through the unmarked intersection.

While sitting on my suitcase at the base of the Pyrenees, it was starting to get dark and cold. I was concerned I might have to sleep in a field or do an all-nighter sitting on my suitcase. Although it was July, as I traveled to higher elevations, the evenings got colder. I had packed a light windbreaker but no sweater or jacket. I failed to take into consideration that winter is twelve months in the higher elevations of the Pyrenees Mountains.

Finally, an old pickup truck stopped. A man and two boys were in the front seat. It was like the *Saturday Evening Post* cover picture. Between the boys were about twenty loaves of French bread. In the back of the truck were about ten wooden cages filled with live chickens.

The ten-year-old boy on the passenger side rolled down the window and spoke to me in French. I answered in English. He then spoke in French to his younger brother and the man who was driving the truck. Following their conversation, the young boy spoke to me in broken English.

He explained that he and his brother were both taking English in school, but his English skills were not that good. If I spoke very slowly, he said he could probably understand most of what I was saying. He then said, "The messieurs would like to offer you a ride. We are going into the Pyrenees Mountains to Spain."

I tossed my suitcase in the back with the chicken cages and climbed in the front cab beside the two boys. The older boy was now holding his younger brother on his lap with the loaves of bread between us.

While we were traveling, the boys began asking me questions about my destination and why I was traveling. I told them the story of my trip thus far—omitting the colorful details of the Folies Bergere.

While I spoke, the older boy translated my words into French for the man driving. He smiled as the words were translated and told the boy he thought it was wonderful that I had cared to see so much of France. Within an hour, we arrived at the border crossing between France and Spain. There were two Spanish guards attending the crossing. They greeted the driver and the boys, who they knew on a first-name basis.

Then the guards asked me to get out of the truck. The older boy told me they wanted to see my passport. I explained I did not have a passport. I was in the U.S. Army. I showed him my leave papers. On my leave papers, I put the names of about eight countries that I might be visiting. If the name of the country was not on my leave papers, I would not be permitted to take the MATS flight to that country. Spain was on my papers.

The guards looked at the leave papers and then shook their heads no. Then one of the guards put his hand across his neck as if he was going to slice my neck. I began to get a little worried. The older boy then asked me if I had military ID that goes around my neck. I had my dog tags in my suitcase. I quickly pulled my suitcase from the back of the truck and opened it on the ground. I frantically searched through my clothes. Within a few minutes, I held up the dog tags. Both guards smiled and waved us to pass into Spain.

About twenty minutes later, I had to go to the bathroom. I asked the boys if there was anywhere I could use a toilet. I knew the word had its roots in French. He understood immediately and said something to the driver. Within ten minutes, the truck stopped in front of an old wooden building with siding that had been weathered for decades of little care. The boy motioned for me to get out of the truck. He slid across the seat and got out with me. He realized I would need someone to convey my problem.

When we entered the building, there was a long bar with a bartender and three men sitting on barstools. The boy asked the bartender if I could use the bathroom. He nodded and pointed to a door to my left. I opened the door and saw a pull chain in the center of the room with a bulb above it. I pulled the chain. When the light came on, all I saw was an empty room.

I walked out of the room and said to the boy, "There is no toilet." The boy took me into the room and pointed to two indentations in the floor. When the boy explained my concern to the bartender, everyone at the bar began to laugh.

Your feet slipped into the indentations, and you squatted over a hole in the center of a basin. That was the extent of the French toilet. It was not designed for anyone who desired a comfortable bowel movement or planned to stay and read the newspaper.

After another hour of driving through the mountains, the truck arrived at a very large building. It was beginning to get dark.

As I got out of the truck and was about to pull my suitcase from the back, the young boy said, "Sir, the messieurs would like to know if you would like to spend the night here."

I was delighted and surprised, and I immediately asked if I could pay for a room. The boy shook his head no. He then explained this was a camp for teenage girls and there were about fifty of them staying here. The messieurs felt they would enjoy my company, and they could learn about America.

Nestled in the Pyrenees Mountains is the camp pictured above. In July 1961, thanks to the generosity of a man and his two sons, I had the good fortune of spending the night with fifty teenage French girls. The girls served me dinner on a long wooden table and then encircled me as I ate. They were curious about America and asked me if I might know their friends who lived in New York City. For every one Frenchman that was insulting, there were fifty that were wonderful. As for the women—they were all beautiful.

The boys took my suitcase and carried it into a room. Unbeknownst to me, the man gave me his room, and he slept that evening in a tent with the two boys. I slept in the lodge with fifty teenage girls.

Before I went to my room, the girls served the man, the boys, and me large bowls of a delicious stew. While I was eating the stew at a large wooden table, the girls surrounded me. Some were sitting next to me, and others were sitting on the top of the table. They asked me all kinds of questions. One asked if I knew her friend who lives in New York. Another asked if American women are really as beautiful as the movie stars.

And the last question, which was asked with a smile and a twinkle after the boys and the messieurs left, did I know the messieurs gave me his room, and I would be spending the night alone with all the girls?

Early the next morning, I heard laughing voices at my door. Two of the girls entered my room and shook me awake. They were laughing and said it was time to get up. The messieurs wanted me to have breakfast before he took me to the train station. They explained it would be almost impossible to hitchhike in Spain because there weren't that many cars. Consequently, I would have to take the train to Zaragoza, and there was only one train in the morning.

After breakfast, I walked outside and saw some of the girls playing volleyball. They were hitting an old beat-up ball.

Before I left, I asked the man for the address of the camp. After I returned to Seventh Army headquarters, I immediately went to the Post Exchange and purchased a volleyball. I sent it to the camp along with a thank-you note. The messieurs sent me the picture of the camp along with a note thanking me for the volleyball.

Chapter Forty-eight

SPAIN AND ENGLAND

*How much a dunce that has been sent to roam
Excels a dunce that has been kept at home!*

—William Cowper, *The Progress of Error*

The train ride to Zaragoza, Spain, was very slow. In Spain everything shuts down in the afternoon for siesta time. When the train pulled into a station about fifty miles from Zaragoza, all the passengers slouched in their seats, put their heads down, and went to sleep. The train was motionless. I walked onto the platform in an attempt to purchase some food from a vendor, but they all had shut down. There were no renegades to break the tradition in Spain: everything stops for siesta.

When the train finally arrived in Zaragoza, I took a taxi to the U.S. Air Force base. I explained to the military police at the gate that I was interested in catching a MATS flight to Madrid. I was in luck. A flight was leaving for Madrid within the hour.

The pilots who flew the plane into Madrid gave me the names of a couple of hotels and restaurants that had special rates for U.S. military personnel. They told me not to even attempt to hitchhike in Spain. Taxis were cheap, and that was the quickest and best mode of transportation around Madrid.

They also informed me there were daily military air transportation flights from Madrid to London.

After three days in Madrid, I had seen a bull fight (which was bloody), visited a famed museum, and had dinner at a four-star restaurant that gave discounts for U.S. military personnel. I was into my second week of leave and ready to move on. Up to this point, I had spent less than $100.

The military police at the Madrid air base were a bit more disciplined. I had grown a small goatee. I was told to shave it off before boarding a plane out of the air base in Madrid. I immediately shaved and proceeded to get cleared for a flight to London, which would be my last stop before returning to Germany.

Upon arrival in London, it was raining and gloomy. I took a taxi into London and found a hotel within walking distance of Buckingham Palace and the Tower of London. I spent more money in London than all the other places combined. It was the last country on my itinerary. Consequently, I decided to treat myself before returning to military life.

I visited all the major tourist attractions in London including Westminster Abbey and Trafalgar Square. I watched in amazement as people fed hundreds of pigeons, which subsequently shit all over the square. The place was a dung hole, but tourists flocked there by the thousands.

On my second day in London, I spent about four hours in Westminster Abbey. This famous and beautiful national church is located near the House of Parliament. I learned from my tour guide that the church once served as the place of worship for an ancient monastery. It is officially known as the Collegiate Church of St. Peter. When the tour was completed, I walked along the side trying to grasp the significance of the collection of cadavers of some of history's most powerful leaders and greatest poets.

At one of the stone burial vaults, a young lady was making a rubbing of the life-size brass sculpture that adorned the top of the stone sepulcher. I asked her why she was making the rubbing. She smiled and said because someday we will no longer be able to make them.

At the time I thought it was a strange answer, but history has shown her to be correct. For the most part, the pigeons have left Trafalgar Square, and making rubbings in Westminster Abbey are no longer free to the public.

Before I left London, I rode a double-decker bus, bought a Harris Tweed sport coat, and was invited by an Englishman to join him at a pub for a yard of beer. I learned how to drink from what appeared to be a long-stemmed hourglass.

On my return flight to Frankfurt, I was accompanied by eight other passengers. We sat across from one another. Once again, this MATS plane was originally designed for paratroopers. The seats were metal, and there was one very small bathroom.

As we were flying across the English Channel, the plane began to shake and dip up and down because of the turbulence. One of the air force personnel handed each passenger a barf bag. I closed my eyes while the woman sitting across from me puked her guts out. When we finally reached the German coastline, she had a full bag. I was shaken, but my stomach was still intact.

After our plane landed at the Frankfurt Air Force base, I stayed the night at the transit barracks and then returned to Stuttgart the next morning with the military courier. In the course of two weeks, I traveled across France, visited two cities in Spain, and did some shopping in London.

I began my journey with $300 and still had $80. I accomplished what I had planned—to see as much of Europe as possible on the cheap. I knew the U.S. military personnel would enjoy reading this story.

Chapter Forty-nine

Dewayne Allen

A man must eat a peck of salt with his friend before he knows him.

—Cervantes, *Don Quixote*

Shortly after my return to Seventh Army Headquarters, while walking from my room to the dining hall for dinner, I noticed a man in his twenties dressed in civilian clothes and carrying a backpack. He seemed to be lost, and he did not have the appearance of being in the military. He slowly walked toward one of the buildings, then turned, and began walking toward another. For about five minutes, I followed him with my eyes. Finally, I realized he was unfamiliar with the base.

I approached him and asked if I could be of some assistance. He introduced himself as Dewayne Allen. He was a student from Utah who had decided to travel in Europe, as most students do—on the cheap. Unfortunately, he ran out of money. He tried contacting his parents to have them wire him money, but they were on vacation. He would be unable to reach them for two weeks.

I asked how he planned to live for two weeks. He said he could only put it in the hands of God. He said he hadn't eaten in two days and slept wherever he could find shelter. I had a feeling I would be doing God's work for two weeks.

I knew there was a barracks on the U.S. Army base for personnel who were in transit. Musicians, sports teams, USO personnel, and military personnel who were visiting for a short time stayed at the barracks. I took Dewayne to my room and gave him an opportunity to get cleaned.

After he was finished, I suggested he walk with me to the transit barracks. When we arrived, I told him to wait outside and let me review the situation. When I walked into the barracks, the place was empty. Not one person was there. A few feet into the barracks was a room with a metal cot, sheets, blanket, and pillow. The room had been prepared for the officer of the day.

I left the room and walked upstairs. When I entered the second floor, I was greeted with a large room with about ten metal beds on each side. A mattress was folded on each bed. There were no sheets, blankets, or pillows on any of the beds or in the room.

I returned to the officer of the day's room and stripped his bedding. I took the sheets, blankets, and pillow upstairs; unfolded a mattress; and laid the blankets, sheets, and pillow on top. I knew it would be much easier for the officer of the day to get blankets, a pillow, and sheets than Dewayne.

Mission accomplished, I returned to Dewayne and told him to go upstairs and make the bed. "Stay there and say nothing to anyone, and if anyone questions your being there, tell them you are in transit for a few days." I explained that the officer of the day rotates, so he probably might not encounter the same person for more than a day or two. Within a week or two, hopefully his money problems would be resolved.

Dinner was still being served for another thirty minutes. I told him if he was hungry to meet me in ten minutes in front of the dining hall. I knew most of the dining hall personnel and doubted if there would be a problem getting him something to eat. Many of the military personnel at Seventh Army Headquarters wore civilian clothing.

After dinner, I walked with him to the enlisted men's club. I bought him a couple of sodas, and we talked. He was a Mormon who lived in Salt

Lake City, Utah. He told me Utah possessed some of the most beautiful places in the world. I told him I would try someday to get there. Little did I know, forty years later, I would be competing in basketball at the Huntsman Senior Games in St. George, Utah—a trip I have enjoyed for many years since.

After five days, Dewayne was not able to contact his parents. I knew eventually someone would question his being in the barracks if he overstayed. During the first week, I let him take $50. He promised me when his parents sent him money, I would get it back. We became good friends. While he was there, I shared most evenings and weekends with him. He never tried to convert me to Mormonism.

When the second week began, some of the guys in the cafeteria began asking questions about my friend. I knew it was time for him to depart. I submitted for a five-day leave to Austria. I told Dewayne I would let him take another $75 if he wanted to accompany me to Salzburg. He readily agreed. We hitchhiked to Salzburg and stayed in a youth hostel on our way.

The youth hostel was a large building with an open room. It accommodated mostly high school and college students who were traveling on the cheap. Dewayne had some experience in staying in youth hostels and explained the best method of finding a place to put you sleeping bag down—next to a pretty girl.

We crossed the majestic Alps into Austria and were enthralled by the beautiful mountains and the meticulously cropped farmlands. Our destination was Salzburg, which is on the German/Austrian border. When we arrived, we toured Mozart's home, ate Austrian food, and were welcomed warmly by the Austrian people.

By the middle of August, Dewayne's money arrived from his parents, and he paid me every cent I lent him. Prior to his departure, he told me I should visit Berlin. He sent a letter to a Mormon family who lived in Berlin and told them about me. He asked if they would host me for a long weekend in September or October. They replied yes.

The morning Dewayne departed Stuttgart to continue his junket, I left my office and met him at the entrance to the Seventh Army Headquarters. He had his backpack strapped to his shoulders and a green hat with a feather on his head. He had purchased the hat in Austria. We both agreed it might be easier for him to get a ride wearing that hat.

After we shook hands to say good-bye, I reached into my pocket and pulled out the emerald I had been given in Idar-Oberstein. I handed it to him and told him it was a sign of our friendship. I received it from a man out of the goodness of his heart, and now I was passing it on. After my discharge, I received a letter from Dewayne telling me he was to be married, and the emerald that I gave him would go in the center of his family crest.

A Host Family in Berlin

The latter part of September, I took the train to Berlin. I stayed for three nights in Berlin with a wonderful lady and her two daughters who were eighteen and twenty years old. One daughter worked days, and the other daughter worked nights. I had a constant chaperone who spoke English. They were wonderful to me. I was almost ready to join the Church of the Latter-day Saints.

One day, I asked my companion if she would take me to the Berlin Wall. The Berlin Wall had not been removed at this time, and East German soldiers patrolled their side with machine guns and dogs. The East German soldiers walked very close to The Wall.

When my companion took me to see The Wall, I decided to walk up to The Wall and chip a piece of masonry for a souvenir. I had no idea the Wall was constructed about twenty feet into East German territory. The young lady that I was with remained about thirty feet back from The Wall.

When I began chipping at The Wall to get my souvenir, she began hollering at me to get out of there. As I was chipping at The Wall, an East German guard on the opposite side of The Wall approached. He held a German shepherd on a leash, and a gun was slung on his shoulder. I could just barely see him over The Wall. As he came closer, I raised the piece of stone souvenir I had just taken, so he could see it. Then I made a quick retreat to where my friend was standing. She proclaimed I was crazy. Nevertheless, she wanted to show my souvenir to her mother and sister.

The Saturday evening before I left Berlin, both girls took me to a Berlin nightclub. The three of us slid into a cushioned mahogany booth, which was enclosed for privacy on three sides. At the opening, there was an illuminated number. There was a dial telephone mounted on the wall inside the booth. I looked at the girls and asked, "Why is there a telephone?" They started to laugh. They told me they would not get any calls because they were with me, and I would not get any calls because I was with them.

It was the ultimate pickup place for young people in Berlin. If there was someone you wanted to make conversation with, you just dialed their booth number then described the person you wanted to speak with. It was an interesting method of allowing patrons to introduce themselves without the fear of rejection.

Chapter Fifty

German, Beer, Wine, and Women

When you stop drinking, you have to deal with this marvelous personality that started you drinking in the first place.

—Jimmy Breslin

When I returned to Stuttgart from Berlin, it was the latter part of September 1961. Basketball season would be starting in October. I was scheduled for discharge on January 15, 1962.

I immediately began preparing for my next story. I knew the warrant officer was not going to recommend me for any promotions because he believed I was involved with his mistress to the point where he read me the riot act about fraternizing with German nationals. My solution was to go into the office as little as possible.

The last week of September, I traveled to Munich for the biggest beer-drinking festival in the world. I knew this feature article would be of interest to almost all the U.S. military personnel.

One of the photographers begged to accompany me. I did not have a need for a photographer, but I arranged for him to take the trip with me. He arranged for a military vehicle for us to use and for the gasoline. I submitted for seven days of temporary duty in Munich for both of us.

The City of Munich had already agreed to provide me with plenty of photographs of the Oktoberfest. The Oktoberfest promoters knew their festival would be enthusiastically received by my readers. What could be better than a few thousand American GIs drinking to the welfare of the citizens of Munich?

Some of the figures I compiled for my story on the 1961 Oktoberfest are as follows: 6 million people attended, 2.6 million liters of a specially prepared 32 percent proof beer was consumed, and 1.4 million links of bratwurst were eaten. When I was there, the festival covered sixty-five acres and had seven huge beer tents each with a seating capacity of over ten thousand.

The festival has been held annually since 1810 with the exception of the periods covered by the two world wars.

My friend and I hoisted mugs of beer while sitting at a long wooden table with German lasses on each side. Between 1,500 and 2,000 beer mugs are stolen every year from the beer tents. There were three or four large German bands in each tent. As the music played, the people in the tents would sing, lock arms, and sway back and forth. We locked arms with some of the young German ladies and kissed after each drink.

While I was absorbed in the atmosphere, I nevertheless remained cognizant of my need to write a story. Munich's Oktoberfest: *the* place to be on assignment.

The House of Three Colors

After I returned from my trip to Munich, a German friend of mine took me to a five-story building called the House of Three Colors. When we arrived, there was a line of American servicemen waiting to walk through the five-story brothel.

My German friend insisted we take the tour of the building. He remarked, "You will never see anything like this again." There were a number of prostitutes in the Stuttgart area who peddled their wares to military personnel. I was not one of the military personnel who assisted their business.

The French soldiers stationed in Germany, according to guesthouse rumors, had the best arrangement. Women were periodically flown in from France to assist the soldiers with a high testosterone level. Providing the French soldiers had not been reprimanded, the madam's assemblage of fine body parts was available.

Following a ten-minute wait in line, we entered the first floor of the brothel. It was arranged like a hotel. When the prostitute was available for business, the door was open. The line slowly snaked through five floors of women lying on beds displaying their merchandise. The higher up you went, the more expensive the ladies were.

A Streetcar Named Desire

A month later, while riding at night on a streetcar in Stuttgart, I had an unusual experience. The car was packed with people, and I was standing and holding on to a metal bar. The standing passengers were squeezed tight.

There was a lady in front of me who kept pressing the back of her body into me. I had a twenty-minute ride before my stop. I wasn't sure what the woman's intentions were. All of a sudden without warning, the interior lights of the streetcar went out, and it was black. When it happened, the lady turned and faced me and squeezed her body into me. She never spoke.

When the lights returned, the streetcar began stopping. When it had come to a stop and the doors opened, she grabbed my hand and pulled me to get off with her. She said in perfect English, "Come with me." She took me to her apartment and led me to her bedroom.

After we made love, she got out of bed and opened the closet door. I was stunned. A first sergeant's jacket was hanging on the inside of the door. I pointed to the jacket and asked with a shaky voice, "Where is the sergeant?"

She said, "Don't worry, he is on a military exercise, and he will not be home for three more days." Within minutes I was dressed and out the door.

Chapter Fifty-One

SEVENTH ARMY BASKETBALL

Winning is not everything. It is the only thing!

—Vince Lombardi

The basketball season for the Seventh Army team began in November. I had an ideal situation from November until my scheduled discharge in January: eat breakfast, check in at the office to determine if there were any news media that needed attention, and then off to the gym for the remainder of the day. Life was good.

I practiced basketball about every day except Sunday. We played five on five, three on three; we ran wind sprints, and we performed a series of drills every other day.

Although a bit ragtag in the beginning, the team came together. We had four ROTC lieutenants: two who played college basketball and two who played college football. Most of the teams we competed against also had former college basketball players.

The draft was still in effect, and very few athletes requested Vietnam. Although I was scheduled to be discharged in January, I remained part of the starting five.

In December, I was notified that my service discharge date would be extended until March 12, 1962. The police action in Vietnam and the rattling of sabers by the Soviet Union in Berlin were responsible for the extended stay.

At the time of my notification, I was issued an M1 rifle and four grenades. I had not shot a rifle in two years or pulled a pin on a grenade since basic training. Yet the army felt it was necessary to issue me these weapons.

The plus side of my extension: it wiped out my active reserve and allowed me to finish the basketball season.

Colonel and Mrs. Stegmaier drove from Ludwigsburg to Stuttgart a number of times to watch me play. They were wonderful people.

The Stuttgart Stallions won the league championship and the subsequent tournament while compiling a 19-0 record.

WILD HORSES — The Stuttgart Post Stallions won the Stuttgart Post league and tournament while compiling a 19-0 record. The nine Horsemen are: standing, (L-R) Don Radican, Vincent Tyler, Otis King, Don Mason, Doug MacVay, kneeling (L-R) Bruce Parker, Ben Murillo, Jack Compton and Hal Barend.
US Army Photo—Tate

Chapter Fifty-two

MONROE COMMUNITY COLLEGE

Liberty without learning is always in peril, and learning without liberty is always in vain.

—John F. Kennedy

I returned to the United States via a troop carrier much like the one I came over on. On this trip, everyone's mood was positive—we were going home. About 90 percent of the military personnel on the ship were being returned to the United States for discharge. I completed my military service where I began it: Fort Dix, New Jersey.

During my departure screenings, I was asked if I had any medical problems as a result of my military service. I mentioned I had the piles. The doctor said I was welcome to complete a report, but if I did, I would have to stay another few days to get medical clearance. The thought of staying another few days in the army did not appeal to my yearning to be free. I was looking forward to returning home and told the doctor to forget I even mentioned it.

With my discharge in hand and duffel bag over my shoulder, I proceeded walking to the exit of the base. I showed the MP my discharge papers and then continued walking away from the military post. I looked back only once to see the sign that read U.S. ARMY FORT DIX. It was a pleasant sight to be leaving behind.

It was a strange feeling being thrust back into civilization after years in a military environment. Fortunately, I was stationed in Germany where the people accepted the American GI and in many cases welcomed them because of the economic benefits they brought.

For the American soldiers stationed in Vietnam and Cambodia, the problems of making the transition to civilian life were tenfold what mine were. They had a hostile environment to live in and a hostile environment to return to.

When I left Fort Dix and the U.S. Army, I knew what I had to do. My task now was to find a way to accomplish it.

Shortly after my discharge from the U.S. Army, I submitted my application for admission to Monroe Community College in Rochester, New York. Donald Smith, the director of admissions, told me it was questionable for me to be accepted at MCC because my high school grades were mostly Cs and Bs.

He asked if it was possible for me to get a letter of recommendation from one of the military officers I served under. I immediately sent Colonel Stegmaier a letter soliciting his help. The colonel sent a letter to MCC and copied me. The letter gave me a new life.

In his letter, the colonel recalled when I first came under his command. He said I was a young man who was misguided. When I left his command, he felt I had developed into a person he could be proud of.

He described my duties and some of the projects I had accomplished while serving under him. Shortly thereafter, MCC sent me a letter of acceptance to the first class at Monroe Community College.

The college began in an old three-story high school building on Alexander Street in Rochester, New York. In 1962, the entering freshman class exceeded a hundred and fifty. In 1966, the pictures in the MCC yearbook of the senior class totaled about a hundred. Today, MCC has the largest student population of any college in the Greater Rochester area.

Making the transition from the U.S. Army to civilian life was difficult, but returning to school after being away from any academic discipline for four years was even harder. I knew at the outset the next two years would challenge my resilience and my physical and mental capacities.

There was no GI Bill to help with my expenses because Congress did not pass the legislation until 1966. Unfortunately for me, Congress did not make it retroactive to cover any of my undergraduate tuition. Consequently, I had to put together a plan quickly.

I needed a car, insurance, books, and money to live on. I had some money left after my discharge from the army, but that would only buy me a few months. I needed two years minimum.

My first stop was Sage-Ruddy in Rochester. With my stock certificate in hand, I walked into the brokerage office and immediately requested a stock broker to sell my Spooner Mines and Oils. After expenses, my original investment of $1,000 netted me about $6,000. Not a bad investment for 4¢ a share.

My brother-in-law, Howard Austin, steered me in the direction of a Ford dealer in Rochester where I purchased a blue Ford Falcon. After I sold my stock and purchased the car, I drove to MCC and paid my first semester's tuition. I asked a lady in the MCC financial office if I could pay for the whole year, but she told me MCC would only take one semester's tuition at a time. I might not be asked to return the following semester. I had not given much thought to the possibility of flunking out of school. In retrospect, the first-year class had about a 40 percent dropout rate.

From the time of my discharge until I moved to Buffalo to attend the University of Buffalo in 1964, I lived with my parents at Fifty-ninth Third Avenue, Braddock Heights. Traveling from Braddock Heights to Monroe Community College was about thirty miles each way. Fortunately, the Ford Falcon was very good on gas; in 1962, a gallon of gas cost 31¢.

My only other expense during my first year: rent. My mother wanted me to pay rent for living at the house, but my dad, who felt I had helped them financially when I was in the army, put the kibosh on that. Even though I had no obligation to pay rent, I still found ways to contribute during my first year. My social life was the other expense—it involved a beer with the guys or a date that drank beer.

My dad spoke with Al Skinner, the Monroe County sheriff, about getting me a part-time job. The sheriff informed my dad that he would probably want to change his registration from Democrat to Republican. The following morning my dad made the change. I was notified a week later that a position would become available in April as a night watchman at a newly constructed sewer plant in Greece.

There had been some vandalism at the plant, and the sheriff thought it would be an opportunity for me to have a job until the plant was officially opened. With hope for the future, I had to make my money last for eight months until I could begin work for the Monroe County Sheriff's Department.

My first semester at MCC was a feeling-out period. I tried to bond with my professors. Some were likable and took time to talk; others were standoffish and felt it was beneath them to afford students more than a rationed amount of time. And there were those who prided themselves on sadistically setting the bar at an unreachable height.

Richard O'Keefe was a history and political science professor who thoroughly enjoyed teaching, and his students reflected his enthusiasm. Maynard North was a German language professor who enjoyed having the reputation for being the most difficult professor on campus. At the time of my discharge from the army, I had a German vocabulary, which afforded me the opportunity to converse with Germans who spoke no English. I was one of the lucky ones in Professor North's class—I received a C. The majority of the class got Ds and Fs. He had a profound negative impact on the lives of many students at MCC.

Having navigated my way through the first semester academically and socially, I joined the Veterans' Club and played intramural basketball with a team called the Zygotes. The intramural basketball team finished the season undefeated. I had no desire to even attempt to play on the college team because of the amount of time I needed for my classes.

At the beginning of my second semester, I decided I would add a few more semester hours to my schedule. I opted to carry about twenty-four credit hours. My goal was to graduate in three years and save the money. In retrospect, it was not a wise move. Academically, I was OK; but physically, I was not getting enough sleep.

One morning in April 1963, I drove to MCC. I walked into the building and began to climb the stairs. About six steps up, I could not lift my legs to go any farther. I sat on the steps for a few minutes and then walked back to my car and drove home. I walked into the house and told my mother I wasn't feeling good. I needed to sleep. I did not wake up for three days. I had mononucleosis.

I contracted the same disease two additional times while attending MCC. Mononucleosis took advantage of a body that had been maxed out. After being diagnosed for the third time with mononucleosis, the doctor advised me that I had better make some changes to my lifestyle. He told me there was an increase in the number of leucocytes in my blood, and there was swelling and pain around my spleen. He felt I could be on the threshold of contracting leukemia.

During my second semester at MCC, I began to retain and focus better. The dust was slowly dissipating from my brain. Life was beginning to open. My classes were enjoyable, and my social and work life was an A+.

Come to My House

I had dated a number of women while attending MCC. One memorable event took place on a Friday afternoon at the beginning of my third semester. A young lady named Sue asked if I would like to go home with her. Her parents were away at a convention, and they were not expected back until Sunday. I readily accepted the invitation.

About 7:00 a.m. Saturday, she started shaking me to get out of bed. Her parents had just come home unexpectedly, and they were knocking at the front door. Fortunately, Sue had put a chain lock on the door, and they could not get in. She hollered toward the front door, "I'll be right down. I am just getting dressed." I was totally naked.

She pointed to an old double-hung window, which was about a foot above the second-floor roof. "Climb out the window," she demanded. She wanted me to take my clothes and go out on the roof. I stood looking at her in disbelief.

"The roof," she said, "is the only way you can get out of the house without my parents seeing you." And she added, "My dad will kill you and me if he finds you here. Now hurry! Get out! I will try to keep my parents downstairs as long as I can."

I put my underwear on and then grabbed my clothes and shoes. I squeezed out the bottom of the double-hung window. With only a pair of Fruit of the Loom BVD shorts on, I exited the window. Sue immediately closed the window and pulled the drapes shut. So much for love.

It was only about fifty degrees outside. With my body shivering from the cold, I sat on the roof and quickly put on my clothes and shoes. I then slowly crawled to the edge of the roof and looked down. It was about a twenty-five-feet drop—enough to kill a person. I saw a downspout at the end of the roof and eased my legs off the roof. I tried to grasp the metal downspout.

When I finally mustered enough courage to slide my whole body off the roof, I was pulling on the gutter with both hands while my legs were squeezing the downspout. Within seconds of hanging on to the gutter, the end of the gutter began to bend down. I quickly moved one hand to the downspout while holding on to the gutter with the other hand. My feet were still about twenty feet above the ground. Fortunately, there was grass below.

As I released my hand on the gutter and grabbed the downspout with both hands, the downspout broke from the gutter. There were three metal straps holding the downspout against the house. When the downspout broke from the gutter, the first metal strap came loose with a pop, and the downspout bent downward. Because of my body weight, within seconds the second metal strap snapped and made a noise. The downspout bent down farther with me still hanging on. About six feet from the ground, I let go and dropped to the ground. There was a considerable amount of noise when I hit the ground, and the downspout shook.

I picked myself off of the ground and ran toward my car, which was parked on a street behind Sue's house. She asked me to park there because she did not want her neighbors to know she had an overnight guest.

The next day at MCC, Sue complained I made too much noise and broke the downspout. We mutually respected a termination of any further relationship.

All-college Beer Blast

During December 1962, I was eating lunch with Don Schneider in the MCC cafeteria. Don and I were both students and members of the Veterans' Club. We had become good friends.

He told me he was running out of money, and I explained that my money was on the short. We brainstormed about possible ways of making money. Finally, we decided to be adventurous and throw a beer party. We reasoned college kids love beer, and they love to party. Together, we had about $300 to fund our venture.

We discussed our plan with members of the MCC Veterans' Club, and they agreed we could use the Veterans' Club name as the sponsor of our party. In turn, we agreed to hire veterans to tend bar and pay them $25 each. We also agreed to donate some money to the Veterans' Club if the venture was really profitable.

We rented the Polish Falcon Hall (which accommodated about five hundred people) and hired a band. Within a week, we had the beer arranged—ten full kegs (Genesee Brewery's city sales manager was a great guy). He gave us the beer on credit.

The night of our party, there was a bad snowstorm. While we were expecting close to five hundred people, only about two-hundred and fifty showed. After paying all our expenses, we each made about $200. We were disappointed, but it was a beginning.

Undaunted by our meager profit, Don and I regrouped and planned for another beer party. We decided this time we would eliminate the weather problems and have the party in September. In addition, we would cut the admission price from $3.00 to $1.50, hire a band, provide all the beer for free, and rent a hall that would accommodate four thousand to five thousand people. This party was going to be the biggest beer blast ever held in Rochester, New York.

To launch a successful beer blast the magnitude of what we planned required a lot of planning, luck, and hard work. Don and I once again offered jobs to the veterans and offered the same proposition to the club that they previously accepted. One of the largest halls at that time in the Rochester area was the Ukrainian American Club. It had a large hall on the first floor and an equally large room below it with a long bar. We estimated the hall could accommodate five thousand people.

Don and I met with the manager and explained we were having a beer party, which would be sponsored by a Veterans' Club from a local college. The manager had a Saturday evening open in September, and we agreed to take it—we paid him the rental fee of $50 in advance.

At Genesee Brewery we again met with the city sales manager. We knew our credit was good because we paid him the day after our first party. This time, we explained, the party would be considerably larger. He asked how many barrels of beer would be needed—we agreed on thirty-seven full kegs. The manager gasped and said, "That is going to be one hell of a party. You don't expect to finish all thirty-seven barrels?" I replied that it is always good to have a little more than you need.

The advertising was our next challenge. While Don was getting one of the girls in the art department to design a flyer, I was trying to convince the girls working in the business office to provide us with free copies if we provided the paper. Emblazoned across the top of the flier were the words "ALL-COLLEGE BEER BLAST—$1.50 / MUSIC & ALL THE BEER YOU CAN DRINK."

Within days, thousands of flyers appeared on every college campus in the greater Rochester area: MCC, St. John Fisher, Nazareth College, University of Rochester, RIT, and State College at Brockport. Don and I visited each campus and posted the flyers on bulletin boards, in the women's and men's restrooms, in college cafeterias, and lounges. I agreed to go into the women's restrooms while Don stood at each door to ensure no women entered while I was taping the flyers on the interior of the toilet doors. Our rationale: it made good reading for a captive audience.

The evening of our party, we arrived about six. The manager of the Ukrainian-American Club was so nervous he was stuttering. He just kept asking, "What are you going to do with all that beer?" We arrived at the club after the Genesee Brewery truck had unloaded all thirty-seven kegs. I tried to explain that it was just to make sure we did not run out of beer. He did not buy it.

I then focused my attention on the side doors of the Ukrainian-American Club. I asked if there was some way we could lock them, and the manager said no. They had to be left unlocked because of fire emergency.

We had a problem. I could see hundreds of kids sneaking in every side door. I asked Don to get some cardboard. We quickly made four signs with arrows pointing to the main entrance and the words Beer Blast Entrance. We took duct tape and put the signs on every side door.

By the time 8:00 p.m. arrived, about four hundred college students were lined up waiting to get into the hall. The band was raring to go—it was their first gig. By 9:00 p.m. there were about two thousand young men and women in the hall—dancing, drinking, and having a ball. An hour later, we doubled the number, and the manager refused to allow any more in until some left. With music and free beer, no one was leaving. We had a line of kids waiting outside to get in until midnight.

Because it was a very high-crime neighborhood, Don would leave periodically for his home with boxes full of money. The money came in like water.

Love Pays

At the time, I was dating three different college students. They all came to the party expecting to get in for free—I charged them each $1.50. My conquest. One of the three girls was Sally Manfer, my former wife.

Sally's mother gave her a blank check that she had signed. It was for Sally to purchase books at Brockport State College where she was a student. Sally's wallet got lost at the party. After she called her mother to inform her that the check was lost or stolen, about 1:00 a.m., Sally's mother came stomping into the club to rescue her daughter.

The place was a mess. Beer cups were all over the floor, and beer had spilled in numerous places on the floor, making it somewhat slippery. Some of the kids were sliding in the beer and pulling each other down on the floor. It looked like a picture from *Mad Magazine*. That was the scene she walked into. She immediately began asking questions to determine who was responsible for the party.

When I saw her, I asked Don to speak with her, and I quickly went downstairs. Don told Mrs. Manfer the sponsor was a Veterans' Club from the University of Rochester. She then searched for her daughter through the kids hugging, kissing, and slopping beer. After she finally found Sally and they left the hall, I was alerted that the coast was clear.

When I was downstairs, one of the bartenders informed me they were running out of beer. I watched as a young man lay on the floor with his head lying on the brass rail and his mouth open. Another student had lifted a keg of beer onto the edge of the bar. He was tipping the keg to allow for the beer to run into the prone man's open mouth. They were going to squeeze every drop they could out of the kegs. I felt a sense of relief. The manager would not allow us to let any more into the hall and the beer had been exhausted—now we could close.

Mobilee Pizza

During the sixties, students had difficulty getting student loans before their second year. Don and I both qualified for student loans, and we planned to use some of our college loan money to finance a pizza business.

Many of the students at our first beer party asked for food. Unfortunately, there was nothing available. After much consideration, we decided to go into the pizza business—a mobile pizza business. The name of our new business was Mobilee Pizza. (We wanted to Italianize the word "mobile").

Don and I scoured junkyards until we found an old Cadillac morgue vehicle. It had been used for transporting cadavers. We bought the Cadillac, licensed it, and gutted the back portion where the caskets rolled into the back. We installed a stepped plywood floor and a counter by one of the side windows. In the counter, we made cutouts for stainless steel containers for the sauce, cheese, and pepperoni.

The plan was to hire someone to make the pizzas. The person we hired would sit on a swivel chair at the counter. To the person's right would be a propane pizza oven and a large cooler containing the mozzarella and premade pizza shells.

We constructed a very large sign, which read Mobilee Pizza, and mounted it on top of the Cadillac. We introduced the idea of mobile pizza to America before Domino's or any of the other pizza companies.

Within a month, we had the pizza business fully operational. We had established suppliers for the premade crusts and mozzarella. Our only problem was the sauce. We kept changing the recipe until finally we had an acceptable sweet sauce. When our sauce samplers stopped cringing, we stopped trying.

The day before our All-college Beer Blast, we hired an MCC student to man the pizza business. We rehearsed our pizza business debut. It was our plan to pull the Cadillac hearse onto the sidewalk in front of the Ukrainian-American Club about two hours after the party started.

A few hours before the party was to begin, the student we hired was having a problem with the sauce; he had put too much oregano in the sauce. I told him not to worry. "The kids will be so drunk they will eat the pizzas." I was very confident the pizzas would sell.

Financially, the evening was a huge success. Even while we were preparing to close the beer hall, the fellow we hired to make pizzas sold out his entire inventory of pizza.

The following morning, I drove to Don's home to split the money. Our only outstanding expenses were Genesee Brewery and the pizza equipment. After we allocated the money for our expenses, we took the balance and split it fifty-fifty.

I stood up from the kitchen table where we had been counting the money, gathered all my cash in my hands, threw it up in the air, and stood under it. Don's mother looked at me in amazement. She thought I was totally crazy.

The following Monday, Mrs. Manfer called the NY State Liquor Authority and wanted to know who was responsible for the drunken party. When Don and I met with the city sales manager for Genesee Brewery that Monday afternoon, the NYSLA had already been to his office. He told them nothing about us. After we paid him for the thirty-seven barrels, he suggested we lay low for a while. That was out last beer party.

About a year later, I was at Lake Ontario with Sally and her family for a picnic. The family had forgotten to bring paper cups. I had about five hundred paper beer cups left over from the party in the trunk of my car. I offered to get some. When Mrs. Manfer saw the cups, her face turned about four colors—she realized I was responsible for the beer party.

Don and I both worked to keep the pizza business going after our last beer blast. We met with a number of student deans in an attempt to get permission to bring our pizza wagon onto their campuses. While we were meeting with the dean at the University of Rochester, he pulled from his desk one of our College Beer Blast flyers and asked if we were familiar with it. We both looked at it somewhat stunned and shook our heads no. None of the colleges granted us permission to sell our pizzas on campus.

Subsequently, I purchased Don's share of the pizza business and continued to run it until I started school at the University of Buffalo the following fall. I delivered pizzas to the nurses' dorms and set up shop at the Rochester ice-skating rinks. One snowy evening, I even delivered a free pizza to Don Mill, the local weatherman for one of the Rochester TV stations. He was broadcasting the weather in the middle of a Rochester street, and I pulled up with my Mobilee Pizza hearse. I stopped the wagon next to him and handed him a pizza I had just made. I knew I would not have much time before the police made me move, but the gamble and free pizza brought me free TV coverage.

At one of the Rochester ice-skating rinks, I parked the pizza wagon on the road adjacent to the rink. An elderly man walked to the pizza wagon with his two grandchildren. He asked me for three pizzas. After I served them the pizzas, the man handed me $50 and said, "Keep the change. I hope you make a million."

When I left for the University of Buffalo, I couldn't find anyone who wanted the business, so I took the hearse back to the junkyard where we originally purchased it—they paid me $75.

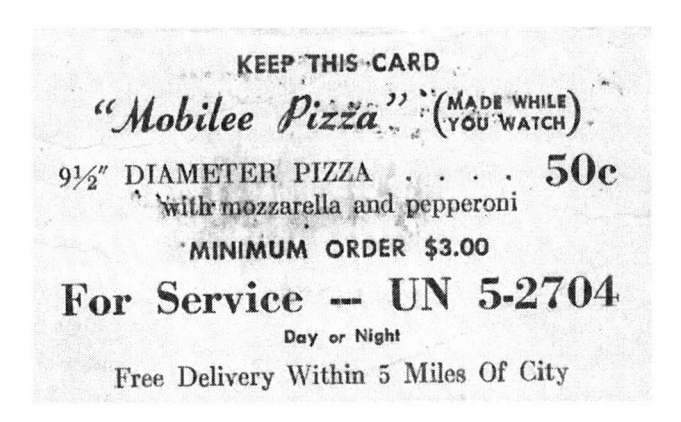

```
           KEEP THIS CARD
    "Mobilee Pizza" (MADE WHILE
                     YOU WATCH)
  9½" DIAMETER PIZZA . . . . 50c
       with mozzarella and pepperoni
          MINIMUM ORDER $3.00
  For Service -- UN 5-2704
              Day or Night
     Free Delivery Within 5 Miles Of City
```

The Zygote intramural basketball team was about to complete a second year of undefeated competition when the MCC physical education director asked if I would consider helping the Monroe Community College basketball team. Three of the team's starting players had just been declared academically ineligible. They were in need of help. I agreed, but I knew it would be difficult to be accepted by a group of guys that had played most of the season without me.

In retrospect, it worked out fine. We won the majority of the final games, and I got to be friends with a fellow player: Douglas Taylor.

The University of Buffalo

Doug Taylor and Rich Meter shared an apartment with me in Buffalo while we were attending UB. Both were former MCC students who transferred to the University of Buffalo.

In Buffalo, getting to the UB campus from our apartment was always an adventure. There were many cold Buffalo mornings when my Ford Falcon refused to start. Together, we would jump start the car and be on our way to class. At the University of Buffalo, I continued to take a heavy academic load with the hope of completing my undergraduate work in three years.

I contemplated playing for the UB men's basketball team. I spoke with the coach and worked out a number of times with the team. Just before it became time for me to make a decision, I broke my ankle playing basketball in a pickup game.

That winter, with winds blowing and snow flying, I walked the UB campus on crutches. Occasionally, I would enlist the support of a friendly face who would help me carry my books.

I had been dating Sally Manfer while attending UB. She would drive to Buffalo on weekends to see me. I planned to finish my undergraduate work and then apply for an MBA program. Sally's mother saw it differently. She wanted our relationship to end if I did not agree to marry her daughter during the summer or fall of 1965. We married on September 4, 1965.

I graduated from the University of Buffalo in February 1966. It took me three and a half years to finish my four-year degree.

Thus ends the first twenty-seven years of my life. These twenty-seven years have set the foundation for my life. Not unlike the first twenty-seven years, the subsequent years have been filled with happiness, sorrow, excitement, love, gratification, success, and failures.

I never played life by the rules, but like a jagged rock in a turbulent sea, I came out polished. I credit having learned things the hard way for growing me into the person I am today.

Although poor, my parents taught me to respect the rights of others and to find a place in my heart for God.

My friends, teachers, and coaches taught me an appreciation for education, hard work, and achievement. My children taught me to love.

Epilogue

Alberta Barend Austin (sister) was born on April 3, 1931. She currently lives in Greece, New York. She graduated from St. Joseph's Vocational School, Rochester, New York. She married Howard Austin, who joined the Greece Police Department and eventually became a detective. Howard died in January 2000. Alberta and Howard have two children: Michael and Patty of Rochester. Alberta went to work for General Motors in Rochester and remained there until she retired.

Raymond Barend (brother) was born on December 25, 1935. After high school, he was employed by E. I. du Pont before joining the Rochester Fire Department. Prior to retirement, Ray was communications training coordinator for the Office of Emergency and EMS Communications for thirty-nine fire districts in Monroe County. After moving to Bristol, New York, he was elected councilman, and then supervisor for the Town of Bristol. He was subsequently elected Chairman of the Board of Supervisors for Ontario County. Ray married Elane Steidle. They had four children: Ray, Linda, Penny, and Heidi. In addition to caring for their children, over the course of three decades, Ray and Elane made a home for seventy-three foster children. His wife, Elane, and son Raymond have since died. His three daughters live in the Greater Rochester area.

David Barend (son of Harold Barend) graduated with honors from St. Bonaventure University and received a law degree from Boston College. While at St. Bonaventure, David honed his skills as a stand-up comic and had his own radio show. Despite the fierce rivalry between BC and Notre Dame, he married Sara Brann, a Notre Dame alumnus.

They have two daughters: Jillian and Sadie. They live in the Greater Boston area where David practices criminal law and Sara teaches.

David recently coauthored a book entitled: *Things That Might Annoy a Yankee Fan.*

Beth Ann Barend Albright (daughter of Harold Barend) graduated with honors from St. Bonaventure University and received a graduate degree from Roswell Park Cancer Institute. After Rosewell Park, she enrolled in a graduate program in art therapy at the College of New Rochelle. She subsequently was certified to teach and is presently teaching biology in the South Bend Indiana School system. She married Tony Albright, and they have two children: Dylan and Riley Ann.

Samara Ann Barend (daughter of Harold Barend) graduated with high honors from the University of Pennsylvania. At graduation, she received the Althea K. Hottel Award—an honor bestowed by the graduating class on one student for their contributions to the university and the graduating class. While attending UP, she interned for Senator Moynihan, who brought to her attention a project he had been working on for forty years to no avail: the conversion of NY Route 17 into Interstate 86. She was the catalyst that drove the project to succeed.

USA Today selected her in 1999 as one of the top twenty college students in the country. While attending Harvard's Kennedy School, she ran as a Democrat for a congressional seat in the very Republican Twenty-ninth District of New York. She lost by 8 percent. Had she won, she would have been the youngest woman ever elected to Congress. Samara lives in New York City and is Vice President and Strategic Development Director for Public-Private Partnerships in North America for AECOM. She and friend Jennifer Ivan founded Minds of Steel, a nonprofit with a mission to help youth combat mental illness with physical fitness.

Ken Asmuth graduated from Hilton High in 1958. Shortly after graduation, he joined the U.S. Navy and served three years in San Diego, California. After the navy, he was employed by Otis Elevator, Rochester, New York, for five years, and then accepted a position with Eastman Kodak in the

Elevator Division Department. He subsequently became manager of the Elevator Division Department. He has three children: Tamara, Keith, and Kip.

Jerry Barker graduated from Hilton High in 1958. After graduation, he joined the U.S. Navy. He married Sue Griffin, the daughter of Greece police sergeant Bob Griffin. Jerry subsequently joined the Monroe County Sheriff's Department. Prior to retirement, he was appointed chief of detectives. After retirement from the sheriff's department, he became director of security for the Greece Ridge Center. He and Sue reside in Greece, New York. Jerry and Sue have three children: Theresa, Karen, and Scott.

Bill Boothby graduated from Hilton High in 1958. In his senior year of high school, he was selected to the All-county First Team for basketball. He graduated from the University of Rochester. Bill became a partner with PricewaterhouseCoopers during his thirty-eight-year career with the company. Later in life, Bill acquired Parkinson's disease. He died in July 2010. He was predeceased by his first wife, Rebecca Stiles. They had one son, David.

Jim Elkins graduated from Hilton High in 1958. Following graduation he joined the U.S. Coast Guard for four years. While serving in the coast guard, he married Shirley Hayes in 1960. From 1962 until his retirement, he worked for General Motors. Jim was a general supervisor, plant coordinator, and manufacturing consultant. Jim has six children: Lisa, Joe, Jim, Todd, Pam, and Ed. His wife, Shirley, has since died.

Ronnie Lupo left high school before graduation and joined the U.S. Coast Guard for four years. After his military discharge, he was employed by Ridge Construction, Rochester, New York. Subsequently, he joined Local 46 of the International Sheet Metal Workers Union. He married Elaine Quinn in 1955 and had three children: Carl, Regina, and Bonnie. Ron presently lives in Venice, Florida, where he is a member of the Nam Knights of America Motorcycle Club. The club sponsors numerous charitable fund-raisers including the funding for training dogs needed to assist wounded veterans.

Donald Schneider joined Local 46 of the International Sheet Metal Workers Union after Monroe Community College. He has been retired for eighteen He lives with his wife, Marge, of forty-seven years in The Villages in Florida. He still loves pizza but has not had a beer in forty years. Don and Marge have a son, Dan, and a daughter, Leslie.

Barbara (Van Dorn) Pedeville graduated from Hilton High in 1957. In 1962, she married Frank Pedeville. For the past thirty-five years, she has been employed by the Roman Catholic Diocese of Rochester, where she is presently Director of Management and Staff Services. Barb has four sons—Michael, Scott, Todd, and David—and nine grandchildren. Her husband, Frank, died in January 2009.

Joe Tolhurst—it was an honor to have been invited to Joe's ninetieth birthday celebration in 2011 at his home in Syracuse, New York. He is considered by many to be the finest basketball player in St. Lawrence University history. Joe was a coach and athletic director at Hilton High School.

About the Artists

Marian Simpson

The picture on the front cover is a reproduction of an oil painting by Marian Simpson. The painting is part of Harold Barend's private collection. It was chosen for the cover because it symbolically represents the contents of this book.

Marian Simpson, who studied art at Syracuse University and the Pittsburgh Art Institute, has taught workshops in almost every state. She has won hundreds of awards for her artwork. Many of her creations have been purchased by corporations throughout the world.

....

Jennifer Pacheco

Throughout the book, there are ink drawings by Jennifer Pacheco. An educator, journalist, author, and artist who created *Love Notes: Experiencing the Natural Areas of Binghamton University* (Binghamton University Press, 2000). Her illustrated book features poetry, prose, and illustrations. Jennifer graduated from Binghamton University with a BA in English and an MAT in teaching English.

CPSIA information can be obtained at www.ICGtesting.com
Printed in the USA
BVOW082116021012

301965BV00001B/5/P